Maybe they could sleep in the same bed tonight without it being too awkward.

Maybe this could work, Gracie thought as she looked to where Austin stood beside the window, big and calm and about as perfect as a man could be, except for a small scar beside his left eye.

He must have shoved his fingers through his hair, because it lay in sexy waves. She wanted to straighten it out, but that would be a big mistake.

Hands off, Gracie. You haven't been attracted to a man in six years. Why start now when you're so close to the end?

What appealed to her, though, was underneath the facade. Austin gave too much. She was a stranger who'd picked his pocket. He should have given her a night in jail.

Instead, he'd shown compassion, and it had her yearning for things that could never be.

She glanced at the bed. Maybe it would still be awkward. She hadn't been attracted to a man in years, probably because she'd been focused on survival. But Austin had taken care of that. She was warm and fuzzy when she needed her defenses the most. If she wasn't careful, she would let her guard down.

Don't forget who you really are. This man must never find out the truth about you.

You're almost home free.

Dear Reader,

Privacy is becoming a precious commodity in today's world. We seem to know everything about everyone around us. The public craves the latest news about celebrities, and we are often pressured by those around us to become involved in social media.

I began to wonder what would happen to a woman who had reached her breaking point and decided to just opt out of today's society. How difficult would her life become?

This is the story of one such woman's journey.

As well, I wanted to follow the escapades of a couple of characters from previous novels—including Austin Trumball from *No Ordinary Sheriff* (Harlequin Superromance, May 2012). Many readers have asked me what happened to him. Here is his story.

There are also two young characters who were separated when they were only twelve years old through no fault of their own—Finn (Franck) Caldwell and Melody Chase from *These Ties that Bind* (Harlequin Superromance, November 2011). I wanted to explore what would happen to them if they met again as adults.

I loved writing these characters in my earlier books and have enjoyed creating happy endings for them as adults, but not before giving them plenty of conflict to overcome first!

Mary Sullivan

MARY SULLIVAN

No Ordinary Home

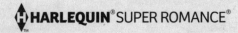

HARLEQUIN® SUPER ROMANCE®

Recycling programs
for this product may
not exist in your area.

ISBN-13: 978-0-373-60877-5

No Ordinary Home

Copyright © 2014 by Mary Sullivan

Printed in U.S.A.

ABOUT THE AUTHOR

Mary started her life living in a large city, and she loved it. Her early career was as a darkroom printer—a career ideally suited to her temperament. She left both the city and the job to start her family. Along the way, darkrooms became obsolete when computers took over. Searching for a creative alternative, she found writing. In particular, writing romance novels, which she enjoys thoroughly. She moved to smaller cities and then the country and then back to a big city, and the novel writing has followed her everywhere! These days she strives for a balance between her public life as an author and her private life, but she always loves to hear from readers. Don't hesitate to contact her through her website, www.marysullivanbooks.com.

Books by Mary Sullivan
HARLEQUIN SUPERROMANCE

Other titles by this author availabe in ebook format.

Thank you to all of the staff at Harlequin, who are unfailingly polite and lovely.

Thank you to every copy editor, line editor and proofreader who fixes my mistakes for me.

Thank you to every member of the art department for giving me stellar covers time and time again.

Thank you to Megan Long for helping me to make this the best book it could be!

CHAPTER ONE

AUSTIN TRUMBALL STOOD under the sickly green fluorescent lighting of a Wyoming truck-stop diner waiting for a table, with the devil eating a hole through his belly. He shouldn't have waited so long to stop for lunch.

The smell of charbroiled burgers and greasy fries seeped into his hair and clothes. Short-order cooks called for servers to pick up orders. Waitresses yelled back, "Hold your horses," or "Coming!" Not-so-nimble fingers slid into Austin's back pocket and lifted his wallet.

The brazen act carried out so clumsily startled a laugh out of him.

Not only did the pathetic amateur lack skills, he had no idea he'd just robbed a cop.

Austin walked like one, talked like one, scoped out his surroundings like one, but the thief had failed to scope *him* out. Big mistake.

Leaning forward, he murmured to his buddy Finn, "Be right back," and spun around just as a boy ran out the front door. Austin followed without calling. The biggest mistake people made was screaming they'd been robbed or yelling to the thief to stop.

What sense was there in warning a criminal you were coming after him?

Outside, a flash of dark clothing rounded the far corner of the building.

Light-footed, Austin followed around to the back.

The boy stood beside a Dumpster that reeked of garbage left sitting too long in the sun. He stuffed Austin's credit cards into his pockets and tossed the wallet into the bin. It hit the side and bounced onto the asphalt. Good thing, or Austin would be tossing the boy into the trash to fish it out.

The kid wasn't even smart enough to watch his back, but actually stood and counted the money instead of hightailing it out of there. No shortage of stupid here.

Using the stealth he'd learned on the job, Austin snuck up right behind the boy just as he breathed, "Two hundred dollars," as though he'd won the lottery. The boy was young; his voice hadn't even dropped yet. Austin shook his head, disgusted with today's youth. Or with their parents. What would drive someone so young out of his home, onto the road and into a life of crime?

The boy's skinny neck peeked out from beneath a dusty baseball cap, narrow enough that Austin would have sworn he could circle it with his hands. The thought made him realize just how vulnerable this kid actually was.

Didn't matter. The boy had robbed him. He was going to jail.

Austin grabbed the back of the kid's hoodie. The thief let out a high-pitched yelp. "Who—?"

"That's my hard-earned cash you're counting." Austin shook the boy.

"Crap on a broomstick." Kid couldn't even swear properly yet. Truly pathetic.

Austin spun him around then dropped his hand from the shirt. His jaw dropped, too. This was no green kid, definitely not a thirteen- or fourteen-year-old boy, but a twenty-something woman.

A woman?

After that observation came another one more interesting, considering she was such a poor thief. This woman had been around; she was pretty, but in a hard-knocks seen-too-much kind of way, skin baked by the sun, jaw defiant. Certainly no pushover.

The bill of her baseball cap shaded her eyes. A person's eyes, Austin had learned, said everything about them. He needed to see hers. He knocked the hat from her head. Startled pale blue eyes shadowed with darkness dominated a hungry face.

"Hey," she yelled and caught the cap before it hit the ground.

He had time only for impressions—high cheekbones, full lips, roughly shorn black hair to match coal-black eyebrows arched like birds' wings ready to take flight—before she came to life, exploding like a Thoroughbred out of the gate.

She was fast. He was faster, and snagged her sleeve before she got far. The fabric tore in his hand, but he managed to grasp her arm.

"Noooo." Desperation rode shotgun with terror in her scream. "Let me go. I won't do it again."

"Damn right you won't, lady. You're going to jail."

The second she realized she wouldn't get far— he was six-one, after all, and she all of five-five, if that—those big hollow eyes filled with more panic than Austin could remember seeing in anyone. In his hometown of Ordinary, Montana, they had homeless people, those who were needy, but this level of despair was something else altogether.

She bared her teeth like an animal, came alive in his arms and fought like a keening cyclone, elbows and knees everywhere at once.

"You aren't going anywhere," he said, calm because he had control. "I can read you like a book." An autobiography. By the time Austin had turned twelve, he'd perfected the fight-or-flight response to a fine art, until one good man had tamed him, and another had given him a stable home, even if only briefly.

The woman cast her eyes about, looking for escape. There was none. He'd backed her in between the wall and the Dumpster. She growled and clawed his face.

"Enough!" he shouted, grasping her forearms and spinning her around so her back was against his torso, her wrists locked in one of his hands. He'd been gentle so far because he hadn't wanted to risk cracking one of her bird bones, but nobody scratched him and got away with it.

He swiped his stinging cheek. Blood dotted his palm. That was a piss-off.

"Listen, stop fighting me. I'm bigger and stronger and this is going my way."

"I won't go to jail." The raw anguish in her voice struck a chord with him—panic used to be both his best friend and his worst enemy—but he ignored it. This thief was getting what she deserved.

"How much would you have charged on my credit cards if I hadn't felt you taking my wallet?"

"Nothing. I needed cash for food."

"Then why didn't you throw them away with the wallet?"

"What?" She sounded surprised. "You actually want some other stranger picking them up and using them?"

"You trying to tell me you pocketed my cards so no one else would use them?" How naive did she think he was?

"Yes."

"You think I'm stupid? That I'll believe that crap?"

Her slight frame bowed away from him like a willow branch, as though she could break free just on the strength of her willpower. Despite her weakness, her helplessness in his arms, tension resonated in her. She might be down, but she wasn't out. Not yet, but he could tell how close she was to the end from the tremor that ran through her body as though she'd just run a marathon. Her legs shook and he was holding up much of her weight. What there was of it.

He admired her fight, her unwillingness to give in, even if he wouldn't cut her a break.

"Let go." She strained against his hold.

He didn't budge. "Nope. You just broke the law, lady. Where I come from, we punish people for their mistakes."

"I didn't have a choice."

"Everyone has choices. You just have to make the right ones."

"Spoken like a man who's never wanted anything." Her bitterness rang loud and clear. "You've obviously never been starving."

He thought of how many times Cash Kavenagh, when he'd still been sheriff of Ordinary and Austin's Big Brother, had caught Austin Dumpster-diving behind both the restaurant and the diner on Main Street scrambling for leftovers. Austin's stomach had been so hollow he'd thought he would die if he couldn't find something, anything, to cram into his mouth.

More times than he could remember, Cash had bought him food because his mom had spent all their money on booze and cigarettes. Big Brothers weren't supposed to buy their Littles gifts, but Cash had.

Once, he'd caught Austin smoking up behind Chester's Bar and Grill, because any escape for Austin from the numbing drive of keeping his mom's head above water was a blessing. But Cash had caught him and warned him away from drink and drugs with a simple lesson. He had tossed the twelve-year-old into a jail cell for the day so Austin would see how it felt.

If Austin got into trouble, who would take care of his mom? As much as the routine of the child taking care of the mother had worn thin, he loved her. She never would have survived on her own. Not then. He knew she could now. She didn't agree with him.

That day, Cash had stepped out of the sheriff's office for a while and had returned with the best winter coat Austin had ever owned, and mittens and a hat, too. The guy had achieved godlike status that day. No one, certainly not his father, had ever cared enough about Austin to give him anything.

Cash had scared him straight, and had cared for him enough that Austin had stayed straight ever since.

"Don't make assumptions," Austin ordered. "I've gone hungry, but I never stole a wallet in my life."

She struggled in his arms. "Bully for you."

Austin chuffed out a laugh and tightened his grip. "That the best you can do? It's pretty lame."

"I might be a thief, but I don't swear."

"You're strange."

"And you're holding me too tightly. What are you? Some kind of perv looking to cop a feel?"

She was trying to get a rise out of him, probably hoping he'd get so mad he'd let go so she could get away. Not a chance. People said rude things to cops all the time. This was nothing.

"I'm not a pervert, but you were right about the cop part."

He appreciated how she stilled in his arms, got a

kick out of shocking her. Good. Maybe she'd think twice before robbing someone again.

"Gotcha," he said. He could feel her pulse in her wrist under his thumb, and her panic sizzled like bacon on a griddle.

"What do you mean?"

"I'm a cop. You just robbed a sheriff's deputy."

"Crap," she whispered, not sounding so tough now.

"You picked the wrong person to rob this time."

"There is no *this time*. I've never stolen a wallet before in my life," she said, defiant, and he believed her. No experienced thief would have been so clumsy.

"Why did you do it?"

He sensed her pride warring with misery before she bit out, "I'm hungry."

In those two words, he heard the stark terror he used to feel. He heard a hell of a lot more than just, *I missed lunch*. Her tone whispered, *My body hurts and I'm scared I might never eat again*.

She didn't smell clean. She needed a shower and to shampoo her short, greasy hair. Her cheap, ill-fitting clothes needed a good launder. Her breath wasn't so great, either. He knew homelessness when he smelled it.

"If you need money, get a job."

"Easy for you to say. Do you have any idea how hard it is? Even when you want to?" Her voice cracked, but she forged on. "I don't have money. I went in there for breakfast. I wanted food, but I wasn't asking for charity. I told them I would work for it. They wouldn't let me wash dishes. They wouldn't let me sweep the floors. I even offered to clean their toilets. I wasn't asking for a freebie, but they kicked me out anyway."

He eased her out of his arms, but held on to one wrist while he studied her. The hollows under her cheekbones and the dark circles under her eyes tugged at him. He remembered how exhausting hunger was.

But he'd been a kid. She was an adult. On close inspection, he figured she had enough miles on her tires to be nearer to thirty than twenty. So how had she fallen so low?

Everyone had a story, and sometimes the fall wasn't such a long drop. His mom came to mind. With that thought, Austin knew he wouldn't press charges.

When he'd caught her, he'd scared her. When he'd mentioned jail, he'd witnessed an unholy terror shoot through her. Maybe she'd learned a lesson today.

Before he went back inside, he needed his stuff back.

He held out his hand. "My money."

She stared at the bills crumpled in her fist. During their struggles, she'd had the presence of mind to hold on to them. Slowly, as if it physically hurt, as though her fingers were crippled with arthritis, she opened her hand enough to pass him the money.

"Here," she mumbled, but her eyes said *mine*. No doubt about it, she had a fierce need.

He bent down to pick up his wallet and opened it. "Give me my credit cards."

She pulled them out of her pockets. Only when he was certain he had everything did he let go of her wrist.

"You telling the truth? About this being your first time stealing?"

"My first time stealing a wallet."

Right. Of course she'd stolen before. Wallet robbing didn't start in a vacuum. "What else have you stolen?"

"Two date squares from the counter of a diner. Two days ago. They wouldn't let me work, either."

"And you didn't get caught?"

Her eyes slid sideways and down. *Here it comes, whatever lie she's concocting.* Then her gaze shot to his. She'd decided on honesty. "I nearly got caught. I had to run into a field with a bull in it to get away from the waitress."

It sounded like a joke, but she wasn't laughing. Neither was he. As petite as she was, she could have been torn apart by a bull in a rage.

"He didn't charge?"

"He tried to, but I was fast and climbed up into a tree. He butted it, but I held on until he lost interest and left. I climbed out onto a branch and jumped off over the other side of a fence. Then I ran for it."

She'd been taking too many chances.

He turned the subject back to what he really wanted to know. "When was the last time you ate?"

"Those date squares."

"Jesus, are you shitting me?"

Her mouth tightened. Pride. He understood pride. "I'm serious."

No wonder she'd stolen his wallet. He wanted to wrap her in his arms and cradle her to a safer place.

Whoa, buddy. She's nothing and no one to you.

She touched a spot deep inside him that he'd thought long buried, the kid who'd gone without too many times. The kid whispered, *Help her.*

His adult self shouted, *Don't.*

He fought the urge to tuck her under a protective wing.

Don't do it, buddy.

He'd been taking care of someone else all his life. Now, when he'd wrangled and scratched and clawed his way out of Ordinary, Montana, for his first vacation ever, when his only problems should be deciding what fishing rod and bait to use tomorrow, or whether to buy the cattle he was checking out when they got to Texas, he was actually contemplating getting entangled in this woman's issues.

You got a screw loose or something, buddy? Leave her be. Did you hear me? Leave her be. She can be someone else's problem. You don't need this.

Damn right I don't. I've got two weeks of footloose and fancy-free to take advantage of.

Even as his thoughts whirled, he knew he wouldn't turn his back on her, and wasn't it a piss-off that he was so honorable? That he couldn't keep himself from helping any wounded or sad creature who crossed his path? Life would be a heck of a lot easier if he could just walk away.

He sighed, giving in to the inevitable rush of mis-guided decency. Damn.

"Come on." He headed back around to the front of the diner. When he didn't hear her behind him, he tromped back.

"You coming?"

She stood where he'd left her, rigid, her intelligent brow furrowed.

"Are you arresting me?"

"No."

She relaxed her spine and eased her fists open. "Then why do I have to follow you?"

"I'm going to feed you."

A frown knit those raven's-wings eyebrows to-gether. If she'd been on the road for any length of time, he figured her distrust of strangers was hard-earned.

"I can't let you walk away hungry," he admitted.

"Why not?"

Might as well tell her the truth. She'd figure it out soon enough. "Because I'm a hopeless sap."

She still didn't seem to believe him.

"Look, I know you probably see the worst of peo-ple on the road, but you can trust me. I come from a small town, where we treat others kindly."

For some reason, that won her over. Her frown cleared.

"Are you coming to eat, or what?"

She might have had a pack of hounds on her tail, she shot forward so quickly, ready to follow wher-ever he might lead if it meant a meal.

Yeah. He could read her like a book. He knew how hunger felt when you'd gone past the point of a grumbling stomach to sheer hollowness, to the ceaseless physical ache. To dreaming about food, thinking about it endlessly, obsessing about it, until it shut all else out of your mind.

He didn't need the reminders of a hard past, should leave her here and be on his way, but God, she was thin. Holding her had been like wrapping his arms around a sapling.

He stepped away from her abruptly because the last thing he wanted was more memories coming back to haunt him. They got worse before they got better.

She stumbled and he caught her arm. "What's wrong?"

"I wrenched my ankle when I jumped out of the tree."

"How far did you jump?"

She shrugged, lips tight. Fine. She could keep her secrets.

For a tough woman, she needs a keeper.

Damned if that's going to be me. I'm sick of that role. I'll feed her and get rid of her. No "taking care" of her beyond one hot meal.

Even so, he led her around front to do exactly that—take care of her.

FOOD.

Food had dominated Gracie Travers's every waking moment for days, weeks, every minute, every painful second.

Hunger was a vicious, angry rat gnawing at her stomach walls. Relentless. Overwhelming. Unwilling to give her a moment's peace.

She'd been through rough patches before, but nothing like this. No one would hire her to do even the most mundane, unskilled work. She wasn't asking for a paycheck. Just for food. Nothing else. Just a meal.

Food.

She didn't *want* a handout. She could work. *Would* work. In her former life, she'd been known as a hard worker. She still knew how to be one. She just couldn't get a real job.

She couldn't work full-time. She had her reasons. She certainly wouldn't share them with a cop.

Food.

Every time her stomach cramped, all of those years of taking her blessings for granted haunted her.

Things hurt so badly now that she wondered if her internal organs were starting to eat each other. How did starvation work? What did it do to the body that made it hurt so much?

The scent of charbroiled burgers drifted out of the diner's vents, so strong she gulped it.

She kept pace with the man who said he would feed her, but hobbled because her ankle still throbbed.

There were so many things Gracie should be worried about right now. Was the guy really a cop? Had he been lying about not arresting her? About wanting to feed her? Why would a guy she'd stolen from want to help her?

Ahead of her, he walked with a long, confident stride, his shoulders broad and square.

What would he expect in return? She'd fallen so low lately she'd actually stolen food two days ago and a wallet five minutes ago, but that was as far as her crime spree would take her. Did he want her body in exchange for food? She wouldn't do *that*.

Despite the questions, the one word that overrode all of them—*food*—won out.

She chased the tall, handsome stranger around to the front of the building. *Tall, handsome stranger* sounded like something out of a palm-reading session or a romance novel. Ha. As if there truly were happy endings in real life. She knew better.

What did he want in return?

If this guy wanted to feed her, fine and good, but she would owe him what *she* chose to owe him. She would polish his shoes, do his laundry if he gave her the chance, or wash his car, but he would take nothing from her other than what she chose to give. She was long past the point of letting people take advantage of her.

But what if he wouldn't feed her if she didn't give in to his demands? Where would she be then?

Her head hurt—from the hunger, but also from the endless uncertainty. It was time to stop running. In two days, she would.

Only two more days to go.

In two days, she would say goodbye to the road forever. No more running.

So close.

She stepped into the diner, desperate for the comfort of a full belly. Her lizard brain just wanted the food this stranger offered. Her developed brain would have to worry about consequences—and how to deal with them—later.

The smells overwhelmed her, of hot fat, bacon, eggs frying. Toast. They'd burned a slice or two. Even if burnt to charcoal, she would eat it. With or without butter. Or jam. Oh, jam. How long had it been?

Another scent teased her. The man beside her smelled clean, more than clean, as though the soap he used was part of him, oozing from his pores like the purest thing on earth.

She hadn't showered in weeks. A month, even? At the last gas station, she'd washed her underarms using cold water, a cheap paper towel as rough as sandpaper and industrial hand soap. Her armpits had burned afterward. They still itched.

Grease and dust coated her hair. What could she do about that? When you were hungry, shampoo was a hell of a lot less important than food. And conditioner? A luxury. She hadn't used it in a couple of years.

She hadn't really cared until this man with his disheveled blond hair, clear blue eyes and broad shoulders made her want to comb her hair. Maybe put on a little lipstick.

She'd given up on all of that six years ago. Cripes. Had she really been on the road that long? Only two more days until the end of her journey. Another couple of days and her money problems would end. For too many years, she'd been running *from*. Now, she was finally traveling *to*.

Inside the diner, the stranger talked to another man and Gracie's instincts for self-preservation kicked in. Did this guy think she'd be good for an afternoon three-way?

She might be homeless, she might have fallen lower than she'd ever been in her twenty-nine years, but she was not, never had been and never would be a prostitute. Not even for food.

She stomped out of the diner.

A second later, a hand clamped down on her shoulder and spun her about. For a big man, he sure could move quietly.

"I thought you were hungry. Why are you running off?"

"I saw you talking to your friend. Did you think I'd sleep with you both in exchange for a meal? I'm not a whore."

He reared back. She'd offended him. "I didn't think you were. I was just going to feed you. What kind of guy do you take me for? I'm a cop."

"Cops aren't always lily-white."

"Neither are homeless women who hang around truck stops and steal wallets."

Shame flared in her chest, hot and unwelcome. She used to have a conscience, before life and desperation had taken over. She shouldn't have touched this man's wallet, or stolen those date squares two days ago. Gran would be disappointed in her. "I told you I've never done it before. This was the first time."

"I think you're telling the truth and that's the only reason you aren't already sitting in the back of a police cruiser." He hooked his thumbs into his back pockets. "Figured you just needed a good meal. That's all I'm offering."

Gracie wanted to believe him, not because she trusted anyone anymore, or because she had any naive belief in the innate goodness of humanity— a lot had been burned out of her by experience— but because if she didn't eat soon, she was going to pass out.

"And the other guy with you?"

"He's a good man." He didn't need to add *too*. She could see in his face he was probably exactly who and what he said he was.

"Let's pretend we trust each other for the hour it'll take for lunch." He watched her steadily, like a poster boy for good health.

Shaggy, dark blond hair framed a face carved by a hard, but loving hand. Sharp, intelligent and wholesome with a generous side of sexy. *GQ* could put him on its cover and women would swoon. Blue eyes drooped down at the outer corners in a languid parody of sensuality, but the awareness in their depths was anything but lazy.

He differed from the people she saw on the road— too many truckers with potbellies from hours spent sitting behind a steering wheel, or the obesity of housewives and kids who watched too much TV or spent too much time at computers.

But this guy? He exercised a lot.

"Let's start over." He stuck out his right hand. "Austin Trumball."

She didn't want to touch him, because she knew she was unworthy of him. If she hadn't stolen his wallet, he would never have given her the time of day, not only because she was down and out, but because she had *chosen* to be that way, a position most didn't understand. If he knew that, he'd boot her to the curb.

The choice had been hers and she had long ago accepted it as the right one. Lately, though, as she'd grown so thin her ribs were prominent, she'd had her doubts.

Now here was this man offering not only food, but also decency. *Accept,* she ordered her pride. *Take his free meal and then move on.*

Keep a wary eye, but trust him long enough to eat.

She shook his hand. "Gracie Travers." Why was it that after so long on the road, she still stumbled when she said Travers? She should be used to it by now.

His warm fingers wrapped around hers, hard and assured. She hadn't been warm in years, not even in the middle of summer. Not even on a beautiful July day as hot as this one.

He shook once, all business, then let go of her hand. She felt the loss of his heat.

"Let's eat." He turned back to the diner and she followed without hesitation this time. She wanted a meal, just one big, hot meal to get her through the next two days until she made it to Denver. Then she would be home-free for the rest of her life.

The day after tomorrow, she would turn thirty. Her money would be hers, free and clear. She needed to get to a bank. Denver was the closest large city.

What she wouldn't give to stop moving, to find a small place to live—nothing ostentatious, just a modest roof over her head and three square meals a day—but that would require a permanent job. To get one she would have to provide a social security number. Once that happened, her freedom would be gone, and *that* she wouldn't give up.

If she could access her money, her problems would be solved. She could buy a new identity. She could buy a small house somewhere. If she lived normally without extravagant spending, she would be okay for life. No one would ever need to know who she really was.

Inside the crowded restaurant, Austin's friend sat in a booth. When he saw her beside Austin, the corners of his mouth turned down.

"What are you doing?" he asked. "Who is she?"

"She's having lunch with us. I invited her. Her name's Gracie." He gestured for her to slide into the booth across from the other guy. She did. "Gracie, this is Finn Franck Caldwell."

She nodded to him while Austin slid into the booth beside her. He took up a lot of room. She studied both men. About the same age, she guessed, or close to it.

Early thirties. Finn wasn't as big as Austin, but he looked equally as fit.

It didn't take a genius to see Finn wasn't happy she was here. Tough. As if that was going to hold her back from a free meal. At least, Austin had assured her there were no strings attached. She wasn't yet sure she believed him 100 percent.

A harried waitress brought menus. "Coffee?"

"Yes," they all said and she returned a minute later with a full pot.

Gracie doctored hers with plenty of sugar and cream, sipped it, sighed and sipped again. Nothing had ever tasted better than this hot drink sliding down her throat.

When she opened her eyes, she found both men staring at her.

"What?" she asked, defensive.

"Nice to see someone appreciate a good cup of coffee, that's all." Austin had a strong voice, deep and rich like the coffee in her cup. He could make a fortune with that beautiful voice. "What do you want to eat?"

All of it.

She studied the menu. "How much can I spend?"

"As much as it will take to fill your belly."

His friend still hadn't said anything. He didn't have to. The flare of his nostrils signaled his disapproval.

"I'm paying him back," she shot at Finn, because she wasn't the deadbeat he thought she was.

"How?"

She turned to study the bench hog beside her. Cripes, he was big. "What do you need?"

Finn snorted and she glared at him. "Not that."

She turned back to Austin and glanced at his messy hair. "You could use a haircut. I'll do that."

Without waiting for a response, she gave her attention over to the menu as though it were the Holy Grail. She couldn't waste another minute talking. The sooner she ordered, the sooner she could kill the pain in her gut. Perusing the options, she blinked to clear mistiness from her eyes. Not tears. No. She was just tired, but God, look at the choices. Saying yes to one thing meant saying no to another.

When the waitress returned, Gracie ordered steak and eggs, because she would need the protein to get her to Denver. Not many truckers picked up hitchhikers anymore, not like they used to. How could she blame them? The world was a dangerous place.

She thought back to when she was a teenager flirting with veganism. These days, she was far more practical. She needed meat.

This afternoon, and for the next few days, she'd be hoofing it toward Denver. As always, she broke the trip down into segments. If she could make it as far as the next small town by this evening, she might be able to work a full day tomorrow and get herself a cheap motel room for the night. Maybe grab a hot shower before continuing on to Denver and visiting a bank. She should look respectable for that.

If someone would hire her for the day, that is.

The meal came with hash browns and toast.

"Do you have rye bread?"

"Sure, but I have to charge you an extra dollar for it."

Gracie avoided looking at Austin. "Make my toast rye, and bring marmalade. And I want rice pudding for dessert." She would need the iron from the raisins. "And a large glass of milk." Lately, she'd been worrying about calcium. Were her bones weakening because she wasn't getting enough? Would she pay for it later in life?

Her head still pounded, especially as she wondered whether she'd made the right choice in running away. Then she thought of her mom and dad, and that jerk Jay, and the circus her life had been, and her regrets faded.

Better to be on the road than to be involved in *that* again, but some days she was so tired she just wanted to quit. Then she would remember she already had. How did a person go about quitting…quitting?

Get your hands on your money.

That will solve your problems.

CHAPTER TWO

GRACIE ATE LIKE a half-starved animal, which Austin guessed she was. Man, could she pack it away.

"Careful," he warned. "Don't make yourself sick. You're putting all of that into an empty stomach. You'll fill up too quickly."

"I can take care of my own stomach." She stopped eating. "Sorry," she said. She must have realized her tone had been caustic and remembered that he was paying for her meal. Austin almost laughed. He figured if she'd been on the road awhile, on her own, she'd learned to take care of herself pretty well.

She was a prickly one, all right.

"We going to get a move on soon?" Finn nursed the last of his coffee. Both he and Austin had finished their meals, but then they'd ordered less than Gracie had, and she was still plowing through hers.

Finn was still watching him, as he'd done all through lunch, but Austin had avoided his gaze. Now he met Finn's cynical glare head-on. Finn's left eyebrow sat cocked. The man could carry on whole conversations with his unruly eyebrows.

That raised brow said everything he wouldn't utter in front of the woman. They'd been best friends for more than fifteen years. Austin could almost read Finn's mind, imagined every word he wouldn't say out loud.

Are you for real, Austin? We're on the road, on vacation, and you pick up a stray? You can't stop yourself from helping people, can you? Not even on vacation.

Ready to defend his actions, Austin halted at the quirk of Finn's lips, because the man was glancing from his scratched cheek to the small woman beside him.

Again, man, really? You let that little thing get the better of you? Some cop you are.

Austin wanted to say she was stronger than she looked, but shame had him holding his tongue. And a certain odd loyalty to the woman he'd only just met. Then his humor kicked in and he grinned and shrugged.

Finn grinned, too, and the tension between them eased.

It would be a shame to let a woman, a stranger, come between a pair of good friends.

Even so, at the moment, Austin's loyalty was to Gracie, because of her hunger and poverty. Finn had never known a day of need in his life. Austin had. He understood desperation. He totally got despair.

To his credit, Finn had held himself back from asking what had happened while he'd waited for Austin inside the diner.

"As soon as Gracie is finished we can go." Austin

turned his attention to her. "Where're you going from here?"

She shrugged. He didn't like the thought of her on the road, even if she was tough enough to handle anything that came along. He wondered if she fully understood the dangers to a woman alone in these places.

If she'd robbed a different kind of man, if it had been late at night with fewer people around, she might have been in more trouble than she could handle. And behind the building, no one would have heard her scream. The thought chilled him. She might be stronger than she looked, but hunger had left her depleted.

"Where did you sleep last night?"

She shrugged again. He grasped her wrist and repeated the question.

She put down a spoonful of rice pudding and wiped her mouth with a paper napkin. She'd been raised to have manners. He'd noticed her speech was good, her grammar correct, better than his. She hadn't been raised poor. He'd bet on that. So, what was her story?

"I know you're feeding me and I appreciate it," she said, tugging on her wrist until he let go, "but where I sleep is nobody's business but my own."

"You made it mine when you stole my wallet."

"She *what?*" Finn leaned forward, expression fierce. "Why haven't you called the cops? Instead, you're feeding her?"

Austin raised a hand to placate his friend. "She

stole my wallet, but I caught her and got everything back." Finn looked angry enough to spit bullets. Or maybe that should be tranquilizing darts. After all, the guy was a veterinarian. Naw. The way he was staring at Gracie was pretty lethal. Austin figured he'd better appease him. "She apologized—didn't you, Gracie?"

She nodded. She'd returned to her pudding and her mouth was full. Good thing. It prevented her from lying. Or maybe she lied easily. He knew nothing about her.

"Where are you headed?" he asked again. "Where are you sleeping tonight?" Last thing he needed was a woman depending on him—he'd had a bellyful of that, more than one man should have to bear in only thirty-one years—but he couldn't help worrying. The world was a dangerous place, especially for a woman on her own.

"I'm trying to get to Denver. I'm hoping to hitch a ride from here to the nearest town."

She was heading to Denver? So were they.

Finn must have seen the wheels turning in Austin's mind because he shook his head. "No. No, no, no. Stop thinking what you're thinking, Austin."

Finn had sat through enough of Austin's griping sessions to know exactly how hard Austin's life was with his mom. Finn's eyebrow shot up again. *Don't take on another needy woman, man.*

Sensing the tension, Gracie's head shot up. "Are you heading to Denver?"

Austin nodded.

She swallowed the last gulp of her milk. "Can I hitchhike to the next town? I'll be no trouble. You can drop me off there and I'll find my own place to sleep. I promise," she said, her voice full of both desperation and hope. "Just give me a ride that far. I can make my own way to Denver later. I'll be no trouble. Honest."

Finn groaned. Austin knew why. They'd been best friends since high school, and he knew Austin inside out. He knew there was no way Austin would—could—say no.

"Okay, but only as far as Casper. We're stopping there so Finn can visit a friend." They could drop Gracie there. The last thing, the very last thing Austin needed was a woman hanging on to him.

GRACIE SAT IN the back seat of Austin's old SUV doing sums in her small notebook. She wouldn't pay him back for the gas since they were going this way anyway, but she would pay him back for everything she'd ordered at lunch.

She remembered to add the extra dollar for rye toast.

This ride to the next town would give her ankle a chance to heal. Things couldn't have worked out better.

Fascinated by the bantering between the men in the front seat, she eavesdropped shamelessly. She'd been on the road so long she didn't know what a normal friendship felt like. Thinking back, she couldn't remember having had one.

The friends she'd had as a child had all been adults and transitory, coming and going as careers and jobs changed.

These men had a strong friendship. She sensed how deep and real it was and it filled her with envy.

Finn talked; Austin listened. She'd learned this lesson about relationships—in many, one was the talker and the other the listener, one the social butterfly and the other happy to take a back seat.

"No way will they lose this year," Finn said. "Even on their bad days, they're miles better than the Broncos."

She'd lost track of the conversation, something about sports teams, but she'd missed which sport they were discussing, distracted by a gurgling in her stomach. She rubbed it.

In the rearview mirror, Austin glanced at her. She settled her hand back into her lap. The man didn't miss much. Good cop. That was all she needed, to have this guy pester her with an *I told you so.*

"They're an awesome team," Austin said. "Even if they did lose this year. They could go all the way next year."

If he said *I told you so,* he would be right. She should have eaten less food more slowly.

Finn popped the lid on a can of nuts and, one by one, tossed them into the air and caught them in his mouth. "They choked, man. No way will they take the championship this year."

He offered the can to Austin, who shook his head.

He ignored Gracie, she noticed. Just as well. Her tummy gurgled and roiled.

Austin's response was quiet. "We'll see. They lost. Let's get past it and hope for a better result this year." The voice of reason. He probably made a good cop.

Teams. Athletes. She knew nothing about sports, or popular culture, or TV shows. Ironic when you thought about it, because—

A stomach cramp had her hissing in a breath. Fortunately, Austin hadn't noticed. Or had he? His eyes flickered to the mirror and back to the road.

She studied his profile. Where Finn was lean, quick and full of nervous energy, and a couple of inches shorter than Austin, Austin could probably out-calm the Dalai Lama. He didn't have the Dalai Lama's charming wit and smile, though. She knew. She'd met the man once, and had been enchanted by him. It had been difficult for her, though, with him so pure and kind, and her a fraud.

What held Austin back? What caused the sadness that lurked in his fine blue eyes?

"What's so great about this herd we're going to see?" Austin asked. Everything about him, even his strong, straight profile, was serious.

"I went to college with the owner. A great guy. He's giving up his hobby ranch. Needs to sell the herd." Finn tossed peanuts into his mouth then offered the can to Austin again, who shook his head and pointed over his shoulder to her in the backseat. Finn offered them to Gracie, reluctantly. Odd as it was for someone who'd been starving a short while ago, the thought of eating even one left her nauseated.

She shook her head.

"Knowing this guy—" Finn turned around again "—those cattle will be top quality and in good shape."

"Can't wait to see them." Ah, a spark of excitement lit Austin's voice. So, they were on a trip to see some cows. She wondered why, so eavesdropped some more.

The gist was that these guys were apparently on their way to Texas, where Austin was going to buy a herd of cattle. So…Austin was not only a sheriff's deputy, but also a rancher?

"You want a mouser for the barn?" Finn asked. "I've got a real little cutie in the office right now."

What office?

"No one's adopting her. All everyone wants these days is kittens." He ate more peanuts. "I don't want to put her down. Worst part of the job is putting down healthy animals just 'cause they don't have a home."

Finn was a veterinarian?

"I'd really like to find her a home."

"You can't take her to your dad's ranch?" Austin asked.

Finn grinned. "Dad would kill me if I brought home another stray. He knows how much I love animals, but put his foot down after the last dog I brought over."

Austin smiled. "Yeah, I remember all the strays you took home even before you became a vet."

Ah. So he really *was* a vet. He had at least that going for him even if he was a jerk in other ways.

"Sure." Austin shifted gears. "I'll take the cat."

A satisfied grin lit Finn's face.

Finn made a joke about a bunch of cows in a field they were passing and Austin laughed—so the man *could* laugh—the affection between them palpable.

Again, that pang of envy.

Even before Gracie had run away, there had been few people she could trust. There'd been Gran and… that was it. No one else.

Now Gran was gone and Gracie was alone.

The men laughed and she pulled her gaze away from the fields flying past the vehicle.

Her stomach cramped. Crap, she felt sick and shivery. Her stomach churned.

It cramped again, hard and sharp.

"Stop the car," she croaked.

"What?"

A strong breeze rushed through the open windows, but it wasn't enough to stem the rush of bile into her throat.

"Stop the car," she shouted.

Austin jerked the steering wheel and slammed on the brakes. The car fishtailed on the gravel shoulder.

Gracie just managed to scramble out and make it to the ditch before losing her lunch.

She retched until there was nothing left, and she wanted to cry. All of that food wasted when her body needed it so badly.

She heard footsteps on the road behind her, calm and measured. Had to be Austin.

She felt a hand on her shoulder.

"Here." A hand held a tissue in front of her face.

Embarrassing. It wasn't bad enough the man had to see her as a homeless person, now he had to witness this indignity?

"Sorry," she said.

He rested his hand on her back while she retched one more time, his touch reassuring. She wiped her mouth.

"You have any gum or mints?" she asked.

"Yeah." He removed his hand. She missed the warmth. She heard him walk to the car. He returned a minute later with a pack of gum.

"Thanks." She took two sticks because her mouth tasted like crap and the gum was sweet and minty. The chewing and her saliva helped to settle her stomach.

She wiped her damp forehead and brushed sweat from her upper lip. When her legs stopped shaking, she returned to the vehicle with Austin keeping step beside her.

"You okay?" he asked.

"Yeah. Just sorry I had to lose that food."

He climbed into the driver's seat while she got into the back. She had to give him credit. Not a single *I told you so*. There was something to be said for the strong, silent type.

Trouble started, though, once they reached the small town midway to Denver when Austin parked on the street near a small hotel and Gracie walked into a back alley to sleep for the night.

"What?" Austin gaped. "No way am I letting you sleep in an alleyway."

"Letting me?" Gracie asked, voice dangerously quiet. "You bought me lunch. You gave me a drive. I appreciate it. That doesn't give you rights, or any say in what I do or where I go." She set her knapsack on the ground on the far side of a Dumpster, where she could hide from the prying eyes of anyone walking past.

Austin followed her. "You can't sleep here."

"I can and will. It's a warm night." Although the sky had darkened on the drive and thunder rumbled in the distance. Gracie walked to the back door of a store that fronted onto the street they'd parked on, where bales of compacted cardboard had been put out for recycling.

Taking a folding knife from her back pocket, she slit the baling wire and dragged a couple of large boxes to set up a bed for herself.

"You're going to sleep out in the rain when I'm offering you a place to stay, free of charge?"

"That's right. I'll cut your hair in the morning. That's for lunch. I can't afford to pay you back for a hotel room."

He stood arms akimbo and brow as thunderous as the approaching storm. "I'm not asking for payment."

"I know, but I wouldn't feel right if I didn't give you something in return."

"You don't like taking." His quiet tone said he understood too much.

"No," she answered. "I don't like owing anyone anything. Not one dime. I like my independence."

Fat drops of rain fell, settling the dust and the stench of garbage. She ignored the rain. What Gracie couldn't ignore, though, was the cramping in her gut. At that moment, it returned with a vengeance. It wasn't going to be vomit this time. She could vomit in an alley, but the runs were another thing altogether.

Crap. Double crap.

When another sharp pain hit, she suppressed a groan. More than shelter from the rain—she had spent many nights exposed to the elements—she needed a washroom. She wasn't going to have a choice. The cramps in her stomach became fierce. She would have to take a hotel room and figure out later how to pay Austin back.

"Okay, thanks. I'll take the room." She picked up her knapsack and quick-stepped out of the alley.

He didn't question her change of heart. Maybe he thought it was his manly powers of persuasion. "Wait in the car," he said. "I just have to pick up a few items." He stepped into a pharmacy just down the street.

Gracie climbed into the backseat. *Hurry,* she thought, squeezing her knees together.

Tension sizzled between her and Finn.

"You don't like me, do you?" she asked.

"I don't like what you represent."

"Which is?"

"People looking for a handout."

"I told Austin I would cut his hair for the food he bought me for lunch. It wasn't my idea to get a hotel room. I tried to sleep in the alley tonight, but I'm learning he's persistent when he's got his mind made up."

Finn snorted. "Yeah, he's stubborn."

He turned around in his seat to pin her with a glare. "I'm giving you fair warning—you hurt my buddy and there won't be a truck stop in the States where you'll be safe from me."

Finn might look easygoing, but he had a sharp edge. She didn't blame him. If she had friends, she would be just as fierce in her defense of them.

"Warning duly noted." Not that she needed it. She had no intention of hurting Austin because they would be parting ways tomorrow morning.

An itchy silence reigned until Austin returned and dumped a plastic bag onto the backseat.

They stepped into the foyer of a small hotel and the heavens opened up behind them, rain drumming hard on the sidewalk, Gracie secretly glad she'd agreed to stay in the hotel. She would have been drenched sleeping outdoors.

Austin and Finn went to the desk to sign in. Gracie shifted from foot to foot. Her stomach hurt. She couldn't wait for a room.

"Excuse me?" she asked the clerk, who checked out her old clothes, her dirty backpack. Yeah, yeah, she knew how bad she looked. "Is there a washroom on this floor?"

He pointed down a hallway. "Past the elevators."

She managed to make it to a toilet before her stomach voided.

AUSTIN STOOD AT the front desk and watched Gracie run for the washroom. She couldn't even wait until he rented her a room.

He tried not to shoot her an I-told-you-so look as she ran off. Putting all of that food into a severely empty stomach had been a bad idea.

It took him a moment to catch what the desk clerk was saying.

"What do you mean you don't have rooms with singles?"

"There's a ranchers' conference in the area this week. Rooms are booked for miles around. We have only two small rooms left, both with only a double bed."

"Okay," Austin said to Finn. "I'll get one for us and one for Grace."

At the thought, a shiver ran through Austin. He could imagine the two of them sleeping like a pair of two-by-fours clinging to the edges of the mattress. There weren't many limits to their friendship, but this was one of them.

They were both big men and a double bed wouldn't hold them. Austin had a double all to himself at home and spent most of his nights sprawled across the thing.

He shivered again. He couldn't sleep with Finn.

Apparently, it weirded out Finn, too, because he stared openmouthed. "Are you nuts? I love you, man, but there's no way I'm sharing a bed with you."

"Is there any way you can set up a cot in one of those rooms?" Austin asked the clerk, thinking that Gracie could sleep in a bed and he could take the cot. Or vice versa.

"We're all out. You're lucky to get these rooms because of a cancellation we received ten minutes ago. This is a small hotel. We don't usually see this volume of traffic."

The clerk waited for his decision.

"There are two rooms," Finn said. "One for you. One for me. Leave that woman to find her own accommodations."

Aware of the clerk listening in, and probably speculating, Austin pulled Finn aside. "I can't leave her to sleep outside. Listen to that rain."

"So what? She smells like she's been doing exactly that for a while. Maybe the rain will clean her up."

"And give her pneumonia."

"She's not your responsibility."

"She's in the washroom right now probably puking up her guts. She'll be weakened and unable to defend herself if she needs to. She could get robbed or raped."

"Seems capable of taking care of herself."

Austin's anger flared. Finn didn't have a clue. "You've never gone hungry. You've always had a good home. You've never slept in dirty sheets let alone outside with nothing over your head. You've never even camped without a tent. Am I right?"

Finn had the grace to look sheepish. "I know. I get how fortunate I am. I really do." He pointed at Austin, nearly jabbing him in the chest. "But you're getting sucked in again."

"No. I'm not."

Finn held up his index finger. "Your mom. You've spent thirty-one years taking care of her."

"Technically, only twenty-five. She didn't fall apart until my dad died when I was six."

"Your *dad?*" The sarcasm in Finn's voice rankled.

Austin didn't talk about his dad. Ever. "Don't go there," he warned. "Besides, Mom wasn't much use on her own. I couldn't have left her to live alone until now. You know that."

Finn shrugged because they'd debated that point to death. Austin knew his buddy thought he should have walked away years ago.

He held up another finger. "How about the kids?"

The kids were a group of teens in Ordinary with whom Austin spent time shooting hoops and making sure they stayed out of trouble. He planned to help by giving them jobs on his ranch when it was up and running, by teaching them skills they would need when they got out into the world. They had nothing, reminding him too much of himself at that age.

"That's good work that keeps them off the streets. Besides, if it's so bad, why are you going to help teach them about animals once I get the ranch?"

"Because I like animals and kids, not because

I'm neurotic about helping every sad-eyed waif who comes along."

Finn had hit the nail on the head. Despite Gracie's tough shell, a sad-eyed waif lingered inside. Finn wasn't as oblivious and unaffected as he pretended to be. There was more depth there than met the eye. Just as there was with Gracie.

Finn held up a third finger. "Roger."

Ordinary, Montana, was small but had a couple of poor old drunks whom Austin threw into jail periodically just so they could sleep indoors. He'd organized a system of sorts to find them beds every night during the winter—in the back room of Chester's restaurant, in C.J.'s barn for a few nights, wherever Austin could get them a spot. One of those homeless men was old Roger, who'd fallen apart after his wife of forty-two years had died. He had no one on this earth on whom he could depend but folks in his hometown. What was so wrong with Austin taking care of him?

Guys like Roger had mental health issues. Who knew what Grace's problem was?

"Gracie needs help, Finn. She was desperate enough to rob me. She said she'd never done that before and I believe her."

"You're a sucker. You're supposed to be on vacation, taking a holiday from helping people." Finn paced in the foyer to offset his nervous energy. "Don't do this to yourself."

"Do what? I'm giving her a bed for the night and

breakfast tomorrow. That's it. Nothing more. Then we'll go our separate ways."

"That woman is trouble. She even has us fighting."

"Fine," Austin said, testy. "Let's stop fighting. You take one room and I'll take the other with Gracie. Okay?" He didn't like the idea, but it had to be done. He'd already told her he would get her a room for the night and he wasn't a man to go back on his word. If he had to, he would sleep on the floor, even if that thought held as much appeal as a bad case of fleas.

Finn didn't respond, just nodded, but it looked like he was maybe biting the inside of his cheek so he wouldn't argue more. Or so he wouldn't laugh.

Austin punched him on the arm.

"Ow. What was that for?" But Finn laughed openly at Austin's discomfort.

Austin sighed. How had the night come to this?

Grace came out of the washroom down the hall, pale and sweating.

Damn. Great start to their vacation, the two of them bickering over a woman Austin didn't even know, and that woman looking sick as a dog.

GRACIE COULD HAVE cried, her gastric distress a waste of calories she desperately needed. She didn't know how long she'd stayed in the washroom before she was done, but was finally able to emerge with her hands washed and her face rinsed with cold water.

In the lobby, she found the men waiting, Finn's expression an odd mix of triumph and dismay, while

Austin looked tense and unable to meet her eyes. What was going on?

Once they got to their rooms and Gracie saw the double bed in the hotel room—and Austin dumping his hockey bag onto that bed—she ran for the door, shooting at him over her shoulder as she left, "I told you I wouldn't pay for lunch with sex."

Austin followed and slammed the door closed before she could leave. "For God's sake, be quiet before someone calls security."

He looked genuinely offended. "I don't want sex," he shouted. "This is all that's available." He slammed his hand against the wall. "I'm not asking you to sleep with me. How many times do I have to say it? Who'd want to go to bed with someone as skinny as you, anyway?"

His remark hurt. She might be homeless, but she was still a woman. He explained about the hotel having no more rooms left with single beds or with two doubles. Not even a spare cot. Nothing. This was it. Or the alley, but that wouldn't work. She suspected she wasn't through yet with stomach problems.

She heard Austin's frustration and saw it in the way he scrubbed his hands over his face.

"Okay. Fine." She moved away from the door.

She didn't know why he wanted her to stay, except for this strange feeling that he couldn't let her go off on her own. Foolish man. She'd been doing it for years.

He sweetened the deal with two words. "Hot shower."

Getting clean won out over all of her objections. Oh, to not have to use heavy-duty cleaning solvents in gas stations.

"Here." He handed her the bag of stuff he'd bought.

She peeked inside then stared at him, tried to glare, but couldn't pull it off because she wanted what she held in her hands too badly to turn it down. He'd bought her pieces of heaven. She laid them out in a row on the bed. A brand-new toothbrush and a tube of toothpaste. Dental floss. Body wash. She snapped up the lid and inhaled. Strawberries. Matching body lotion. Hand cream. Skin cleanser. Facial moisturizer! Shampoo and conditioner that smelled like coconut and pineapple.

Oh. Oh. It had been so long since she'd had any of this stuff.

"Okay," she said, but her voice cracked. She cleared her throat and said, "Okay," again, because she'd become too emotional too quickly, his thoughtfulness so sweet, so unexpected, it left her speechless. She shouldn't take any of this, but as far as she could tell, it was freely given. In six years, the only times men had offered her anything had been with the understanding that she pay for it in ways she wouldn't.

Austin hooked his thumbs into his back pockets and stared at the carpet. "I hope it's all okay. It's not the most expensive stuff out there."

"It's perfect." And it was. In her former life, she'd bought only the best. Until doing without, she hadn't realized how truly fortunate she'd been. This, though, was an unparalleled gift. Who *was* this guy? Why would he care so much for a stranger?

He'd set the bait securely. Of course she would stay. They would make the sleeping arrangement work somehow because there was *no way* she wasn't having a long hot shower tonight. "I'll sleep on the floor. You can have the bed."

The weird hum Austin made sounded noncommittal.

"If it reassures you at all, I'm not any happier about this than you are." Austin gestured toward the double bed. He rummaged in his bag and pulled out a fresh shirt. "You want to shower before dinner or after?"

"I guess you'd prefer before?"

"Yeah. We'll be going to a nicer restaurant than a truck-stop diner. You're pretty ripe."

She gathered the things he'd bought her, but hesitated just outside the bathroom.

"I won't come in and attack you. You're safe with me." She registered his hurt tone at being silently questioned; she'd already seen that he was a decent man.

Gracie entered the small bathroom and closed the door behind her. She locked it. Wrong. That only added insult to injury. In an act so foreign to her that it required a leap of faith she hadn't taken since she'd run away six years ago, she unlocked the door. Right.

AUSTIN HEARD THE lock click and disappointment hit him. Then Gracie unlocked it and he smiled. Progress. He listened to the shower turn on and stay on for a long time; Gracie must be making full use of the hot water. Good. She needed it and it would give him a chance to call his mom. He picked up his cell, but didn't dial right away, just stared at the wall, steeling himself.

Tension that hadn't been there five minutes ago tightened his neck. He rolled his shoulders, but it didn't ease.

He should have checked in earlier. *Should*. Too much of his relationship with his mom was clouded with too many *shoulds*.

Well, you didn't call earlier, so quit with the guilt trip and do it now.

No phone call had ever been tougher to make. A moment later, she answered.

"Hey, Mom. It's me."

Silence. What else had he expected? People didn't change overnight just because others wanted them to.

"How are you? Did Deputy Turner stop by today?"

A long hesitation followed, but he wouldn't break it. The ball was in her court.

Finally, he heard, "He came by," in the small voice he knew too well. He could hear the subtext as clearly as a bell: *I'm helpless. I need you.*

It tugged at him, but he hardened himself.

"Good. I'm glad he visited."

"He didn't bring me anything."

"No reason he should. The milk would still be good. You'll have enough fresh fruit and vegetables for the next few days."

"He said you shouldn't have gone and left me alone."

Austin doubted that. Turner had been one of the ones urging him to get away. Mom must have misinterpreted something the deputy said. Deliberately, no doubt.

"Mother." Austin kept his tone firm. "You're not an invalid. You're only fifty. You *can* take care of yourself. You have no diseases, no dementia."

She made a sound that was hard to characterize. It might have been a humph. He'd called her on her so-called helplessness in the past, and yet he still took care of her.

Breathe deeply. Hold. Exhale the guilt.

"Listen, I have to go," he said. "I'm meeting Finn for dinner."

"Go. Have fun." Her clipped words came out loaded with resentment.

Holding his anger in check, Austin decided he'd better cut the call short. "I'll call again tomorrow. Good night, Mom."

He tossed the phone onto the bed. Better than throwing it at the wall.

For years, he'd been trying to rehabilitate his mother, to prop her up, and he was exhausted from taking care of her. It had to end soon. He was sick of it. She—

A sound of distress from the bathroom caught his attention.

Gracie! In her weakened state, had she fallen? He barged in.

CHAPTER THREE

GRACIE STOOD BENT over the toilet with a towel wrapped around her, shivering and retching.

As far as Austin could tell, nothing was coming up.

"You must be pretty well cleaned out by now." He rubbed her back, all of the knobs and bones and sharp edges along her spine. Too bad she'd lost her lunch. She sure needed the calories.

Austin grasped her shoulders and held her steady while she retched some more. "Don't think you're going to lose anything else. I think you're done."

She nodded. "Why are you in here?"

"Heard you retching."

"Crap on a broomstick," she said like it was some kind of badass imprecation. Austin grinned until she burst into tears.

Aw, goddamn, he hated to see a woman cry. He held her and patted her back awkwardly, because this wasn't how he usually held a woman. He never hugged strangers. At least she was clean now and smelled like flowers and coconut.

She hiccupped and cursed again. "I don't *do* this," she said and he could tell she wanted to sound fierce. Hard to do when her teeth chattered like a pair of maracas.

"Don't do what?" He led her into the bedroom.

"I don't cry. Ever. I haven't in…" He wasn't sure but he thought she was doing calculations in her head. "Six years. I haven't cried in six years. This is so dumb."

He rummaged in his bag and pulled out a hoodie and a T-shirt. "Put these on."

He turned his back while she dressed.

She hissed, "Don't go thinking I'm weak just because I cried." He heard the zipper rasp on his hoodie.

When he turned back to her, her cheeks were bright red, hot against her pale skin. Nothing worse than having a woman cry and then having her get angry 'cause you saw her doing it.

"I don't think you're weak." He watched her dig through her bag until she came out with a comb. "You're one of the strongest women I've met."

From the way she looked at him, she didn't know what to do with his compliment. She entered the bathroom and he followed. She dropped the comb into the sink and poured a few drops of body wash on it.

Good. He'd hate to see her using something dirty to comb her clean hair.

"What was the crying about?"

She studied him in the mirror, pale eyes challenging, embarrassed but tough. "That food wasted. I needed it, really need the nutrition. It's been a rough couple of days."

More than a couple, he guessed.

Her face went hard-edged, as though she had to be superstrong now that he'd seen her vulnerable.

Note to self, Austin. Do not, I repeat, do not show pity.

Man, she was tough. A couple of the women he'd dated in Ordinary would have played the pity card for all it was worth. Not this woman.

"I need to brush my teeth." Her stomach made gurgling noises. "I'd better not go out to dinner."

Despite the sadness lurking in her eyes, the clear regret at missing another meal, Austin kept his tone neutral, saying only, "I don't think you should, either. Stay here."

He left the bathroom and heard her brush her teeth. While she finished cleaning up, he called room service. She might not be able to go out for supper, but she should eat something, or she would be starving by morning.

GRACIE LEFT THE BATHROOM, wishing she could hide in there all night.

How humiliating to have cried in front of Austin. She hadn't cried since she'd learned of Jay's infidelity. Once she'd gotten that out of her system, she hadn't planned to ever cry again for the rest of her life.

So why today? And why in front of a stranger?

Because I've almost reached the end of my road—and my rope—and I'm exhausted.

Hunger had left her depleted. No other explanation for it.

She stopped and stared. Austin had lined the middle of the bed with the spare pillows in the room and had put an extra folded blanket on top of her side of the bed. He'd even turned down the covers.

Such thoughtfulness. Oh. Waterworks threatened again. *Stop it. What's wrong with you?*

Nothing! I'm not going to cry, okay? I'm just really, really moved.

Maybe this would work. Maybe they could sleep in the same bed tonight without it being too awkward.

Austin stood across the room beside the window, leaning on the frame, big and calm and about as perfect as a man could be, except for a small scar beside his left eye.

He must have shoved his fingers through his hair because it lay in sexy, rumpled waves. She wanted to straighten it out, but no. That would be a *big* mistake.

Hands off, Gracie. You don't need to be attracted to a man right now. You haven't been for six years. Why start now when you're so close to the end?

What really appealed to her, though, was underneath the great facade. Inside that broad chest beat an understanding heart. The man gave too much. She was a stranger who'd picked his pocket. He should have given her nothing more than a night in jail.

Instead, he'd shown compassion and it made him too attractive, had her yearning for things that could never be.

She glanced back at the bed. Maybe it would still

be awkward. She hadn't been attracted to a man since Jay, probably because she'd been preoccupied with survival, but Austin had taken care of that for tonight, and that made her warm, soft and fuzzy when she needed to keep up her defenses the most. If she wasn't careful, she would let her guard down.

Don't forget who you really are. This man must never find out the truth about you.

You're almost home free.

She had a long way to go before she could relax into her new, safe life. She didn't need anyone getting in her way.

Lucky for him she was too sick to complain about it. She had both her pride and her independence to consider. She didn't need anyone to take care of her. She'd grown sick to death of handlers in her old life.

A residual rumble overturned her stomach. Yeah, all right. She would let him take care of her, but only for one night.

She crawled under the blankets and pulled the covers over her like a cocoon, running her hand across the cheap comforter with the ubiquitous bland design. In her old life, she'd slept in the best hotels, but no bed had ever felt better than this one did.

She hadn't realized how fortunate she'd been in some areas of her old life until it was all gone.

Someone knocked on the door and Gracie assumed it would be Finn, but a bellhop came in with a tray, setting it onto the small table and leaving after Austin tipped him.

Food.

"What's that?" she asked. "I thought you were going out with Finn."

"I am. This is for you. Sit up."

For her? How much was she going to owe by the time they parted, and how was she going to pay him? One haircut wouldn't cover it. Whatever the bellhop had brought in smelled good and her stomach grumbled. Austin was going out to dinner. If she didn't eat the food, it would go to waste.

She sat up and leaned against the headboard.

Austin brought a steaming bowl to her. "Here." He grasped a pillow from his side of the bed and put in on her lap then set the bowl on top of it.

Chicken soup. It smelled even better than it looked.

"Take a few sips. Make sure it sits well in your stomach. I also ordered a poached egg and toast."

She hated poached eggs, but she would eat it. Gladly.

He folded his arms across his chest while his cheeks turned pink as though his own kindness embarrassed him. The masculinity of his biceps exaggerated by his crossed arms in contrast to the vulnerability of his blush charmed her. "I don't really know what you like, other than eating too much too fast."

"I was starving. You would have eaten the same way if you were in my situation." The words spurted forth hot and defensive before she realized he was teasing her.

"Sorry," she mumbled.

Unflappable, he ordered, "Try the soup."

Did nothing upset this guy?

How about having his wallet stolen?

Oh, yeah. He hadn't liked that. Otherwise, though, he looked like he could withstand a cyclone, mayhem and anarchy all at the same time and still keep his cool.

Even when she'd robbed him, he'd seemed angry, yes, but she'd only feared being sent to jail and the notoriety that would cause. She hadn't worried that he'd hurt her. And wasn't that strange considering she hadn't known him.

His posture, his demeanor, everything about him screamed *decency*.

She sipped the soup. It slid warmly down her chest like sunlight pouring through an open window. It hit her stomach with a resounding *aaaaah.* "It's good." Just as the bed felt amazing, she didn't think soup had ever tasted as good, even though it was modest. She sipped more, eating it carefully although she wanted to inhale it.

While she ate, Austin went into the bathroom and showered. When he came out, hair damp and smelling of soap, he asked, "How does your stomach feel?"

"Good. Stable. I think I'll survive."

He lifted the cover from a plate on the tray and brought it to her.

"Sorry it's not much. I didn't want you throwing up again."

"Me, either." She took a bite of toast. After she chewed and swallowed, she asked, "Why are you being so nice to me?" She didn't mean to sound cynical, but life on the road had taught her a lot about people, and their often questionable motives.

Sliding his wallet into the back pocket of a clean pair of jeans, he shrugged then strode to the door, all without meeting her eyes. "See you later." He hustled out into the hallway as though she'd threatened to shoot him.

So, he had secrets. Fair enough. She had hers, too.

Going slowly, she finished her meal. When she got out of bed, her legs gave out and her ankle ached.

She'd let herself go too long without nourishment.

Taking baby steps and small movements, she retrieved her knapsack from a chair then got back under the blankets and opened it. She didn't have much time. Austin could be gone for a few hours, or as little as one, and she had work to do.

First, she took out her notebook and snagged the room service menu from the bedside table. She calculated how much the meal had cost Austin and then added what she thought he would tip.

Men tended to tip better than women, and he was a generous guy, so she guessed the tip would have been good.

She added the total to the sum she already owed him and returned the book to the outside pocket of her knapsack.

Shoving aside her old clothing, she pulled her laptop from the big inner section. Crazy to own a laptop, even if it was ancient, and not sell it for food, but this machine fed her soul. It also brought in the only bits of money she earned while on the road.

With a little luck, the room would have Wi-Fi. Most did these days.

She booted up her computer and opened her blog then eased herself out of the harsh reality of her life and into her fantasy world.

When she was ready, she started to type.

Dear readers,

I'm sitting here in (Where should she be today?) the Langhe region of Italy on a stone terrace looking out on (she glanced around the generic hotel room, bland by anyone's standards) the Nebbiolo vineyards with their soft hillsides in the distance, the evening sun turning them to gold. I'm sipping a glass of the excellent local Barolo, which is made from the grapes grown below. Heavenly. Day after day, grapes bathe in the warm, magical sunlight particular to the Mediterranean and scent the region with their sweetness. Then the little darlings are plucked and made into the delectable wine for which the region is known.

I sit here contemplating how good life is, how one needs little more than the sun on one's face and a glass of wine for all to seem right with the world. The ennui of daily life fades to nothing and one is left in a state of bliss.

She cast long tentacles into her memory to fill out the post, unearthing details of her own trips to Italy years ago, memories flowing from her fingertips like old friends. Those were the days. Only they weren't. All of the beauty of the land couldn't erase everything around those trips. The people. The circus atmosphere. The dreadful hoopla. Here, in her blog, she shared only the best. When she felt she had shared enough, she closed off.

Tomorrow will find me in La Morra and the day after in the Barbaresco wine region, where I will visit Neive, a picturesque town, and later will sample the delightful Spumante in Alto Monferrato.

Until then, fellow travelers, be well. *Arrivederci.*

Lina Vittorio

Gracie Travers posted the blog—yes, the room had Wi-Fi—turned off her computer and sighed.

Thank goodness for her alter ego, Lina, who gave her a rich pretend life. Where would she be without her fantasies to lighten the unrelenting darkness of her reality?

She had once traveled those very roads in Italy, but that was a long, long time ago, with the few golden moments committed to memory. She'd been a girl then. Now she was a twenty-nine-year-old woman, alone, with no one to depend on but herself. That suited her just fine, most of the time, except for those rare moments when it wasn't enough. When she wanted more. When loneliness could no longer be kept at bay.

Stop it, Gracie. Save the pity party for a night when you aren't sitting cozy and warm in a soft bed.

If wishes were horses, she would either really be in Italy, or she would live in the home of her dreams, nothing grand, just a roof over her head and regular meals. Despite her upbringing, she wasn't spoiled. She really did need very little, only the basics. *Food.*

Now so close to the end of her odd, self-imposed lifestyle, she had reached her limit. She could no longer tolerate the moving, having no place to call home, without anchor, companionship or loved ones. In her travels, she'd envied each and every couple she met and the homes they lived in, whether large farmhouses on rural land, or tiny urban bungalows on postage-stamp lots.

She wanted to belong, but on her own terms, and so she kept on traveling.

She'd been on the move for too long and it exhausted her, but what else could she do? She had only one talent and had already tapped it dry. Too early. A burnout and she wasn't even thirty yet.

Crap, she was tired. She closed her eyes to rest. Just for a minute.

"WHAT THE *HELL* are you doing?" Finn eyed Austin across the restaurant table with the mulish jut to his jaw that had been there since Austin had picked up Gracie. Finn was a good guy in general, solid, salt of the earth and all that, but he could get mad like nobody's business. "Haven't you had enough of taking care of a woman? You need to cut yourself some slack and just have a good time."

Austin figured Finn had a right to be angry. This was their buddy fishing vacation. They'd both needed this for a long time and had turned themselves inside out to make sure it happened, Finn by getting a veterinarian from the next county to cover his calls, and Austin by dealing with his mother.

"Let it go, Finn."

"I can't. You're being irresponsible."

Austin couldn't have heard that right. "Irresponsible? Me? I'm the most responsible guy on the planet."

"Yeah, okay, maybe that was the wrong word. How about impulsive?" Finn amended.

Impulsive fit. It never had before, but it did where Gracie was concerned.

Her hunger, her need, resonated with him, but there was more. He liked the fight within her, her drive for independence and her refusal to give in. He even kind of understood why she'd stolen from him. But, cripes, the woman needed a long-term goal to get herself into a safer life.

"You shouldn't be doing this, man."

No, he shouldn't, but Finn had his own thing going on, too.

"What about you?" Austin asked.

"What about me?"

"We're on vacation, but you're going to see a girl you knew nearly twenty years ago. Why?"

"She needs help."

"So does Gracie."

"Gracie is a stranger."

"So's your friend."

"Nope. We've been in touch for ten years."

"But you haven't seen her in twenty."

"So what? When I told her we were going to Denver, she asked me to stop in on the way." He picked at his food. "Don't you remember how great she was?"

"I wasn't in your orbit at that time. I was a year younger than you and you were new in town. I heard a bit about it, but not much." He'd been too busy trying to find sustenance and keep body and soul together.

"But you know the story, right? It was huge. The paper carried it for a week."

Austin didn't remind Finn that the only newspapers he ever saw as a kid were at the bottom of trash bins covered in garbage. He shook his head.

"Her mom was driving past my dad's ranch just as a deer jumped out. She crashed into the tree at the end of our driveway and the car caught fire. Man, I'll never forget how brave my dad was that day. Melody's mother got thrown from the car, but Melody was trapped in the backseat. Dad didn't hesitate. Just reached right into the fire and pulled her out. Saved her life."

The waitress hovered ready to pour more coffee, her eyes on Finn. He'd inherited his dad's good looks.

"That's cool." Finn's father was cool. Austin, yet again, felt the lack of a father figure in his life. Every boy should have a father. Austin had had two of them. One had died when he was only six and the other hadn't wanted him.

Not that he cared.

Really.

For the tenth time, Finn glanced across the street.

Austin checked out what he kept looking at. Storefronts. What was so interesting? Ah. The apartments above them.

"She's in one of those, isn't she? That's why you chose this restaurant?"

Finn nodded.

"Are you going to see her after dinner?"

He shook his head. "She isn't expecting me until tomorrow. I'll go across after breakfast."

Finn had a lot of confidence. So why the edginess? "Why are you nervous about seeing her?"

"She left town suddenly. One minute she was there and the next gone. I never had a chance to say goodbye."

"You're angry about that?"

Finn's mouth angled grimly down on one side. "You know what? You see too much."

"I had to learn to be perceptive." Living with an alcoholic did that to a kid.

"Yeah, I'm still angry," Finn admitted, "but I want to see her, too. We've been writing letters for over ten years. Well, she writes letters. I email my responses. Had enough writing in college." He placed his cutlery across his empty plate and pushed it away. "Melody's no stranger. And she isn't a pickpocket. There's no similarity between our situations."

Austin shrugged. Maybe not.

He felt Finn watching him. Finn knew him about as well as anyone did. He probably thought he knew what Austin was thinking.

"This has nothing to do with my mom." Even to Austin's own ears, he sounded defensive. "This is nothing like dealing with Mom."

"No? You take your first vacation ever. We're barely more than a day away from home, and you pick up a stranger. A mighty sad one, I might add."

He thought of Gracie taking small sips of the soup he'd ordered when he knew she wanted to gulp it down. He thought of her tears when she'd lost the last of her lunch. Yeah, sad, for sure. But strong, too, with a lot of pride. He liked that about her.

"She's got problems, Austin. That woman is trouble. Why'd you bring her here?"

Good question.

Figuring he might as well be honest with his best friend and himself, he answered, "I don't know."

FINN STOOD IN front of his hotel-room door and watched Austin walk down the hallway to his own room, hating this tension between them. They'd been best buds for a dozen years. They weren't normally like this.

It was that woman's fault.

"Hey!" he called, not sure why except wanting to get back on good terms with his buddy.

Austin turned around, walking backward to his room at the end of the corridor. "What?"

"Don't forget to keep a hundred bucks handy for when I catch the biggest fish on this trip."

"In your dreams." Austin grinned and spread his arms. "That hundred bucks has my name on it."

Austin entered his room and Finn stepped into his own, breathing a little easier. Things were good. No permanent damage done.

He should have been honest with Austin. He wasn't nervous about seeing Melody. Nope, not nervous. Terrified.

Holy freakin' Batman was he scared.

Ever since the day a couple of weeks before his twelfth birthday when he'd watched his dad pull Melody out of a burning car, he'd been fascinated by her.

Every kid had pivotal moments in his childhood. That had been one of his. Man, oh, man, to see Remington Caldwell as a hero. To see that girl pulled out alive, but with her hair afire. To watch his dad put out the flames with his bare hands.

It didn't matter that he hadn't known at the time that the guy was his father. He had been a hero to Finn ever since. What a bonus it had been to learn, a couple of weeks later, that the great courageous man was also his dad.

His mom, a nurse, had made him visit Melody in the hospital. He'd dragged his heels. What boy his age wouldn't have at being forced to visit a sick girl?

Melody had been a revelation. Despite all she'd gone through, she'd had more character and spunk than any other kid he'd ever met.

Even in a hospital room with a turban of bandages

around her head, she'd been beautiful and strong-willed. She wouldn't let him get away with any of his "boy" crap, and he'd respected that.

Hell, he didn't even know what color her hair was.

Finn sat on the bed, took his wallet out of his pocket and slipped out the photo taken of him and Melody in her white turban of bandages at his birthday party at Grandma Caldwell's house.

They perched on each side of the bed, flanking his grandma. Grandma C looked down at Melody with a drunken smile, courtesy of the stroke she'd suffered. In that not-quite-right smile there was affection. Even Grandma had liked Melody right away.

At one point during the party, Finn had run in from outside to find them asleep, Melody curled into a tight little ball against Grandma's side.

Something in his boy's heart had melted, shifted. Nothing had been the same since.

He smiled down at the photo. He hadn't looked at the thing in years, had refused to. He'd been so damned angry with her for leaving the way she had, without a word to the boy who'd fallen for her hard.

Then, after a nearly ten-year silence, a letter had arrived. From Melody. From the girl who epitomized perfection. And Finn had fallen all over again.

Those letters were damned fine. The woman could write. She could probably sell snow to the Inuit. She'd melted his resistance and he discovered that inside his grown man there was still that twelve-year-old boy who'd never stopped waiting for Melody Chase to return.

In the past ten years, her letters had come from a P.O. box, not a home address. Until this evening, he hadn't known if she lived in a house, an apartment or a condo. She'd shared her dreams, her fears, tidbits about her life as a journalist, but not enough else, and he was starving for more. He didn't know where she'd been, or why she had waited a freakin' decade to contact him.

Where *had* she been? What *had* she been up to? Had she been safe? And that had always been at the root of his anger, of his unreasonable urge to see a girl he really barely knew. Was she safe? For years, he had worried.

And then, a letter.

How are you? Where are your comics? Why can't I find them in the bookstores? On the internet?

And then, her heart-rattling, *I've thought about you. I think of you.*

And his heart had exploded, expanded and then rearranged itself into familiar patterns. Or not, like a bone reset, but not quite aligned. He'd been off-balance and wanting to see her ever since.

She hadn't allowed him to visit. He didn't know why.

A month ago, she'd changed her mind.

Come. I need help.

And here he was.

And tomorrow morning, he would see her again.

GRACIE'S EYES POPPED OPEN. She came awake suddenly, unsure what had disturbed her. A quick glance around the room confirmed that she was still alone. She caught her computer a split second before it slid from her lap to the floor.

Then she heard it—Austin's voice in the hallway. Crap! She tossed aside the covers and had only just gotten the laptop back into her knapsack when he came through the door. What would the guy say if he knew she owned a computer?

She tried to look casual. "Hey."

"Hey, yourself." He looked from her to her bag and his eyes were full of suspicion. Maybe he thought she did drugs. Not her. She was one of the lucky ones. She'd survived without them, and without alcohol, too, unlike many of her colleagues. She'd chosen a more literal escape from reality—running away and living on the road.

Austin's cop's eyes bothered her. She didn't like it when he looked at her with pity, but she didn't like this hard edge, either. She wanted that sweet, caring tenderness of earlier.

Come on, Gracie. You know how to act. You can do better to put off his suspicions.

"How was dinner?" That sounded more natural. She wandered back to the bed and slid under the covers. "Where did you go?"

"Mexican restaurant down the street."

"Mexican." She heard the longing in her own voice. She loved Mexican. "What did you have?"

"Enchiladas."

"Oh." She adored them. She salivated. "Were they good?"

"For a small town, yeah, surprisingly good." He tilted his head. "You sure do like to talk about food."

"I think about it, dream about it, fantasize, plan when I can eat again. Yeah, it's a big part of my psyche these days."

He nodded as though he understood, but how could he? He had a good job and, she presumed, a roof over his head. She doubted he ever went hungry or wore hand-me-downs, or worse, ate something found in the garbage. He couldn't possibly relate to homeless life.

"Did the meal stay down?" he asked.

"It stayed down, probably because it was small. I nodded off after I ate. That helped."

"Are you still hungry?"

"Always."

Humor crinkled the corners of Austin's eyes. He had nice eyes, blue and bright, warm when he let down his cop's guard. He picked up the phone from the bedside table. "What do you want?"

"Anything."

"You mean that, don't you?"

"Yes. I'll eat anything you order. Except maybe raw fish. I doubt I could keep that down right now."

Austin's smile lit up his face like fireworks piercing the night sky. She could sell tickets to the women staying in the hotel and make a bundle. Lordy, lordy.

"Doubt it's on the menu," he said.

Gracie returned his smile, surprised how good it felt to be playful with this man, to not be serious and worried every second of the day.

"Grilled cheese okay with you?"

"That would be good, yeah."

He ordered a sandwich for her and a big bag of chips and a soda for himself. After they arrived, he pulled off his cowboy boots and settled himself on top of the covers, leaning against the headboard and shoving chips into his mouth while she ate a sandwich made with two cheeses on whole wheat bread, forcing herself to slow down and savor each bite. The last thing she needed was to screw up her stomach again.

Austin picked up the TV remote. "Let's see if there's anything on worth watching."

When Gracie finished the sandwich, Austin caught her licking butter and grease from her fingers. She flushed. "I'm sorry. My manners have slipped while I've been on the road."

"How long has that been?"

"Since I—" The sentence came to a screeching halt, like tires squealing before a car wreck. His casual tone had nearly sucked her into betraying her secrets. The ambience of the room, the low lighting that cast a soft glow on one end of a dark room, the camaraderie of two people sitting on a bed watching TV together as friends do, had lulled her. The situation was so unusual for her that she'd been seduced into trusting this stranger.

Frantic, she rebuilt the mental barriers that had slipped. Even so, part of her still wanted to pretend she could enjoy some of this time together. The pillows running the length of the bed between them offered the illusion of safety. She could appreciate his company without fear of him wanting more.

He flipped the channels, pausing briefly on a couple doing the dirty.

"Um," she murmured. "We should watch something other than porn." It had been so long, she couldn't remember how making love felt. This man stretched beside her, in his confident easy male glory, made her sap run.

None of that, she ordered her unruly libido.

"Probably a good idea to switch." He sounded subdued. "Let's see what else is on." He flipped channels.

"Hey! The Television Food Network. I want to watch."

"You would. Naw. Let's find a movie."

They settled on *The Bourne Identity*. "This movie's great," Austin said.

"Macho spy thriller full of action. No wonder you like it."

"Matt Damon looking pretty buff. No wonder *you* like it."

"He's okay." She tried to sound nonchalant while her eyes were glued to the set. Buff understated it. He didn't hold a candle to Austin, though.

She never saw the end of the movie, just quietly slipped under the covers when sleep claimed her. She thought she felt someone pull the covers over her shoulders.

CHAPTER FOUR

THE HEAT AGAINST his chest and belly burned with a flame Austin hadn't felt in too long. His thumb stroked skin as velvety as the leaves of the geraniums he'd planted in pots in the spring, for his mother. Not that she'd noticed.

The woman in his arms smelled of coconut and exotic flowers.

His lips found her neck, her tiny mewls of pleasure a waterfall of delight.

He came awake slowly, the dream too good to give up, his hands caressing and exploring soft skin. She curled against him as though she could burrow inside of him. Whomever he'd slept with last night sure was affectionate.

Slept with!

His eyes flew open.

Gracie lay nestled against him as sweetly as a puppy against its mother. There was nothing sexual in the way her fingers curled around his arm, or the way her forehead lay in the curve of his neck, but it was morning, he was male, and she female. His first thoughts had been sexual.

If she knew, she would hate him for it. He knew

she didn't want him to think of her as vulnerable, but he did. She was. What would she think of him if she knew he wanted her?

He shouldn't have made that nasty remark yesterday about her being too thin, but he'd been sick of her accusing him of being interested in only one thing and he'd snapped. What would she think if she woke up now and noticed that his body sure didn't mind her being so thin?

Before she could feel the effect she had on him, he eased out of bed. Like a trusting puppy, she followed him, murmuring in her sleep, her hand caressing his arm. He found the gesture poignant and sweet, his thoughts changing, no longer sexual, but tender. He should move, get away from her, but he liked this natural, honest woman with her prickly defenses down.

The pillows he'd used to separate them had been tossed to the floor sometime during the night. He was pretty sure it hadn't been by him.

She didn't stir. He glanced at the clock. Seven.

The sun shimmering through the sheer curtains lit her face with a soft glow. Her hair, clean now and blue-black in morning sunlight, framed high cheekbones, a sharp chin and a stubborn jawline. Those fierce raven's-wing eyebrows were less intimidating in sleep.

Her cheeks glowed pink against alabaster skin.

She cleaned up well.

Looking younger and not as hard-edged as she had

yesterday, was this the real Gracie? Or was yesterday's tough woman the real one?

He didn't know. She had secrets. That much he could tell. She could keep them. He hardened his heart against the tenderness of a few moments ago. He didn't need to carry anyone else's burdens.

He grabbed a clean T-shirt and underwear, and yesterday's jeans, and went to the bathroom to shower and get dressed. No sense having her wake up and catching him semi-aroused. She would stop trusting him.

So what? After breakfast, he would never see her again. He and Finn would be on their way to fish until they were sick of it.

GRACIE LAY STILL until she heard the bathroom door close and the shower turn on. Then she exhaled the breath she'd been holding since she'd rolled over and tried to follow the warmth of arms that had let her go too soon.

When her mind had registered where she was, who she was with and what she was doing, she had lain still with her eyes closed. Awkward.

Austin had rocketed out of the bed, probably propelled by her trying to cuddle with him, and most likely disgusted by her skinny body.

Tough.

People got thin when they didn't have enough to eat.

She rubbed her arms. The room wasn't cold, but she wanted him and his heat back anyway.

Those few moments before she had realized she was in the arms of a man she shouldn't be with had been glorious.

It had been too long.

Which one of them breached the barrier Austin constructed yesterday evening? Probably her. A cuddler by nature, she missed it more than anything else, maybe even more than regular meals.

Jay had been good at cuddling. That was about the only positive memory she had of him, and about the only compliment she could give him. It had taken her four years to discover just how big a mistake she'd made when she married him. She hadn't known him at all. Since the divorce, she hadn't looked back.

She missed his hugs, though. Any human contact, in fact. Sensory deprivation was a tough thing.

She wanted to touch people. She'd had too little of it in her past life. Maybe that's why she'd been drawn to Jay, and willing to overlook his flaws for too long, because he'd offered a warm pair of arms and a solid chest to cuddle against. Not to mention she'd been young and naive enough to believe his lies.

She crawled out of bed. She didn't want to. It was the first clean bed she'd slept in in a long time. The first real bed, clean or otherwise. Her pillowcase smelled like a tropical island from her hair.

She pulled on her pants, so Austin wouldn't see how skinny her legs had gotten. She used to have shapely legs. They were strong from all the walking, but too thin, pared to the bone by the miles she'd traveled.

When Austin stepped out of the bathroom in jeans and a snug-fitting white T-shirt, he looked good enough to have her consider climbing back into bed with him, and that was a shocker. She hadn't been attracted to a man since Jay.

In fact, she'd thought her libido had died with news of his infidelities. Yes, plural. Devastating.

Boy, had she been wrong. Apparently, her libido had only been dormant and waiting for the right man to bring it raging back to life.

A drop of water fell from Austin's damp hair and landed on his neck.

If she knew him well, if they were a couple, she would walk right over and lick it off and who knew where that might lead.

In those first few months, when Jay had still been wooing her, she'd adored the love play, the giggling, the sex.

Yes, sex. She missed it. Six years was a long time to go without.

Stop. Austin isn't for you. No man is. Stop thinking about love games and desire. You can't have them.

No sense getting maudlin and wishing for things that couldn't be hers. Time to screw on her head right, to put the practical ahead of the whimsical.

It was time for her to hit the road. Before she did, she was taking one more shower and washing her hair again, just for the pure pleasure of it.

She didn't say a word when she passed Austin and closed the door behind her. Neither did he.

Did he feel as awkward as she did?

She had gone to bed with a stranger, and had awakened in his arms. Oh, those arms. Oh, that warm touch.

Get a grip, Gracie.

As though she might not be able to use conditioner for another year, she slathered it on, even though her hair was short. She cut it regularly. Herself. It showed.

When she finished washing and dressing, she forced herself to look in the mirror. Austin's body had reacted to her purely as any man's would to waking up with any woman. What man would want *her*—an escapee from a Charles Dickens novel, a waif with big eyes in a too-narrow face, who wore ragged clothing and picked pockets for a living? Well, not for a living, but that was what she'd done to Austin yesterday.

Too bad he'd been a cop.

Too bad he was a decent guy.

She'd met every kind of person on the road. She could have stolen a wallet from a jerk, but no, she had unwittingly dipped her fingers into the pocket of the most decent guy she'd met in years. And, in the space of twenty-four hours, she already liked him.

Don't go getting any ideas. It's because he didn't have you arrested when he could have. This is nothing more than gratitude, pure and simple.

Even so, she liked him more than she should, and far too quickly. Holy crapola. She needed to get away from him.

She left the bathroom to find Austin already packed and on the phone.

"Okay, we'll see you in fifteen minutes." He hung up.

He turned from the window. "Good morning."

She said the same thing, just as quietly.

"Are you hungry?"

"Starved."

"What else is new?" he teased, as though they were good friends used to ribbing each other. "Come on. Let's get going. Finn's waiting."

"Go where?"

"To breakfast."

"You know I don't have money. You fed me yesterday and last night and paid for this hotel room. I can't take any more from you."

"What are you going to do about breakfast?"

"Nothing."

"Listen, I'm not going to let you walk away hungry. It isn't in me to do that."

She wanted food. She wanted what this man had to offer with no strings attached. He'd sure proven his decency last night. She'd curled against him and he hadn't taken advantage. Other men would have. But it hurt to take, to compromise her independence. She couldn't do it.

"It's too hard for me to keep taking from you. I'll go for breakfast—thanks—but only if we come back here afterward and you let me give you the haircut I promised."

He ran his fingers through his hair, leaving ridges in the damp waves. "That bad, huh?"

No. Not bad at all. "A bit." She liked it long, but needed to give him something and this was all she had to offer.

"Okay." He stuck out his hand to shake. "Deal."

She took it with a sigh, relief flooding her. She didn't like dealing with people, didn't like owing, and no longer liked giving. Her current motto, *Live and let live, and leave me alone,* had served her well for six years. No need to change it now.

She would cut his hair, then leave. Run. Get away from this guy who tempted her with possibilities that just couldn't be.

He zipped up his bag. "I'm done packing. Let's go."

"What about your other stuff?" she asked.

"What stuff?"

"The shampoo and conditioner, the body wash and toothpaste you bought yesterday."

"Those are yours."

"Mine?" she squeaked. Whole bottles. Not samples she managed to pick up at drug stores. Or tiny travel bottles that lasted through two shampoos.

"You think I want to walk around smelling like coconut and pineapples and strawberries? Go get it and pack it."

Feet on fire, she scrambled back to the bathroom. No *way* was she leaving *anything* behind. She picked up everything he'd bought, but also took the bottles provided by the hotel. In the garbage can, she found the paper from the tiny bar of hotel soap and wrapped the bit that was left after Austin had used it. Waste not, want not.

It all went into her backpack.

When she left the room, he said, "You don't have to carry that with you. We'll be coming back after breakfast to check out."

"This goes with me. I take it everywhere."

"The room will be locked."

"It goes with me." It was a point on which she never compromised. Everything she owned was in her bag. Like a turtle, she carried her home with her. It wasn't much, and it was cheap stuff, but it was all she had.

She walked with him out of the hotel and down the street until they stopped in front of a Mexican restaurant.

"Is this the one you mentioned last night?"

"Yep."

"I'm going to order enchiladas."

"I don't know. It's breakfast. You might want huevos rancheros."

"Ooh. You have a point."

He reached past her to open the door. So strange. No one ever treated the homeless, the nomads of the world, with courtesy. Most times people ignored them, or didn't see them, the invisible of the streets.

With the slightest touch at the base of her back, he directed her into the restaurant ahead of him. It should have offended her. She could make her way into a building on her own, thank you very much, but that feather-light, brief and respectful touch charmed her.

Mr. Decency.

"Finn might already be here," he said.

He wasn't. They got a booth by the window to wait for him.

They spotted him standing across the street in front of a low-rise apartment building, unmoving.

"What's he doing?"

"His friend lives there. He's going to visit her while we're passing through. He hasn't seen her since they were kids." He gestured with his chin toward Finn. "That's why we stopped to stay here last night instead of driving straight through to Denver."

Austin pushed his menu aside. "You should let me drive you to Denver."

"No."

"That's it? No discussion. No *thank you for the offer.*"

Gracie blushed. "I don't mean to sound ungrateful. Thank you for the offer, but no."

The waitress poured them coffee.

"Finn might be a while. Let's go ahead and order."

Thank goodness. The smells in this place had Gracie's mouth watering. She ordered huevos rancheros. So did Austin.

Who was this guy who treated her so well? While they waited for their food, she asked, "What's your story?"

He paused with his coffee cup halfway to his mouth. "My story?"

"Yes. Where are you from?"

"Ordinary, Montana."

The waitress brought a basket of warm tortillas. Gracie took one and bit into it. Heaven.

"Have you lived there all your life?" Her fascination with happy homes and secure childhoods seeped through. She couldn't help sounding wistful.

"Yeah. I grew up there. The guy we're visiting in Denver was the sheriff when I was young. He influenced me to enter law enforcement." It sounded like an ideal life. Lucky guy.

"You said you're a deputy, right? Think you'll ever be sheriff?" She could see him in a position of authority. Easily.

"Probably."

"People have to vote for you."

"I treat the people of Ordinary with respect. They respect me in return."

She studied his face. No arrogance. "You're that sure of yourself? Think you can do the job?"

"I've been trained for it, but I also want to do it. It's my life's work. No doubts there."

His life's work. How did it feel to be so sure of yourself and your future that you'd already mapped out your life? How did it feel to know where you belonged?

"What about you?" he asked.

"What about me?"

"Why are you homeless?"

None of your business.

When she didn't respond, he said, "You're young and healthy with no apparent mental-health issues."

"How do you know?"

"I know." He sounded confident of her mental state, but how could he be? The guy didn't have a crystal ball.

He was right, though. Her mind was sound.

"So? Why are you homeless?"

Thank goodness their meals arrived. She ate without answering.

Holy leaping Batman.

Finn stood in front of the door to an apartment that might turn out to be a Pandora's box, once again channeling the twelve-year-old kid who'd loved comic books, for whom writing and illustrating comics were more important than anything else on earth—and he hadn't even seen the grown-up Melody yet, hadn't talked to her and or seen the changes adulthood had brought.

Back then, he'd had no interest in girls—until Melody had exploded into his life, and had appreciated his work. Had loved it.

He'd wanted to write and illustrate comic books for the rest of his life.

Where had that boy gone? He'd grown up and had left foolish dreams behind. He lived in the real world now, working as a vet with a steady income, not as the cartoonist he'd always thought he would be.

Aw, hell, everyone had to grow up at some point.

He jiggled the keys in his pocket.

Nuts, he shouldn't be this nervous, not as a grown man. His heart raced as though he were a scared kid who'd been locked in a dark basement. Crazy. Someone was playing a nasty trick on him, turning his nervous system into an arcade game, with balls of both excitement and dread careening every which way.

Melody Chase had played a trick on him twenty years ago when she'd run out of his life.

Come on, man, get real. She *didn't play the trick. She was a kid. She went where her mother told her to go when she told her to.*

Yeah, I know, but she never called. She never wrote.

He'd been crazy about her, but in her mind, he'd been what? A footnote? A blip on the radar of her existence? Just a boy who'd kept her distracted in the hospital with card games and cartoon drawings…and that was it? Was that all he'd been to her, while it had taken him too freaking long to get over her?

Yeah, he was still mad, even though he knew it was that twelve-year-old kid's unreasonable feelings that lingered. This wasn't the rational response of a grown man. He raised his hand to knock. He wanted to see Melody anyway, just to see if she was as perfect as in his memories.

How much had she changed? How much had he? Would she like what she saw? Did it matter? God, he'd been such a hopeless kid with a childish crush.

He was a thirty-two-year-old man now, not a boy given to flights of fancy.

He'd had plenty of girlfriends. No need to be nervous.

His knock echoed loudly in the empty hallway.

He'd measured all other women against his childish memories. Not fair to the women he'd dated. Not fair at all.

What if he'd imagined the crush *she'd* had on *him* all of those years ago?

Didn't matter. She was in trouble. She needed him. He was here.

He ran his fingers over his hair, bringing it under control. He should have gotten that homeless chick to trim it.

Footsteps approached the door from the other side. He swallowed.

The door opened…and there she was.

Melody.

Words backed up in his throat. He was a smart guy. He could string sentences together. Normally. Not now. Not a single word came to him other than her name.

"Melody." His voice broke. He cleared his throat.

She'd grown up, not much in height, but in maturity. So pretty.

Her smoky-gray eyes widened, misted, softened. "Finn," she whispered.

If she hadn't invited him here, if he'd met her on the street, he would have known her, would have recognized her striking face, and her full lips—the kind of lips a lot of women spent good money to get. He knew women's lips. These were real.

When his gran had been bedridden after a stroke, he'd painted comics on her bedroom wall to entertain her. Melody had been the heroine in those stories.

No wonder.

She could get any man's pulse racing.

They stared at each other, frozen in a bubble of both memory and anticipation. Tears formed in her soft eyes but her mutinous chin jutted forward. She'd always been a fighter, but what was she fighting now?

Her lips trembled and she pressed them together, defiance so clear on her face that Finn knew she'd fought this battle many times before.

He couldn't stand to watch her like this—defiant, yes, but also vulnerable, as though he might find her lacking in some way. What did she have to feel vulnerable about? Had she guessed he was still angry, even after all this time?

Gently, as though she were a wild and balky horse he had to calm, he wrapped his arms around her. The moment seemed to call for it.

A sigh slipped out of her and she melted against him, holding him close with her arms hard across his back. He sighed. He still meant something to her.

He nuzzled his chin against her soft dark hair, so damned glad it had grown back in after the fire. The damage hadn't been as great as he'd feared.

When she eased out of his embrace, he asked, "Can I come in or are you going to make me stand on this doorstep all day?"

A shaky laugh burst out of her. He remembered that laugh. "Yes, of course. Come in."

He stepped into a sparsely furnished but comfortable apartment. Nothing was cheap. Whatever she'd done with her life had been good. She wasn't in need.

His pulse beat in his ears. She was safe. All of those years of worry for nothing.

After the way she'd left town, he'd always worried. Before rational thought could stop his unruly tongue, he blurted what he'd been sure he could control. "Where the *hell* did you go?"

She'd come into his life in dramatic fashion and six weeks later had left just as dramatically.

He'd missed her, had *ached* for her, the lost friend who had never once, not *once,* bothered to stay in touch with him so he would know where she was, so he would know she'd cared as much about him as he had about her.

She'd never called to let him know she was *safe*.

How dare she disappear for so many years and then contact him ten years later, out of the blue, with letters. Great letters, yeah, but not *her,* and not to say *I'm coming back,* but only to chat. To touch bases. To give him piddly, stingy bits of her life, but not the whole thing.

She didn't answer. He gripped her shoulders and all of those years of worry spewed out of him. "Melody Chase, where the *hell* did you go?"

MELODY STARED AT the boy she'd dreamed about so many times over the years. He wasn't a boy any longer. He'd grown handsome like his father, not as tall, but lean and strong, his arms ropey and muscular. His vet work must include more than just domestic animals. But then, Ordinary, Montana, was a ranching community. He had to be a farm vet, too.

The women of Ordinary must crawl all over him, a modern-day James Dean with darker hair, but the same sexual intensity.

Thick hair curled in a wave back from a broad forehead. His black eyelashes were longer than hers, for Pete's sake, and framed silver-gray eyes.

Where her eyes were a soft smoky-gray, his were keen and sharp, with cleverness snapping like bed sheets hung out to dry in a brisk wind.

He'd grown more beautiful with age, while she'd become more bizarre.

Life wasn't fair.

But then, hadn't that been the story of her life?

Open-heart surgery when she was a kid and getting burned in a car accident at eleven, then spending years on the run, left a woman feeling somehow diminished, *less than* others, especially good-looking men.

He had a right to be angry. She had been taken away from Ordinary suddenly and hadn't contacted him for ten years.

"My mom wouldn't let me get in touch with you." But Melody knew she should have defied her and found *some* way to let him know she was safe.

Finn frowned. "Why not?"

"She was afraid my dad would find out."

"That's a stretch. It's not like the FBI was monitoring my mail."

"No, but Mom always worried. She was paranoid. You don't know what it's like to live with an abusive man. She did."

He relaxed his rigid stance, but only a fraction. "No, I don't."

She touched his arm. She didn't want him angry with her. She needed him, but more than that, she wanted his friendship. She'd lived too many years without friends when she was growing up. Those few weeks in Ordinary had been a lantern glowing in the darkness, with Finn the flame.

"Please, Finn. Sit so we can talk."

She didn't scare easily. She'd walked through hell many times over and had just kept on trudging.

Finn Franck Caldwell didn't scare her—but he did intimidate her with his perfect face and strong, perfect body.

From Finn's first glance when she'd opened the door to him, she knew he found her attractive. He might not, though, if he knew the full truth about her. She, on the other hand, had taken one look at him and had fallen all over again, just as she had as a young girl. Fast and hard. Leaving Ordinary and Finn had been the hardest thing she'd ever done.

Life wasn't fair.

"I didn't want to go. I had to. I had no choice. Mom did what was best for us." She led him to the sofa and sat down. "I loved Ordinary. I would have lived there forever."

"You would have liked growing up there."

Finn sat on the edge of the sofa as though he might jump up at any second. His left leg did a jig. Was he as nervous as she?

"What was wrong with your dad?" he asked. So strange that Finn was here speaking with a man's deep voice. "Why was he so angry that day?"

Melody sucked in a breath and held it. The words *father, embarrassment* and *danger* were all synonymous for her. It had been bad when she was eleven. It was even worse twenty years later.

"Was it a custody battle?" Finn asked. "Did your mom steal you from him?"

"No! My mom's a great person."

He took her hands in his, his grip strong and warm. "Easy. When you left so quickly, we had no way of knowing what had happened. All we could do was speculate. So you all ran away because he was abusive? For real?"

"Yes," she whispered. "Mom said he was awful to her when I was a baby, so she took me away."

Finn grimaced. "Aw, Melody, I'm sorry."

"When we came to Ordinary, it was our third time trying to get away from him."

"What's your real last name?"

She hesitated, wary enough to be crafty, to lie, but this was Finn, her first and only crush.

"Messina." She'd never told another living soul.

He nodded. "Where did you go?"

"All over the northwest. We eventually ended up in Seattle. It's a good city, but I wanted to live in a small town. As soon as I was old enough, I moved down here."

"Why not come back to Ordinary?"

"After the way we left? With my dad showing up at the hospital ranting and raving and the staff having to call the police?"

After the accident, her stay in the hospital had been protracted to give her scalp time to heal and to monitor for infection. She had been allowed out only once to attend Finn's birthday party two weeks after the accident, but then had to return to the hospital that evening. Another week later, her father had come to the hospital. They had panicked. She'd still had bandages on her head when they'd heard there was a man at the front desk looking for them.

That awful, violent surge of panic had been familiar. Her heartbeat stuttered now as she remembered. She'd been terrified. What if her father caught them and hurt her mother? After the initial burst of fear, a cleansing anger had rushed in.

Let him come, she'd thought. If he tried to hurt her mom, Melody would scratch his eyes out.

Mom had panicked, and Melody's nurse, Randy, too, because he and Mom had fallen for each other. Randy had gotten them all out the back door, into his SUV and out of Ordinary. He and Mom were married now and still lived together in Seattle.

Through Randy's grapevine at the hospital, they'd heard about her father's violent confrontation with the police. "See?" Mom had said. "That's why we run."

Melody leaned close to Finn. "How could I have faced you when the whole business had been so sudden and embarrassing. I was deeply ashamed. When you live on the run, you live with shame."

That wasn't the only thing that had kept her away, but Finn didn't need to know the rest.

"As soon as I was old enough, as soon as I knew my dad couldn't take me away from my mom, I mailed you that first letter."

"I was real glad to get it, Melody."

"So? Are we okay? Do you forgive me?"

"Yes."

She wasn't sure she believed him. The word was right, but he still seemed to be holding back.

"Finn, they did what they thought was right. I contacted you when I could. I didn't even know if you would want to hear from me."

His fine intelligent gaze flashed. "I wanted to hear from you. I was always scared your dad had found you and hurt you. I worried a lot, Melody."

"That day in Ordinary was the closest he ever came."

Finn took her hand, his palm sliding across hers like warm sunshine. "I'm glad he missed you."

"Me, too."

"Now you want to see him. Why?"

She willed him to be the same generous Finn she'd known all those years ago, the same great kid who'd brightened her days when he'd visited her in the hospital, who'd helped her to forget her pain.

"I got in touch with my father a couple of years ago. He's this big unfinished *thing* in my life, you know? I've never even met him."

"That's so strange."

"I know. I wrote him this long letter, telling him how he'd made my life hell. How he'd betrayed my mom's love with his violence."

"Did he respond?"

"Oh, yes. He sent back a long letter and, Finn, it was so strange. He said he understood why my mom ran away with me, but that he'd never abused her. That he had always wanted to get to know me."

The confusion she'd felt after reading that letter, her sense of betrayal even though she didn't believe her mom had done this heinous thing, still rattled her. She knew her mom well. She would have never done that.

She picked at a piece of lint on her pants. "That day in the hospital? When he freaked out?"

Finn nodded.

"He thought he'd finally tracked us down and that he'd see me for the first time. When we weren't there, he snapped. He said he isn't normally a violent man. That Mom is lying. But that day, he couldn't hold in his frustration any longer."

"Do you think he's telling the truth about your mom?"

"I don't know. I mean, she's such a good woman. When I called and told her about the letter, she started to cry. She told me to let it go. Not to contact him anymore. That his family would hurt me if I met them."

"Did you stop contact?"

"I mailed him one last letter telling him I didn't want to get to know him. I forbade him to come near me. That was it for a long time, until I got a letter from him three weeks ago. He has cancer. He's dying. It…it changes everything." Urgency coursed through her. What if he died before she got there? They might not have known each other like in a normal family, but he was her only father. Now when she thought she might never see him, she wanted to run to him, to learn who he really was. "If I don't hurry, if I don't visit him, I won't ever meet my dad."

"Which is why you asked me to take you to Texas."

"Yes. I need to see him before he dies. I need to find out who he is." She crushed his fingers. "I need the truth."

A self-reliant woman, she had depended on only herself for the ten years since she'd moved out of her mom and Randy's house. "I know it's selfish of me to ask you to come. I could go on my own. I could fly down. I could take a bus, or rent a car and drive to Texas, but I've never felt so alone, Finn, as when I think about meeting the man who abused my mother. What kind of meeting can it be? An angry one or a sad one? Can there be any happiness?" Doubts and confusion plagued her. What was real and what wasn't? She had to know. "You're the only person I could think of who would support me in this."

"I understand, Melody. No problem. I'm here for you. We can leave now if you're packed. Austin's waiting in the restaurant across the street. We're going to meet him there."

He laughed, strangely. When she looked at him in question, he explained about some hitchhiker his friend had picked up and now here he was about to bring her along on their trip, too.

"You mean you didn't tell him?"

"Nope. He might have cancelled. The shit's going to hit the fan, but he'll get over it. Are you packed?"

"Yes, I have my bag ready."

Finn stood, nervous energy humming through him. "Hey! What are these?" He'd picked up her sketchbook from the coffee table. She jumped. She'd meant to hide it.

She tried to grab it from him, but he held it over her head, reading the captions and the dialogue in the drawings.

His face lit up. "You write cartoons?"

"Comic books." He had inspired that interest in her.

The only time Melody had been in his house, Finn's grandmother had been bedridden because of a stroke. Melody was allowed one day out of the hospital to attend Finn's twelfth birthday party. That's when she'd first seen the drawings. Finn had just finished painting the walls of Grandma Caldwell's room with a comic he'd written—about a princess and a hero who didn't have to save her because she was smart enough to save herself.

Melody had tried to do the same, *had* done the same for years, but she was nearly thirty-one years old and so damned tired of fighting her own battles.

She had a big one coming up, and she needed Finn's moral support. He was the only friend she had these days who knew about that day in the hospital.

"I'm glad to see you doing this," he said. "The story's good. The drawings suck, though." He softened that with a smile.

She sighed. She struggled with them, but she just didn't have his talent. "I know."

Finn smiled. "Grab your bag. Let's head out on this adventure. I'll make sure you don't get hurt, Mel."

She doubted that very much, but at least he would be there if she fell apart.

CHAPTER FIVE

BY THE TIME Austin and Gracie had finished their meals and walked out of the restaurant, with Austin's fingers at Gracie's back, Finn was crossing the street with a woman about Gracie's age, but shorter, with a delicate, rare beauty.

Finn made introductions.

The woman, Melody, shook Gracie's hand and then Austin's.

"I remember when you came to Ordinary," Austin said, leading them back to the hotel. "But I didn't know the full story until Finn told me last night."

"I don't remember meeting you at Finn's birthday party." Melody had a delicate voice to match her dainty look.

"I wasn't there. We weren't friends in those days. We probably hadn't even met yet."

"Oh, right. Finn was still new to town."

Gracie watched Austin study the woman. Did he find her attractive? Not that it mattered.

"Looks like you recovered from the accident pretty well." Austin smiled at Melody. Gracie didn't like that smile. "Finn told me about it."

"Yes, I'm fine."

Gracie turned to look at Melody, because there'd been something odd about her tone. The men didn't seem to notice, but Gracie was pretty sure the woman was lying.

"What do you do these days?" Austin asked.

As they stepped into the hotel lobby, she glanced at Finn, who glanced away for a moment, and Gracie smelled a problem.

Apparently, so did Austin because when he asked, "What's going on?" Gracie heard suspicion in his voice.

Finn looked at him. "She's coming with us."

"What?" Austin stopped walking. "What are you talking about?"

"Melody needs to visit her father in Texas. I told her she could drive down with us."

Austin transferred his attention to Melody. "Wasn't your father the one who showed up at the hospital? The one you were running from because he was abusive?"

Cool as a cucumber, Melody responded, "That's right, but he's dying and has asked to see me." Beneath her delicate beauty, Gracie sensed she had a spine of steel.

"Why would you do that if he was abusive?"

"Because I've never met him."

Austin said to Finn, "We need to talk."

When Finn balked, Austin grabbed his arm and steered him across the lobby. From this distance, Gracie could hear their raised voices, but not the words.

Melody seemed to be studying Gracie. "Have we met before?"

Crap. No, no, no. The question she dreaded. "No. I would remember you if we had. This is my first time coming through here."

"I've lived lots of other places and you seem so familiar. Ever been to Montana?"

"Nope." Yes, she had, but she needed to quash this line of questioning. Quickly. Who knew where it might lead.

"How about Seattle?"

"Nope."

"I have an excellent memory for faces. I really think…."

Oh, double, super crap. She was going to figure it out. The hyperventilation that happened when someone got too close threatened to kick in.

"You know, Gracie, I'm a reporter."

A reporter? Oh, dear sweet God. Nothing worse on this earth. *Nothing*. She couldn't get enough air. The room closed in on her. *A reporter*. She didn't care that some of them told stories worth reading. In her experience, they were invasive and pushy and incessant in their need to know *everything*.

"I write human interest stories and I really feel like…."

Run. Gracie's instincts went into overdrive. Her palms itched. The skin on the back of her neck crawled.

Melody's eyes widened.

There it was—the instant of recognition and it spelled as much trouble as a big bag of TNT.

Melody snapped her fingers. "Hey! Aren't you—?"

"No!" Gracie would never be that person again. If she'd had her way, she wouldn't have been her in the first place. She backed away with her hands in front of her as though she could ward off the awful truth.

Gracie crashed out of the lobby and onto the sidewalk, nearly bumping into a couple who told her to watch where she was going.

"Sorry." She walked as fast as her legs would carry her. She didn't care which direction. Just away. Run, run, run.

She'd changed her hair back to her natural color. She was years older, leaner, harder. Still, she'd been recognized. It had taken Melody only a matter of minutes to figure out who Gracie really was.

Gracie walked fast and hard while her nearly healed ankle started to ache again, outrunning her past. Where to now? How could she get from here to Denver without that woman trying to follow her?

She hunched her shoulders, trying to blend in, to disappear again. To be invisible.

She scooted down an alley. People didn't bother those who lived in alleyways, in the darkness, in among the dirt and trash, the offal that civilization ignored.

She could disappear again. She could become invisible.

She would.

HER BIG BREAK!

At last.

Melody had been searching high and low for the story that would make her career. She'd just found it.

Who would have thought she would run headlong into it here in this tiny town? Why was someone that famous skulking around in the worst clothes, with the trashiest haircut and a drastically different hair color, after being missing for the past five or six years?

What was she hiding from?

Melody smelled a *story* and a darned good one.

Her lips curved in a cat-licking-cream-from-its-paws smile. She needed it. The timing couldn't be better, with her going to Texas to finally meet her family.

When she had still been living at home, she had heard her mom mention her dad's name in a quiet conversation with Randy. Melody hadn't been meant to hear. Gord Grady. She knew her mom was originally from Texas. Had she met him there?

Minutes later, she'd been on the internet searching for Gradys who lived in Texas. She had found her dad all right, easily, because he was a mover and a shaker in Texas. He was known. He had money. Big, huge money.

Lord, the shock of finding out her dad was one of the wealthiest men in the state.

She didn't know how her mom, who had no one, no family, little money, had come to know him, but somehow she had and Melody had been the result.

For hours, she had stared at photographs of the man, a hale and hearty version of her pale, slight self. "My father," she would whisper. "Dad. Daddy."

The name on Melody's birth certificate wasn't Grady, though. It was Messina, her mom's surname, but she'd gone by Chase for years so her dad couldn't find her.

The more she read about the family, and the more she researched, the angrier she grew.

During all the years she and her mom had been on the road, living hand-to-mouth while her mom worked at any job she could find, always afraid, always looking over their shoulders, these people had been living high off the hog.

The day she had learned her father's name, a fire had been lit in Melody's belly. Someday, she would have money of her own, significant money, and would thumb her nose at the high-and-mighty Gradys of Texas.

She would be a success and then those grandparents who had rejected her, that man who had fathered her but hadn't stooped so low as to marry her warm, beautiful mother, that monster who had hurt her mom, would fall all over themselves to get to know the famous Melody Messina. The second after she said hello and goodbye to the Gradys, she was taking back her birth name.

And she would turn her back on them.

She'd been searching for a really good story, something to break her career wide open.

This was it.

With her research and writing skills, and with a story the public was dying for, she could produce a book for which publishers would pay good money, a hefty advance, and that the public would devour.

After all, it wasn't every day one of their favorites came back from the dead.

"YOU PLANNED THIS all along, didn't you?" Austin got right up into Finn's face so he couldn't deny the accusation. "Ever since we decided to go to Texas. You knew before we left Ordinary you wanted Melody to come with us."

Finn nodded with a quick, sharp jut of his jaw. "Yeah, I knew. Would you have let her come otherwise?"

"No. Why can't she go alone?"

"Because she needs a friend with her. She's scared to death to finally meet the man who was so mean to her mother. But the guy's dying. She has to go."

"So? You couldn't have just gone with her on your own? Why drag me into her business?"

"Because we were already planning this trip."

"Wrong. We were planning *a* trip. Not *this* one." Austin's suspicious nature went into overdrive, putting two and two together, stunning him. "You not only knew she would come, but you were the one who suggested going to Texas in the first place. Is your buddy really selling his herd?"

"Yeah, he's selling," Finn snapped. "When he put the word out online on the loops, I thought it couldn't be better. You needed cattle and they were available in Texas. Melody needed to go to Texas. Perfect."

"No, it isn't perfect. I would have just flown down to check the herd and then flown back home."

Finn was supposed to be his best friend, on his side, not manipulating him. Austin had been manipulated all his life. He sure as hell didn't need it from a friend.

"I trusted you."

"You still can."

"Not after this."

Finn lost it. "Do you know how badly you needed to get away?" He pointed a finger at Austin's face, nearly hitting him. "Buddy, some days when you complained about your mom I wanted to choke you to get you to shut the eff up."

Austin flushed. What with the decision to buy the ranch being huge, and his mom adamant that she wouldn't move out of their tin can of a god-awful trailer, Austin had been vocal about her.

He was a sheriff's deputy in town, for God's sake. It was embarrassing that his mother wouldn't let him provide something better.

"So I complained a lot? You still could have gone on this trip with just Melody."

"I was trying to make two friends happy." Finn pressed his hand on Austin's shoulder. "I felt torn, man, between two people who needed something from me. I knew you needed to get away. I knew Melody needed company. I'll say it again, this was perfect."

"There's nothing that can be done about it now."
Austin strode away.

He found Melody alone in the lobby. "Where's
Gracie?" He sure as heck hoped she wasn't in gastric distress again. She needed to keep food in her
belly for when she—

He'd missed what Melody had just said. "Pardon?"

"I said she's gone." Melody gestured toward the
front door. "She left while you were arguing with
Finn. Everything okay? Are we good to go?"

"No, we aren't good to go." He shot her a dis-
gruntled look. She might be an okay person, and
she might be Finn's friend, but she was screwing up
what was supposed to be a great holiday.

Panic rose in Austin's chest and he had no idea
why. Gracie could take care of herself, as she was
fond of telling him. She could get herself to Denver
on her own, no problem. So why couldn't he leave
her be?

"Which way did she go?"

Melody pointed left.

Gracie and her need for independence were wearing him down. Why was everything a struggle with
her? Austin rushed out the door. Street was empty.
Damn. Where was she? He strode past an alleyway
and peered down. Also empty. She couldn't have
been gone more than a couple of minutes. *Where
was she?*

A couple of blocks ahead, he caught a glimpse
of movement, someone turning a corner. He raced
ahead, just managing to catch sight of another move-

ment at the end of an alley, someone turning another corner.

He ran to the end of the alley and found Gracie, trapped by a fence behind a store. No way out.

She jumped when she saw him. "What are you doing here?"

"I could ask you the same thing."

"I'm leaving. I need to get to Denver."

"Thought you were coming with us."

"I changed my mind."

She was lying. "Why?"

"You guys have another guest."

"So?"

"I don't want to impose."

Austin's cop training kicked in. Something else was going on, but what? He didn't care. She was leaving. He didn't want her to.

Why not? It's not like you owe her anything.

He had no good answer. He didn't want her to go without him. That was all.

"There's plenty of room for you."

"I know. It's just that...."

"What?"

When she didn't respond, he took her arm and shook it gently.

"It's just what?"

Still, she didn't say anything.

SHE COULDN'T EXPLAIN without telling him the truth. Like that was ever going to happen.

"Talk to me," he said.

Gracie weighed what she would and would not tell, what that woman would or would not reveal.

She didn't know Melody, but she knew reporters and had little respect for them. Yes, they were just doing their jobs, but always at someone else's expense, all under the guise of the public's right to know.

Her life had been turned upside down by the press, over and over and over again. She wouldn't let it happen now. Not when she was so close to the end of her journey.

She rubbed her forehead, so tired.

She didn't need this.

Tomorrow, she would change the course of her life and then to heck with every reporter in the world.

How could she stop this from happening? That woman was probably on the phone right now with her editor, plotting how much she would write, when the story would run, how much they could make on the story.

Not *the* story. *Gracie's* story.

My story and no one else's.

Self-righteous anger replaced the panic and helplessness she'd felt at the hotel.

Gracie was running, again, and allowing others to control her actions, again, when she should be taking control.

She was sick of not having the upper hand.

If she were near Melody, maybe she could control her, but she sure as heck wouldn't be able to if she were on the run.

Keep your friends close and your enemies closer.
Good advice.

Determined to regain control of her destiny, she jammed her hands onto her hips. "Okay."

Austin's eyebrows shot up. "Okay? Um, what are you saying okay to?"

"I'm going to take you up on your offer of a drive to Denver."

He smiled, and it was sweet and caring. "You are?"

"Yes. You said there's still room for me so I'll take it."

"Come on. We should head out right away."

"I still have to cut your hair."

"All right, we have time for that."

Back at the hotel, Melody sat in a chair in the lobby as Finn paced in front of her. Gracie glared hard at Melody, daring the woman to say a word.

She didn't, just studied Gracie as though she were a specimen in a lab. She could stare all she wanted as long as she kept her mouth shut.

"Are we good?" Finn asked.

"Yep." Austin steered her toward the elevators. "Gracie's going to cut my hair. We'll meet back down here in…?" He glanced down at Gracie.

"Twenty minutes."

"You heard the woman. See you then."

Gracie didn't get why Austin was angry with Finn and Melody other than over being blindsided by Melody's unexpected arrival. Maybe Finn had lied to him.

That would be enough to anger Gracie. She valued honesty.

You haven't been honest with Austin, have you?

I'm not his friend. I don't owe him that kind of truth. My lie is one of omission because my history has nothing to do with him.

Upstairs in the hotel room, Gracie took her small scissors out of her bag, the ones she used to cut her own hair, along with her new bottle of shampoo, and washed the scissors in the sink. She dried them carefully then returned to the bedroom with a towel.

Austin sat on a chair he'd pulled away from the small table in the corner, with his shirt off and his back bare. Holy, holy moly. The man was too well-built and too beautiful. Yes, downright beautiful.

She approached uneasily, regretting now that she'd offered to do this. In her need to pay him back, she hadn't realized that this could be dangerous to her.

Touch. Six years of deprivation. She'd been starving. She craved touch. Had known too little of it, even before she'd run away.

She settled the towel across his back and his broad, muscled shoulders. The warmth of his body seeped into her through the slightest touch.

Good-looking, fit, kind, generous, decent. The man was perfect in every way, or would have been in another time, under different circumstances.

Guard your heart, Gracie.

Thick hair curled at his nape. Now that push came to shove, and she had to do what she had offered to do, she hated to chop it off. But cut it she would, because she owed him.

Her little finger grazed his ear. She thought he shivered. A shiver ran through her. She suppressed it. No sense letting him know he affected her.

"Tell me about Ordinary," she said, searching for something—*anything*—to take her mind off the intensity that was making her crazy, tempting her with treasures that weren't possible for her.

He told her bits and pieces before drifting off into silence.

She cut his hair more quickly than she should have because touching him made her regret things that she couldn't change. Despite the rush, she did a good job, because she'd been trained by the best, just by watching.

When growing up, she'd had her hair cut and styled too many times to count. One of her hairdressers had become one of many unlikely transitory friends, along with a manicurist and stylist.

She brushed off his nape and took the towel to the bathroom to shake the hair out into the tub. After hanging the towel back on the rack, she returned to the room.

Austin hadn't moved. She stepped in front of him. He'd fallen asleep, his face relaxed in repose. She smiled, happy that she had given him a few moments' peace with the haircut.

Dangerously she took advantage, looking her fill, her need to touch overriding common sense. With the tip of her finger, she traced the scar beside his left eye. He sighed, his breath warm on her wrist.

Gracie, stop. You're playing with fire.

I can't stop. Not just yet. This feels too good.

Let me touch some more. Give me just another second to look at this beautiful man and make a memory to carry into the future.

He shifted and her gaze shot to his eyes. They were open and watching her.

She snatched back her hand.

"Finished?" he asked, and he sounded like he'd been running uphill rather than sleeping.

"Yeah," she murmured, breathless, too.

She had thought herself immune to a man's beauty. She'd seen too much physical perfection over the years, most of it artificial and shallow. But this man held a depth of character she hadn't encountered often.

He called to her deeply, which was awful. Nothing could ever happen between them.

AUSTIN SAVORED THE delicacy of her hands on his hair, her warm feminine tenderness, shocking coming from this hard-edged, private woman who consciously separated herself from the world. But for these brief moments, he felt a closeness to her more intimate than tumbling with her in a bout of lovemaking on the bed not four feet away from them.

He was a simple guy who liked beer and a bucket of chicken wings after work, but if he were a wine aficionado, or a poet, he might come up with the right words to describe what Gracie did to him with her callused but gentle fingers.

He'd had girlfriends back home and every relationship had been ended by his mom, even when she hadn't done anything. You marry the family and not just the guy, right? The women who knew him in Ordinary also knew his mom and hadn't wanted to marry into a family that would include, well, the world's worst mother-in-law.

It left him lonely, restless, unfulfilled.

The temptation to not tell Gracie about his life, to just start something here and now brought him too close to pulling her onto his lap and deepening the intimacy with lips and hands.

That would be dishonest. One thing he valued above all else, probably because of his mom, was honesty. As well, he liked that this closeness had come from only fleeting strokes of her fingertips. In the innocence of her touch, he had experienced an eroticism he didn't want to complete with sex. At least, not here and now, in this rare, precious moment of communion.

She caught him watching her.

Austin stared into the palest of blue eyes. Her coffee-scented breath whispered along his cheek.

Everything he felt was too vivid—fierce attraction, unprecedented tenderness, unbridled frustration, even a strong aversion to her homeless state. He kept his emotions under control. No grand passion for him. Not after living all his life with a woman as clingy as Mom, as prone to high drama. A woman who just wouldn't let *go*.

He didn't need more emotion in his life right now. Or ever.

His psyche—or *something*—though, needed Gracie. Not just any woman. Gracie. Why? He didn't know her well enough to feel this kind of pull, but he did.

He stood slowly, trying to figure out exactly who Gracie Travers was, confused by how warm she could be one minute and then closed off the next.

They had to get out of this hotel room, because the war inside him might swing toward liking her altogether too much.

At the same moment he turned away, she did, too, and just as quickly. Okay, so it was unanimous. Neither one of them wanted this to happen.

Good. He was glad. Really.

THE TENSION IN the car was thick enough to cut with a lightsaber. Finn fumed. What was Austin's problem? Why was he making it a big deal just because Melody was with them?

But his conscience quibbled, wouldn't let him get away with his deceit without some acknowledgment.

He shouldn't have lied to Austin. But Melody was here now and he couldn't be happier. Austin would have objected to her coming along. He would have sent Finn on ahead by himself to get Melody and they wouldn't have had this buddy trip they'd wanted to take for years. The one his mom had wrecked twice before with what Finn thought were manufactured emergencies. The one they had already been planning when Melody contacted him. *I need you.*

How could a man with any scrap of decency not respond to that?

Austin might think Finn had been trying to pull a fast one, but Finn loved his friend like a brother. Austin was dying a long, slow death in his mom's house. Finn didn't like the woman and the stranglehold she had on her son, with her helplessness and her need to be taken care of and rescued regularly.

Austin was just too good and honest a guy for a woman like her. Putty in her hands, man.

He needed to get away and Finn had made it happen.

Couldn't Austin see Finn just wanted him to be happy?

He needed to give Austin time to accept that this had been a good solution for everyone. He and Austin were having their road trip, and Melody was getting the support she needed.

If only Gracie weren't here shooting daggers at Melody. What was her problem?

She was just a homeless woman. Melody had a real job and a real life. Where did Gracie get off on thinking she was better than Melody? From the way Gracie was staring at Melody, Finn would say she was thinking exactly that.

If this were his car, she'd be out on the road on her own again.

He caught Melody's eye and gave her a reassuring smile. No way should she have to put up with Gracie's crap.

At least Melody wasn't a freeloader, living off other people.

Gracie, on the other hand, was a user. No two ways about it.

Finn wasn't going to stand by and let her manipulate his buddy the way Austin's mother did.

Austin, I love ya, man, but Gracie's taking you for a ride, big-time, and you're too decent a guy to see it.

After they stopped for lunch, Finn directed Gracie into the front seat so he could sit in the back with Melody, vaguely aware of his urge to protect Melody from the woman.

This close, Melody's light and lemony perfume drifted around him, beguiling his senses and tying his tongue. This close to her, he became shy. Finn Franck Caldwell? Shy? Anyone who knew him would laugh at the concept.

Melody affected him, made him want to be more, to do more.

"So Finn Franck became Finn Franck Caldwell," she said. "When?"

"My parents got married soon after you left. I kept both names to honor both sets of grandparents."

"Why did you become a vet?" she asked, voice soft and cast low, so the backseat became their own private world. "What happened to drawing comics? You were so good. So creative."

"Real life reared its head. I knew I wasn't going to be able to make a living on comics. In one of your letters you once said you wanted to write a book someday and get published. You know how hard it is to hit it big. It's even harder when it's with comics instead of novels or nonfiction."

He didn't know when he had picked up her hand, but found himself playing with her fingers. Her pinky finger was maybe half as long as his. Amazing. She had small, delicate hands, with short, buffed nails. No nail polish. He liked that. No artifice. With Melody, what you saw was what you got.

"I loved working with my dad when he tended animals," he said, "so it seemed natural to become a vet. It's not like I gave up a lot. I love my work."

"Do you have long hours?"

"Sometimes. They're not consistent. I have an office in town, but I'm out on the road a lot visiting local ranches. You don't plan for sick animals. I've missed a lot of dates and family gatherings because of cows giving birth, or cats or dogs hit by cars, and even the odd wild animal tangled in fences."

He stared out at the passing fields. "Dad's retired now, so I cover a lot of the area around Ordinary. My hours will get even longer once Austin gets his ranch going. I'm going to help him out with his animals. Plus, I like to mentor kids in town. It gives them something to do besides get into trouble. It's amazing how universal it is for kids to like animals."

Melody smiled. "I like hearing that passion in your voice. It makes me believe you really didn't give up too much to be a vet."

"I meant it when I said I like my work."

In the distance, the Denver skyline shimmered. They would arrive soon. Too bad. He liked the intimacy of this small cocoon in the back of Austin's old SUV. And he liked holding Melody Messina's hand.

FIFTH WHEEL. SUPERFLUOUS. Out of place.

Gracie stood in front of a very nice suburban home in Denver, while the hosts and Austin and Finn exchanged hugs and high fives.

Gracie was no friend; she was a stranger, and painfully aware of how she looked in her ancient clothes, carrying a backpack that had been hauled back and forth across the country.

She tugged on the hem of her sweatshirt, hiding where the seam had unraveled.

What on earth was she doing here at Austin's friend's house? He'd insisted she would be welcome, but she wasn't so sure. So why had she allowed him to convince her to come, even though she had reached her destination and would be going to the bank tomorrow? She should be downtown scoping out an alley to sleep in so she could go to the bank first thing in the morning. Freedom was so close she could taste it. So why was she here? Maybe it was the promise of the barbecue these people planned to serve. She wouldn't have to starve tonight.

Food.

That familiar and desperate refrain reared its ugly head even though she'd had breakfast this morning.

If she were honest, there was more to it. After so much time alone, without any kind of company, it was good to be with people. With Austin. If only they'd met under different circumstances.

The way things stood, Austin had all the power. He had money. She didn't.

As had been drummed into her as a child, over and over, money was power.

The Kavenaghs answered the door with big smiles. A good-looking couple—Cash tall and laid-back, and Shannon a pretty enough blonde that Gracie would bet she could have been a model when she was young—took Austin into their arms like a long-lost son.

Gracie had learned from Austin that Shannon was a DEA agent. When Cash had moved away from Ordinary to marry Shannon, he had left law enforcement to become a teacher. Apparently, it had been the right decision. Austin said he loved teaching.

They lived the typical suburban life, nice house, big backyard, three kids…and a love between them that was palpable even to a stranger.

When she stepped through their front door behind Austin, nervous, they welcomed her, the lonely homeless girl, with open arms, as though she had as much right to be here as Austin or Finn or Melody.

When Cash, six-one and counting, wrapped his bicep-heavy arms around her, she leaned into an embrace so fatherly and tender her eyes watered. Then Shannon moved in, radiant in middle age, and just as warmly welcoming as her husband.

Austin knew good people. Except for Finn. He wasn't good. He wasn't nice. He'd been angry with her since the moment they'd met. Hypocrite. He didn't want her ruining their buddy trip and yet he had Melody with him.

He'd gotten worse on their drive into Denver, looking at Gracie like she was dirt.

Who cared what he thought? She had to protect herself at all costs, and if that meant keeping a jaded, wary eye on Finn's girlfriend, or whatever she was, then Finn would have to suck it up.

The Kavenaghs's teenaged children joined them after school, the boys roughhousing with each other and their chocolate Lab, Doobie. The daughter chattered with her mother in the kitchen.

"Really, Cash? You named your dog Doobie?" Austin scratched the dog behind his ears.

"Shannon did. Being a DEA agent, she thinks it's hilarious."

They went out onto the back deck overlooking a large yard.

When the boys brought out a football and tossed it around with Austin, Finn and their dad, using two Ponderosa pines at the back of the yard as goalposts, Doobie went nuts, barking and running in euphoric delight. And tripping everyone. Finn scooped him up in his arms, grunting. "You're a big dog, Doobie."

Gracie had to admit his laugh was contagious, deep and straight from the heart.

Finn ruffled the dog's fur and kissed his head and suffered Doobie washing his face with his big tongue. "Cripes, you need to go on a diet." He dropped the dog onto the grass.

"Can we put him inside just for a couple of minutes? Until we finish our game?"

Gracie tried not to let his affection for the animal and his laugh interfere with how much she disliked the man.

"Bring him up on the deck. We have a baby gate we put across the stairs." Shannon stretched the gate between the railing posts, closing off the steps, and Doobie barked a protest. "Quiet," Shannon said, all-business.

Doobie lay down with his head on his paws and his nose under the bottom of the gate, every so often emitting a pitiful whine.

Cash threw a long pass and both Austin and Finn grabbed the ball at the same time. They wrestled for it, rolling on the ground and laughing like a pair of little boys, their resentment over the women joining them on the trip forgotten for the moment.

In their roughhousing, Gracie saw their real affection for each other. She regretted she'd, in her way, come between them. Perhaps here, in this house full of loving people, they could have a break from their conflicts.

Shannon laughed. "Overgrown children."

When they finished the game, seventeen-year-old Evan tossed Finn a Frisbee and slid the gate back. Doobie bounded down the stairs and caught the Frisbee Finn threw for him. They played for another half an hour, Finn's devotion to the dog unflagging.

So he liked animals. He was still a bit of a jerk.

They all sat down at the table while Cash put burgers on the grill.

Doobie lay down in the shade of one of the Ponderosas, the scene so idyllic Gracie blinked to assure herself she wasn't dreaming.

Sixteen-year-old Jake took over at the grill, the scent of meat charring powerful enough to force Gracie's growling tummy into overdrive.

This was real, not one of her wishful-thinking daydreams she often had about families she met. These people epitomized a gracious welcome foreign in her experience.

So this is what a normal family feels like.

Shannon and Cash's boys were tall and good-looking like their father. The daughter, Jessica, could have been a clone of her gorgeous blonde mother. The boys hovered over her, protectively. She batted them away, laughing. Funny that she didn't seem spoiled.

They idolized their dad. He gave them a lot of attention, leaving Gracie to wonder, if this was truly a normal family. Or were the Kavenaghs exceptional?

Shannon asked Gracie to step into the kitchen with her for a second.

"Jessica, you come, too."

Gracie's startled gaze met Austin's. He didn't seem concerned so she followed them both into the house.

Once in the kitchen, Shannon asked, "Gracie, while you're here, would you like to use the washing machine? You could get your clothes clean. Start fresh when you leave."

The heat of shame crawled up Gracie's chest and into her cheeks. She'd washed herself and her hair, but not her clothes. They must smell. Austin hadn't said a word. But then, she couldn't have washed them anyway. She had no detergent and no change for the machines in the Laundromat.

She swallowed her pride, because getting her clothes clean was an excellent idea, and retrieved her bag from the hallway. She followed Shannon to the laundry room.

Shannon filled the washer with detergent and Gracie added her meager wardrobe.

"Why did you want me, Mum?" Jessica stood in the doorway.

"Can you give Gracie an outfit to wear while her clothes wash?" Shannon smiled. In that smile, Gracie detected no pity, only compassion. There was a world of difference.

"Sure. Come with me." They headed upstairs.

"Jess," her mom called after her. "Start the machine after Gracie adds the rest of her clothes."

Shannon came to the bottom of the stairs. "Give her everything."

"Give it to her?"

"Yes. *Give* it to her."

"What do you mean everything?"

Shannon gestured down her body, her hands hovering around her breasts and her groin area. *"Everything."*

Jessica laughed. "Oh, I get it. This will be fun." She took Gracie's hand and practically dragged her to her room. "Mom can't give you any of her stuff because she's bigger than you are, especially in the bust. Dad *really* likes her bust." The girl rolled her eyes. "The way they go at it, sometimes I think they're still a pair of teenagers."

She rummaged in a dresser drawer, then held up matching panties and a bra, pink with ribbons and lace. "What do you think of these?"

"They're beautiful."

"Okay, put them on. They're yours."

"Mine?" Gracie had to be mistaken.

"You heard Mom. For Pete's sake, don't cross her. She likes to get her own way." Jessica leaned close and whispered, "But in a good way. I just like to give her a hard time so her head doesn't get too big."

"I can't possibly take these. They're too pretty and too expensive."

"If it makes it any easier for you, the bra's getting too tight. I was flat for years, but now I think I'm going to be more like Mom than I thought."

She moved to the closet. "Jeans and a T-shirt okay with you?"

"I really—I don't want to take—" Gracie thought she might cry. She breathed hard to settle the unfamiliar emotions flooding her. The sensitivity of the mother in guessing that Gracie had no clean clothes, and the generosity of the daughter were almost too much.

"Gracie, I don't know why you need help, but you do. You should really just take it when it's offered. My mom and dad give me so much. I know how lucky I am. Mom tells me stories about the drug addicts she meets at work all the time."

Jessica's eyes got huge and she slapped her hand across her mouth. "OMG, I didn't mean that you were an addict. I just meant...."

Gracie touched her hand. "Please. It's okay. I didn't think you did."

Jessica sat on the edge of her bed, scrunching the shirt and pants against her chest. "Dad talks about some of the kids he teaches who have nothing. Sometimes he buys them food."

Gracie sat down beside her.

"When they talk about those people, I feel so lucky, so fortunate that I have the advantages I have. Mom and Dad are strong people and know how to help. I don't. Let me do this?"

Throat constricted, Gracie nodded. When she could speak again, she said, "I can't tell you how much I appreciate this. You're a good person, Jessica, and wise beyond your years."

Jessica smiled. "That's so nice of you to say. Now put on the clothes. I want to see if they fit."

She turned her back and Gracie changed clothes, hiding her torn underwear inside her pants so the girl wouldn't see them.

"Okay, let's go."

Jessica turned around. "Oh, wow, that red shirt looks amazing with your black hair and eyebrows."

She ran down the stairs with Gracie close behind her.

"With those amazing black eyebrows, a few piercings, and the right clothes, you could totally do Goth."

Gracie passed a mirror in the hallway. "You know, I never thought about it, but I really could."

It would help with her disguise.

While the washing machine chugged away, Gracie went back outside and took her seat between Austin and Jessica.

"Austin, tell me about the ranch you bought." Cash put a platter of burgers onto the center of the table.

Just as she'd guessed. He had money. He led a normal happy life, so different from her own, which was as dysfunctional as possible.

"Remember the Olsens?"

"You bought the old Olsen place? Good choice. Perfect size for a hobby ranch."

"That's what I figure. I waited a long time for the right size ranch to come on the market. This one suits me perfectly."

"And the kids? What's that all about?"

Kids? Austin had children? Did that mean he also had a wife? She glanced at his left hand, she hoped without being obvious about it. No wedding band. She was sure she would have noticed that by now.

Why would it matter anyway? There was no future for her with any man, let alone one as decent as Austin.

"I like the work you used to do with Big Brothers Big Sisters," Austin said, "but I want to affect more than just one kid at a time. Ordinary's developing a problem with some of the youth. There's nothing for them to do."

Oh, these weren't his own kids.

"So, what's your idea?" Cash passed Gracie the bowl of potato salad dotted with dill pickles and bacon bits. Real bacon. Gracie nearly swooned.

"I want to put them to work on the ranch." Austin took the salad from her and helped himself, but she could tell he barely noticed the food. A glow lit his face and he was about as excited, as upbeat, as she had seen him. "I want them to learn everything."

"Great idea," Cash said. "Love it. It would be good for their pride to be working and learning."

"Exactly. Pay them for their labor so they have spending money. Or teach them skills like animal husbandry that they can apply toward school credits. I'm in talks with the district school board now."

Wow. A real do-gooder. Why wasn't she surprised? He hadn't been able to let her, a wallet thief, go without helping her, had he? She'd been a stranger. The kids he was talking about were probably all people he knew in his hometown.

A person could be judged not only by their actions, but also by the opinions reflected in the eyes of those around him.

Reflecting from these people were warmth, admiration and respect for Austin. Where was Gracie's reflection? She didn't have one.

Gracie had disappeared. She'd left her other persona behind, one she could no longer stand to be, and had headed out on the road in search of anonymity.

She'd found it, all right. She'd been so successful, she'd lost sight of herself.

Who did people see when they looked at her? Who was she?

"Finn's going to come out regularly and teach the kids about animals," Austin said. "Maybe one of them will show enough interest and someday become a vet."

"I was real glad when Austin told me he was going to start helping these kids after he bought the ranch." Finn had finished his burger and wiped his fingers with a paper napkin. "I've been taking a couple in on Saturdays and paying them to clean out cages at my office. But mostly they're there to learn about the animals, as well as just spend time with them. Animals aren't meant to be caged. But I really want them to see how animals work and live on a ranch, how symbiotic the relationship between animals and humans can be. This will be a great opportunity for so many of them."

Austin grasped Finn by the back of the neck and squeezed. "Great to have you on board, man."

Okay, so maybe Finn was a do-gooder, too, but he still didn't hold a candle to Austin.

Doobie had wandered onto the deck and sat beside Finn, who scratched his head idly while he studied Jessica.

"The boys at school must be fighting over you, Jessica" Finn said, smiling. "How old are you? Fifteen? You have a boyfriend yet?"

"No!" both of her brothers shouted.

Jessica sent them a repressive look. "Yes, I do."

"Since when?" Evan put down the burger he'd been about to bite into.

Jake frowned at Jessica and stopped eating, too. "Who? Someone at school?"

"Of course at school. Where else can I meet guys with you two hovering over me all of the time?"

"We're just trying to protect you."

"I don't need protection. I'm perfectly capable of taking care of myself."

"Who is it, Jess?"

"Alex Bradford."

"Alex?" they shouted in harmony.

"Are you serious?" Jake stopped chewing. "That nerd? What the he—heck do you see in him?"

"Intelligence. You macho guys have no idea how sexy intelligence is."

"Hey," Cash said. "I don't want to hear my little girl talking about sex and boys in the same sentence."

Shannon rolled her eyes and shared a private smile with her daughter. Gracie envied them their bond.

Gracie tended to agree with Jessica. Intelligence was a major turn-on, so much more than good looks.

She glanced at Austin and then grinned and winked at Jessica.

The girl had been about to take a bite of potato salad, but stopped and stared at Gracie. Oh, no. Oh, no, no. Recognition. That damned wink. Gracie had done it without thinking and cursed herself roundly.

How could a kid Jessica's age, a teenager, recognize Gracie? Come on. This trip was becoming too ridiculous.

This, *this,* was why she avoided civilization, why she hung out with truck drivers who wouldn't have a clue about her.

First a reporter and now a kid who seemed to know too much.

Was a little anonymity too much to ask for? Was there no such thing as privacy anymore? Darned internet. Everyone knew everything about everyone, while privacy died a fast and painful death.

Gracie needed privacy, though. Craved it like a junkie needs drugs.

"I've been watching a lot of retro stuff on TV lately," Jessica said, frowning because she was obviously working out a problem. "They have all of these great old shows on."

Old TV shows. Goose bumps broke out on Gracie's arms. The burger she'd eaten fell like a bomb to the bottom of her stomach.

Jessica's face lit up as the lightbulb went on. *She knew.* She'd figured it out.

Swarmed, Gracie blinked against bright lights. Too many flashes. Her mother hissed in her ear, "Open your eyes." She pinched her arm. "Smile."

"The lights hurt. The flashing makes me dizzy."

"Just do it," her mother ordered. "Smile!"

Too many questions. Too many orders, directions.

"Turn this way."

"Over here."

Go away. Everyone go away. Leave me alone.

Gracie shot out of her seat, sending it skidding across the deck. She shook her head, a sharp fast denial.

Everyone stared. She could read their thoughts on their faces.

Austin thought she'd eaten too quickly again and needed a washroom.

Finn stared at her as though she was every bit as nuts as he'd been thinking all along.

Evan and Jake glanced at each other and back at her, but didn't stop eating.

And poor, sweet, wide-eyed Jessica looked like she'd done something terribly wrong, and shook her head. *I won't tell,* she mouthed.

Shannon said, "Gracie, you don't have to rush off to transfer the clothes yet."

Austin leaned toward Cash and whispered something.

Cash said, "There's a powder room just to the left of the front door."

"Thank you," Gracie murmured and entered the house. She ran to the bathroom, where she closed the door and leaned against it, gulping mouthfuls of air into her panicked lungs.

When would the fear of the freak show rearing its ugly head again ever stop?

Tomorrow. When she got her money. Tomorrow couldn't come quickly enough.

At a tentative knock on the door, Gracie jumped away from it.

"Yes?"

"Are you okay?" Jessica. No longer a sweet, caring young woman, but a dark shadow at Gracie's back.

Gracie opened the door. "Did you mean it? That you won't tell?"

"I won't tell." She looked small and unhappy. "Mom asked me to help you put your stuff in the dryer."

In the laundry room, Gracie transferred her clothes.

"Why can't I tell people who you are?" Jessica asked. "I'm right, aren't I? You *are*—"

Gracie stopped her before she could say the name. If Gracie had her way, she would never be that person again.

"I just can't. Please don't let anyone know." Her rushing blood roared in her ears. *"Please."*

Jessica lifted her hand as though to comfort Gracie then dropped it, and Gracie recognized the hesitation for what it was. When she'd thought Gracie was just an ordinary person, her actions had been natural. Now that she thought Gracie was *somebody,* she didn't know how to behave. Finally, Jessica did touch her by placing a gentle hand on her shoulder. "Hey, hey. It's okay. It's your private business. If it's that important to you I won't tell anyone, but I don't get it. Everyone wants to be rich and famous."

"Not everyone." She could do with some of the money, but being famous wasn't all it was made out to be. Not by a long shot. "Fame is hell." Especially for someone shy at heart, and who should never have been in the spotlight in the first place.

"I like my privacy."

"Is that why you live on the road?"

"Yes. To get away from the spotlight." To stop being hunted by everyone and his brother, from people wanting, wanting, wanting something from her. Nobody ever thought to give to her, only to take.

Except Austin.

Yeah, he was good at giving.

That was a first for her.

"Gracie, let's just go back outside and enjoy ourselves. Let's not worry about this stuff. I'm really sorry I scared you."

She sounded so miserable Gracie smiled. It was shaky and uncertain, but it was a smile, because she believed Jessica when she said she wouldn't reveal her secret.

They hugged then entered the hallway that led toward the back of the house, the walls lined with pretty embroidered landscapes.

"This embroidery work is gorgeous." Gracie touched one of them, tracing a delicate leaf.

"Mom's work. She loves it. I know, hard to believe, right? The big tough DEA agent doing girly embroidery."

As they stepped onto the deck, buoyed by her release from imminent exposure, Gracie joked, "You're mom does crewel work."

Jessica giggled, but Evan jumped to his feet. "She

does not. The work she does is amazing. She gets drug-dealing scumbags off the street."

Life was a minefield. In Gracie's experience, it always had been, no matter how hard she had tried to be good and to do everything right. At any second, she would step on a landmine and that would be it. Game over. Life ruined. Crushed, she opened her mouth to defend herself, but Jessica got there first.

"Sit down, doofus. She was talking about Mom's embroidery. Hello? C-r-e-w-e-l."

Shannon laughed. "Good one, Gracie."

Evan sat down with a sheepish grin. "Sorry, Gracie."

Gracie liked that he had stood up for his mom. A lot of love here and a lot of loyalty. Only great parents inspire that in their children.

If only she'd known that when she was young.

For goodness sake, Gracie, quit with the "if onlys." Life sucks. Get over it and move on.

But a tiny part of her still nursed envy and longing.

The Kavenaghs convinced her to sleep over. Rather than spend the night in an alleyway—alone—somewhere in the city, she accepted their offer. Tomorrow, she would go to the bank. After that, she would spend enough time alone starting a new life somewhere. For these few additional precious hours, how could she give up the temptation to spend more time with this amazing family? Their warmth seeped into her bones, and she absorbed it like a starving child, learning from them what a good, happy family looked like. If she was ever lucky enough to have her own family, *this* was how she would do it.

She slept in a sleeping bag on the floor of the basement family room. Austin had tried to give her his bedroom upstairs, but Gracie liked having this private space downstairs all to herself. She especially liked the coziness of the fireplace. Even though it was July, Cash had built a small fire in the hearth to help her to fall asleep. She appreciated it.

Before going to sleep, she had work to do. She got her computer out of her backpack. Everything inside smelled clean, like dryer sheets. She turned on her laptop. Fifteen minutes later, she had read all of the comments from her last post and had put the latest story up on her blog. Surprisingly, her blog readership had risen steadily to a couple of hundred hits a day. She liked to respond to loyal readers. Satisfied, she slipped into the sleeping bag and fell asleep.

AUSTIN SAT IN Evan's bedroom in the Kavenagh house, staring at his phone. Evan and Jake were staying with friends so Austin and Finn could have their bedrooms. Melody slept in the guest bedroom at the end of the hallway. Gracie slept in the basement.

It was time to check in with his mom. What with all that had happened, he hadn't called her today.

He knew he had to. These calls were the most difficult thing he did each day.

After putting it off for too long, he finally called.

Nothing had changed since yesterday, the call full of prolonged silences, sniping and attempts to make him feel guilty. Sometimes, he wondered how he could still love her—but he did—and why he bothered to try to please her.

There was no gratitude, only a feeling that he should be doing more.

The solitude and independence of his ranch couldn't come soon enough.

He soothed his mom as best he could, but hung up knowing neither of them was happy with the result.

Austin sat on the edge of the bed and put the phone on the bedside table with as much restraint as he could muster when his feelings were volatile. He could choose his friends, but not his family.

She was his only family, though.

He thought of Gracie in the basement. Did she have family? Or was she as alone as he felt?

If she had family, why was she on the road?

He undressed and lay on his back staring at the ceiling and the shadows cast by the streetlights shining through the open curtains, and thought about the woman downstairs.

In the clean outfit Jessica had given her, she had looked pretty. In the easy social atmosphere of the Kavenagh home, she looked younger.

That woman.

Gracie.

Lord, she tempted him.

CHAPTER SIX

GRACIE AWOKE TO a wet nose on her cheek. She opened her eyes to a close-up view of Doobie's nostrils and laughed. What a great place this house was.

She might never have a husband and children, but if that good fortune ever came to pass, she would fill her home with love. And dogs. And cats.

Breakfast was huge—bacon, eggs, hash browns and toast. Not that it would matter anymore once she got her money from the bank, but she liked having a big breakfast to sustain her for the rest of the day.

Excitement burbled inside of her like the engine of a luxury car revving for a drive—a Porsche or a Lamborghini.

Today was the first day of the rest of her life. In another couple of hours, she would be on her way to a new life. Home-free. Anonymous in the best possible way.

She was in the homestretch now.

If that thought felt bittersweet because she would also be leaving Austin, she couldn't help it. The man couldn't—shouldn't—matter to her. She had met him only a couple of days ago, but he was working his way past hard-won defenses. No man other than Jay had managed to do that, and there was a world of difference between the two men. Jay couldn't hold a candle to Austin.

Apparently, the others would be staying here another night to visit. The temptation, oh, the terrible, nearly irresistible temptation to give in to Cash Kavanagh's invitation for her, too, to stay tonight, had her close to giving in. But she couldn't. Getting more entangled with Austin was not an option. She had too many secrets and a new life to start. On her own.

The scent of the food placed in front of her beckoned.

Food.

She could enjoy these last few moments with these people.

Austin sat beside her and she was aware of his every movement.

She tucked into her meal. After today, she would never have to worry about food again. She would be able to go into any shop and buy as much as she wanted.

"Go slowly," Austin warned. "Remember what happened with the burgers yesterday."

Gracie nodded, but said nothing. She couldn't tell him the truth.

After breakfast *and* a late lunch, she finally whispered to Austin that it was time for her to go. He had offered to drive her downtown when she was ready to leave. She said goodbyes that hurt more than she would have thought possible. She couldn't lay all of the blame for having stayed so late on this warm family who didn't seem to want to let her go. It also lay with her, because she hadn't wanted to leave. But the time had come. The clock was ticking its way toward late afternoon, and she refused to stay for another meal, because another meal would lead to another night and that wouldn't do.

She had waited a long time for this day, when her money would become *hers* and hers alone. No way was she waiting until tomorrow to claim it.

How could she feel so close to these people after only twenty-four hours?

They were warm and welcoming and generous. It might all be an illusion, but she doubted it. How could she not care for them?

Jessica wrote down her mailing and email addresses. "Will you stay in touch? Or if you don't have email, can you send postcards? I'd like to know if you're okay."

"I'll be fine, but yes, I'll keep in touch." *Especially after I get my money and settle down somewhere.* Then she would get a post-office box for keeping in touch with certain people, without letting them know where she was. She hugged Jessica hard. "You take care of yourself and that nerdy new boyfriend."

She didn't say goodbye to either Melody or Finn other than a brief nod. Melody could write whatever she wanted, but she would have no proof. Who would believe her?

Austin followed her to the car. While they drove downtown, she asked the question she'd been dying to ask since yesterday.

"So Cash was the man who influenced you so much when you were young?"

"He was my Big Brother when I was twelve. I didn't have a father and I was getting into trouble. He was sheriff. I think he was afraid I'd get into really serious stuff if he didn't step in."

He glanced at her and then back at the road. "He was right. I probably would have."

"I can't imagine you ever being in trouble. I thought you would have been the perfect Boy Scout."

His mouth thinned into a grim line, alerting her to his tension. The man was more than surface appearances. He had issues roiling beneath that calm exterior. He didn't respond to her joke.

How serious was the trouble he'd been getting into? How bad could Austin's teenaged rebellion really have been? He was a cop now, so it was probably normal kid-pushing-against-authority stuff.

She wasn't going to get anything else out of him. He was closed up tighter than a steel drum with a hammered-on lid.

They arrived downtown. She'd been trying to leave this guy, to get rid of him, since the moment they'd met. Now walking away felt more painful than anything she'd ever done.

When he pulled up to the curb where she asked him to drop her off and cut the engine, she didn't know what to say.

She had never been tongue-tied in her life.

Thank you seemed grossly inadequate for the gifts he'd given her. First, and most important, the food.

What would she have done without all the food he'd bought her?

She'd been close to the end of her rope. How much longer could she have forced her body to run on empty?

Second, there'd been the companionship. He gave a lot without asking for much in return. She didn't know many people like that.

She hated to think that she'd never see him again, but that was exactly how it would be.

"I can't tell you how sorry I am I robbed you."

Austin's bittersweet smile hid something dark, some kind of pain Gracie didn't have a clue how to name.

"I'm not," he said. "I'm just real glad I met you." He drummed his fingers on the steering wheel. "What I don't understand is why you can't keep traveling with us. You can't keep sleeping in alleyways."

"I'm turning thirty today. I can get money that's been held in trust for me."

"Today's your birthday? Why didn't you say so? We could have done a cake. Come on back. We'll have a party."

"No. Thank you." Happiness backed up in her throat. That he would even think of doing that for her left her shaken and grateful. She hadn't celebrated her birthday in years. In the past, getting older had been a bad thing, but today, it was a godsend.

"I need to move on." She touched the handle of the door, but didn't open it. Not yet. Not quite yet.

There could never be anything more between

them. He deserved a far better woman than she, someone as honest as he was, someone who had lived an ordinary life like he had instead of the circus she'd grown up in.

The time had come to say goodbye. Heat seemed to blow through the car and Austin reached to turn down the heater, obviously forgetting that it was July and the only thing coming out of the vents was cool air. The heat had nothing to do with the weather. It arced between them and had since the moment they'd met.

Austin dropped his hand back onto the steering wheel.

The heat was them, their unspoken desires and needs and wishes. Impossible wishes. At least, Gracie thought those wishes were shared, but maybe they were only hers.

"Well," she said and reached out her hand to shake his. "Thank you." In the end, what else could she say?

"Well," he said and grasped her hand in his much larger one, engulfing her fingers with his calm, sure strength. "I guess this is goodbye."

Why did she feel like crying, as if maybe she was walking away from the best man she would ever know? Certainly, he'd treated her well, but so had others. *Some* others. Not all. Not many.

This shouldn't be so emotional, so devastating.

He cradled her hand in his as though it were a precious jewel. Holy mac and cheese, how could a handshake be so devastating? How could it set her heart to fluttering like a young girl's on her first date? How could it feel as though he was absorbing a part of her soul through the palm of his hand?

Austin Trumball, who are you and what have you done to me?

He tugged, gently, and she yearned forward. He leaned close, closer, his breath a caress on her cheek. She held her own breath because she knew what came next, and wanted it. Craved it. Just this once.

Then his lips were on hers, warm and tender and firm.

In his kiss was the heat of summer, the shimmer of sheet lightning, the earthiness of morning dew.

His palm cradled her cheek, his thumb and forefinger angled her chin where he wanted her. His tongue played hide-and-seek with hers, so sweetly.

A dangerous kiss, it whispered intimate promises to her naive daydreaming heart, promises that would hurt when they weren't fulfilled.

She pulled away by increments, not wanting to end a kiss as sweet as Austin's.

End it now, Gracie. Hurry. This is madness.

But she didn't rush. She savored the feeling and only then, with one final brush of her lips, did she let go.

This close, his sensual, lazy-lidded blue eyes were flecked with dark navy. Funny, she couldn't for the life of her remember what color Jay's eyes had been.

She saw her own confusion and longing reflected there.

Once upon a time, she'd been the sweet girl everyone had wanted her to be, and it had nearly ruined her. She had literally escaped a phony world full of nasty temptations and vices. By running away.

In her previous life, and in her travels, she'd learned to build a shell, as hard and as tough as any woman needed to survive on the road. Even so, a gooey, syrupy core of hope hid inside her, every so often peeking around corners with an innocent *Is it safe to come out?* No. Never. She protected it at all costs. Another betrayal could destroy her for good.

She'd seen a lot of bad on the road, but also plenty of couples holding hands, kids sharing ice cream and puppies frolicking with their owners. She'd seen love. She knew it existed.

It scared the daylights out of her, because she'd never known it in her own life, and didn't know how to get it.

Who would want a world-weary, scarred warrior like her?

Who would take her on?

She slid her hand from Austin's, slowly, memorizing the feel of him, to take out one month, one year, one decade from now when she was living alone and hiding from the world, and feeling the lack of love. She almost certainly would live alone. In the future, how could she possibly ever find another man as good as Austin? She would need a memory like this. Of him.

He'd left a mark on her. Had she, invisible, not-sure-who-she-was-these-days Gracie, left her mark on him?

She hoped so.

In the end, there was only one thing to do. Walk away.

"Goodbye," she said and opened the door.

When she got out of the car, she closed the door, but rested her fingers on the handle, holding on for a few more seconds. Why was this so hard?

The past six years had been a series of fleeting hellos and shorter goodbyes. This shouldn't be any more difficult than those.

But it was.

In time, she let go, looking at Austin, hoping for one final glimpse of those beautiful, terrible emotions roiling in his blue eyes, but he stared straight ahead, jaw hard and expression closed. He drove off without another glance.

She watched him until he disappeared around a corner. When she could no longer see him, she raised her hand in a half-hearted wave and then dropped it.

This was right. For the best. She would have had to say goodbye to him in Texas anyway. It would have been even harder after spending more time with him.

Her chest filled with a miasma of loss, regret, tenderness. She might be a little bit in love with the guy, and wasn't that crazy? She'd known him for only two days. Only two? Impossible when it felt like forever.

Get over him. He's just a man, like any other.

No, she couldn't say that he was like *any* other man she'd met.

He was amazing, if too confident in himself and his own ideas.

She smiled. She would never forget Austin Trumbull, that's for sure.

She walked to Denver's largest bank and the race engine inside her revved. For the first time in her life, her money would be hers and hers alone.

She wasn't sure how trust funds worked, but she thought she should be able to get something out today and the rest another time at another bank when she settled down. Her parents had kept her woefully ignorant about money. It was time to learn how to handle it herself. At least she would eat tonight on her own dime.

Before stepping inside, she sat on one of the benches that lined the street and retrieved her little notebook from her backpack pocket, finishing her tally of everything she owed Austin, and then subtracting twenty dollars for his haircut. She couldn't, in good conscience, charge more. She'd learned from the best, but she wasn't a pro.

Boy, oh, boy, food was expensive at restaurants. She owed Austin a lot.

She knew who he was. She knew where he lived. She would mail him a check.

First, she had to get her money.

The lazy summer breeze carried away regret and what-ifs. She straightened her hair and stepped into the bank. This morning, she had clean clothes to wear, all thanks to the Kavenaghs.

Would she ever see them again?

Cut it out. No looking back.

Every step now is a step forward. Today is the beginning of the rest of your life.

She approached a teller and asked to speak to the bank manager.

GOODBYE, MY LEFT NUT, Austin thought. After that kiss? That bit of perfection that should have been a beginning instead of an ending?

The beginning of *what?*

He didn't have a clue, but he couldn't leave her to walk away, not until he knew for sure she was safe. Then he would consider it.

Then, and only then, he would really say goodbye. Maybe. After he explored more of whatever it was that had built between them.

He turned the corner and parked, then strode back to the street to follow Gracie.

He wasn't stalking her, not *per se,* whatever the heck that meant. He just couldn't, honestly couldn't, let her go off alone. He had to know she would be okay.

Without making himself conspicuous, he followed her to a bank then waited in a bus shelter half a block away. If she came out smiling, he would know things were good for her and he could leave her to continue on her journey.

But the sweetness of that kiss… Gracie was a stranger and yet not a stranger. And that kiss was more like a possibility, a beginning, the promise of more, even better, to come.

Could he go on his own way without exploring what could develop?

Could he go off without her when the thought of never seeing her again left him edgy and empty?

Gracie, and her well-being, shouldn't mean anything to him. Finn was right on that score, even if it did make Austin madder than hell when his buddy said it.

He waited ten, fifteen, twenty minutes for her to come out of the bank.

Lack of airflow and the sun beating full-force on the glassed-in shelter made him step out onto the sidewalk. Still no sign of her.

He checked his watch. Thirty minutes gone. How long did it take to access a person's money?

Movement at the bank door caught his attention. Gracie came out. About time. He stepped back into the shelter and leaned against the glass to watch her.

She sat down on the bench in front of the bank, posture slumped and beaten.

Austin pulled away from the wall, easing his hands out of his pockets. Something was wrong. Very wrong.

How could this have happened? How could her parents have betrayed her again?

Millions of dollars gone.

They'd defrauded her of all of her money and they'd known she wouldn't do anything about it. To challenge her parents, she would have to step out into the open.

If she took them to court, she would be thrust back into the spotlight—absolute anathema for her—and crafty manipulators that they were, they had counted on that to keep her from pressing charges.

If her life before she'd disappeared had been a circus, what would happen if she took her parents to court? The feeding frenzy would eclipse anything she'd experienced to date.

She cringed, as though just the *thought* of suing her parents hurt physically, let alone actually doing it.

Oh, dear sweet Jesus, her account was empty.

A full-blown panic struck, icy and terrifying. Her lungs burned with frost. It hurt to breathe, the air passing through her nostrils and down her throat like liquid nitrogen.

Holy Hannah, the life had been sucked out of her. It was twenty years ago and she was a child again doing everything her parents asked of her, but it had made no dent in their indifference to her or in their desire for more from her. Obedience got her no more love than it ever had.

It was six years ago, and she was an adult, but might as well have been a child for all she knew about the real world. She had just learned the truth about her husband—that he had married her for her money, that he had never loved her and that he had slept with other women throughout their five years together.

That night, aching and in despair, she'd packed her knapsack and had walked out of their home—and had been walking ever since. She had signed the divorce papers on the road, barely escaping the trap Jay and her parents had set in trying to catch her that day.

She was valuable to them, but not for herself. Only for what she could do for them, for how much money she could bring in.

She'd learned a thing or two since leaving. She'd learned to be crafty, to be deceitful, and to be distrustful. They hadn't caught her that day, or since.

But she obviously hadn't learned enough. She'd still trusted her parents to leave her money alone. She had thought there would be at least enough to buy a small house. Failing that, she'd thought she could take the money and purchase a new identity then get a job somewhere where she would never be found.

Yesterday, after Jessica had recognized her, she'd realized it wouldn't have worked unless she *really* changed her looks. Her old self, that version of herself that had never been real, was everywhere. Cable television. Same with the internet. Too many old shows and movies were available everywhere these days.

She had nowhere to go. How could she have been so wrong about her parents?

You knew what they were like.

Yeah, but I'd hoped they had changed.

So naive.

Yes.

She couldn't have prevented this. There was nothing she could have done to change this outcome.

She sat on the bench in front of the bank and rested

her head in her hands, hollow, gutted. Oh, dear sweet God, where did she go from here?

Her safety net, her someday-this-will-all-be-over guarantee was gone. She had *nothing*.

Noise coming from the bank caught her attention. She glanced up.

Tellers and customers stood in the windows, whispering, banging on the glass, smiling and waving. Some had their cell phones out, no doubt taking photos. Or shooting videos.

She cursed the day cameras had been added to cell phones. So little privacy in the world now. Didn't people understand what they'd created? How dangerous it was?

The manager had obviously told everyone in the bank who she was. She'd had to show him her real ID to access her account.

The bank was closing. If she didn't leave now, she would be swarmed. Reporters would show up. More gawkers would point fingers. The whole painful, ludicrous process would start again, and maybe this time she wouldn't survive.

Frantic, she stood and started to walk. When she heard whispering behind her, she ran, hard and fast, until it faded.

She no longer had that big *out* in her future, the goal to reach thirty, claim her money and be free for the rest of her life.

Her freedom had been shattered.

She had always known that once she got her money, she would have choices, would be able to buy a phony SSN and birth certificate so no one could find her. Goodbye to the old Gracie and hello to the new permanent Gracie with no more ties to the past.

Her head hurt. She rubbed her forehead, but kept walking.

Every last choice had been taken from her. She had no doubt her parents would find out where she was now that she'd contacted a bank. They would have people watching for her. They could certainly afford to. They had all of her money. She knew them well.

She had to leave Denver, but where would she go? Drifting had lost its appeal. She'd been everywhere, had seen everything. She wanted a home, roots, permanence.

The streets emptied as people rushed home to dinners and TV programs.

One house she passed cast a golden light from its windows, the warm glow like a ray of hope.

Hope. She laughed bitterly. She had none left.

That didn't stop her from staring into the home. The owners hadn't yet closed their curtains for the night.

Gracie loved spying from a distance—not like some sick Peeping Tom, but taking pleasure in seeing the mundane, everyday tasks and turning them into treasures—fixing dinner, straightening living rooms, calling children away from computers and television sets to sit down for dinner as families. The whole worth more than the sum of its parts.

Isn't that how families should be? Shouldn't they enhance each other, not feed off one of their own?

When would it be her time? Given her background, could she ever have a normal life?

Inside the home, a pair of boys wrestled while their mother chastised them—or so it appeared. Gracie couldn't hear a word that was said, but her active imagination took over and created a scene from a movie. She should really write movie scripts. She couldn't seem to turn off the spark in her brain that created stories.

"Honey, can you set the table?" the wife asked, tossing the spinach and arugula salad with olive oil and balsamic vinegar.

"Sure." The husband carried in the steaks he'd barbecued on the back deck. "Should I get out spoons? Are we having soup before dinner?"

"Asparagus soup."

"Asparagus? For the boys?" he derided, but there was humor beneath the words. "Good luck getting the kids to eat it."

She laughed, because they'd eaten it all last week for lunch while her husband had been away on business. Didn't he get how cool their kids were? She put the warm dish of roasted sweet potatoes on a trivet on the table. A squeal from the living room caught her attention. She smiled and shook her head.

"Those boys. Always so full of beans."

"Want me to talk to them?"

"No. Boys will be boys."

"Why are you staring into that house?" At the voice behind her, the daydream shattered.

Austin leaned against a lamppost watching her.

Her modern version of *Leave it to Beaver* faded into the ether. Inevitable, of course; it had never been real.

Why wasn't she surprised to see him? Lordy, the man was stubborn.

"You need to leave me alone." She should have known he would follow her. "Why are you here?"

"I wanted to know you were okay."

He stood with his hands in his pockets and his eyes on the scene through the window.

"You followed me from the bank?" She didn't like that he was still here, still concerned about her. Hadn't he seen her mortified enough by poverty and desperation? She didn't want him to see how far she had really fallen. Didn't want him to watch her hit rock bottom.

"Yes. I saw how you looked when you came out. I gave you time to walk and deal with whatever is wrong and now I want to help."

"Why?"

"Why were you staring into that house?" He'd sidestepped the issue.

Why was she staring into that house?

He could never understand her need to dream, her longing for a little of what she saw around her, but had never known for herself. "I'm not a Peeping Tom. I didn't even realize I was looking. I was just standing here thinking."

"I know you aren't a Peeping Tom, Gracie. I've learned things about you."

Like what? she wanted to ask, but didn't. The less

they shared, the fewer emotional intimacies between them, the better.

"It's not all as good as it looks, you know."

"What do you mean?"

He pointed toward the house. "There are probably cracks in the foundation of that marriage. Those boys might be fighting for real rather than roughhousing. Their mother could be truly angry rather than mildly frustrated. There is no such thing as the perfect life."

But I want it to be real. I want there to be something good to replace what I had.

"Isn't there a better reality out there somewhere?" She hadn't meant to ask that out loud.

"Better than what you have now?" Austin snorted, softly.

No. Better than what I grew up with.

Austin pointed toward her knapsack and worn-out sneakers. "Almost anything is better than that."

"Maybe. Maybe not. We all make our choices for our own reasons."

"Your sorry state is a choice?"

He would condemn her now. "Yes."

His frown didn't look angry, but more confused.

A couple carrying bags of groceries passed on the sidewalk, their nods friendly, but also curious. The woman's floral dress swished around her legs. The man murmured something and her husky laugh brightened the corners of Gracie's dark mood.

Gracie walked away, because they looked odd standing there, as though they had nowhere to go.

Well, that was sure true for her, wasn't it? Absolutely nowhere.

Austin had cattle to purchase in Texas and a ranch to return to, and good deeds galore with which to impress others, but she had nowhere to go and no time to be there.

She had nothing.

Just ahead, two teenagers—the rural version of city punks, Gracie guessed—argued. Looked as if they might break out the fists at any moment.

Austin stepped between them.

Was he crazy? That's how innocent bystanders got hurt. One of the kids might have a knife. These days, it seemed everyone carried a gun.

"Hey," he said, as though he were doing nothing more than helping two friends overcome their differences. "Ease up, guys. What's got you so riled?"

Riled? Sometimes the guy sounded more like a cowboy than a modern-day cop. The kids stopped fighting and turned their hostility on him.

"Who're you?" one asked. Belligerent young punk. A kid on the verge of manhood trying to prove himself. She didn't like Austin being on the receiving end of the kid's macho needs.

Austin didn't seem fazed.

"What the hell do you want?" The other teen pushed toward Austin. "Mind your own business."

"Just trying to keep the peace." Austin stood his ground.

The first kid snorted. "You're a cop, aren't you?"

Austin nodded.

The second kid scoffed, "Man, I could tell that from a mile away."

"What are you fighting about?" In Austin's voice Gracie detected neither anger nor criticism.

"Jimmy stole my bike."

"How many times do I hafta tell you? I didn't steal it. I borrowed it to follow my sister. I don't trust that guy she's dating."

"Who? Sammy? I wouldn't trust that dirt bag, either. Where's my bike now?"

"Sammy took it from me."

"Bastard. Let's go get it."

They turned on Austin. "Next time, mind your own business." They walked away in a huff, but on the same page and with a shared purpose.

Gracie rounded on him. "Why did you get involved?"

"Sometimes the best way to bring two people together is to give them a common enemy. For kids their age, that would be a cop." Austin laughed. "I don't mind being the bad guy if it brings peace and cooperation."

"What if they had ganged up on you physically?"

"I'm trained in this, Gracie. It's what I do."

Despite herself, she was impressed, and her desire to stop having anything to do with Austin made her cross.

"So you have to do it even when you're off the clock?" She sounded peevish, but couldn't stop herself, not when her problems crowded in on her, dark and demanding answers.

She didn't have any.

Heart heavy and leaden-footed, she turned down an alleyway, because dusk was ever so slowly encroaching. Footsteps echoed behind her and she tensed.

"Stop following me. My life is none of your business."

"I'm making it my business."

"Oh, Lord." She stopped walking and confronted him. "Save me from macho men and their need to control."

"I'm not a macho man."

He looked like one, tall and brave. He was more than that, though. He was also insightful. Witness his remark about the occupants of that house not necessarily being as perfect as she had hoped. He'd known what she was thinking. Macho didn't *begin* to truly describe Austin Trumball.

"I don't need to control, but I do need to know you're going to be all right." He leaned against the wall in the alleyway, arms crossed, pose casual, but tension threaded his voice.

The man just couldn't seem to stop taking care of her.

"Nothing happened. Everything is fine."

She chose a spot behind a bale of cardboard, pulling an old sheet out of her knapsack to lie down on, so she wouldn't soil her pretty new outfit. No one from the street would be able to see her here. She would be as safe as she ever was, which wasn't saying a whole lot.

Austin hadn't budged.

"You're going to get tired holding up that wall all night." Gracie spread her thin blanket over her shoulders. It was still early, but she had no food to eat, nowhere to go and nothing to do.

"I'm not leaving until I get an answer." Austin stood like a sphinx, as though he had all the time in the world to wait her out. Ha. Time was all *she* had. Nothing else. "What happened at the bank?"

She didn't respond.

True to his word, he still stood there ten minutes later. She fidgeted, turned this way and that, adjusted the blanket over her shoulders, because it really was too early for bed and Austin's stare was disconcerting, even though she couldn't see it in the darkening alley. She felt it on her, his steady perusal a caress of her hair, a touch on her lips, a brushing across her eyelids.

She shot into a sitting position. "You're really making me mad. Will you just *go?*"

"Already told you. I'll leave after I get an answer."

"No, you won't."

"The only reason I won't is if you got bad news. Did you?"

She shrugged. He interpreted her silence correctly.

"It was bad news at the bank, wasn't it?"

A sigh gusted out of her on a wave of disgust. The man just wouldn't *quit*. "Yes."

He squatted on his haunches in front of her, crowding her, but also surrounding her with his big, safe bulk, his clean scent and his caring warmth.

"What happened? Where was the money you were supposed to have?"

"Gone. Someone spent it."

"Someone? Who? Did someone other than you have access to your account?"

She nodded.

"Why did you let them?"

"I didn't have a choice," she shouted, wishing she could shake this man's irritatingly calm demeanor. "It wasn't my fault."

"How could giving someone else access to your own bank account not be your fault?"

She kept her story to herself because trust was a hard and bitter nugget in her breast.

She sighed long and heavily because she'd run out of options and energy. She truly did want Austin to leave her alone. She needed to be alone to grieve, and maybe even give in to a good crying jag.

"Go," she said. "I want to be alone."

"Goddammit," Austin exploded. "Do you have to be so tough? Can't you just take a helping hand when it's offered?"

"No. I know people. I've seen everything on the road. I don't trust anyone. I'm sorry if that offends you."

She reined in her frustration and lowered her voice. "I learned a long time ago that the only person I can depend on in this life is me. There is no rescue. There are no Prince Charmings."

Not even you.

"I'm strong enough to save myself and I will." She

was being hard on him, so she softened her tone. "You've been generous and kind. I have allowed you to rescue me for two days. You will never know how much I appreciate that you didn't turn me in to the police when you could have." Lord, what a media circus that would have been. Talk about her worst nightmare.

"In the end, though, we're strangers and it's best if we stay that way. I'm alone. I will support myself. I had a plan. It's been blown out of the water, but I will figure something out. I will survive. I always do."

Cripes, she was tired. She needed sleep.

"Please just go, Austin." She sounded as dispirited as she felt. "I'm not going to dinner with you. I'm not going to let you give me another hotel room. I'm certainly not going to go back to the Kavenaghs." And let them see her failure? No way. She was worse off today than she had even been yesterday. Today, she had no hope. Determination, but no idea how she would survive, and too-noble, too-responsible Austin didn't need to know that. She had meant it when she said she would rescue herself.

"Thank you for all you've given me, but we're done, Austin."

He must have heard the finality in her voice because he walked away without another word, not even goodbye. That hurt, and she didn't want to think about why. They didn't know each other. That sweet tender kiss had been a fluke.

She closed her eyes and willed herself to sleep, but sleep wouldn't come. The harder she tried, the more it eluded her. She was supposed to have been through with this life. She was supposed to have her own money to buy her own food, or to rent a room.

Now she was nobody. Who would love her the way she was, homeless and broke, with nothing to offer but need?

What had there ever been to love about her other than her ability to pretend to be someone else? What would any man see in her without her money and her fame?

A mouse ran over her foot.

She should tell it to get lost, but didn't have the strength to do even that.

This situation was never supposed to have been permanent.

After dozing fitfully, she set out on the road early, with the sun just beginning to leak over the skyline.

With a little luck, she would be in the next town before Austin, Melody and Finn set out for the day. Maybe even by the time they had breakfast.

What were they having for breakfast today?

CHAPTER SEVEN

"WHY ARE YOU rushing us?" Finn tossed his bag into the back of the SUV with an impatient flick. "Why can't we have breakfast here? Why do we have to put in mileage first?"

Why didn't Finn quit with his insistent questions? The women had come between them, had eroded part of their friendship, and Austin wanted things back the way they were.

The fault was partly Austin's. Leaving Gracie was turning out to be about as hard as anything he'd ever done. He eased off on his attitude. "I want to get an early start. That's all. Let's just go. Please."

Angry and frustrated that Gracie had hit a huge snag but wouldn't take help from him, he hadn't slept all night for worrying about her.

Didn't his friend understand that he needed to be away from here? That he needed to put distance between himself and Gracie? If he didn't, he just might rush down to that alley, take her out of there by force and feed her breakfast whether she wanted it or not.

"Get in the car." Austin stowed his bag in the back and slammed the door. "Please." Yeah, he wanted to get out of town, but he didn't want to talk about it.

Last night, what choice had he had but to leave Gracie? What else could he do? Toss her over his shoulder? Physically drag her back to the Kavenagh house, where she would be safe and sound?

We're done with each other.

While he'd been looking at possibilities for the future, she'd been trying to get rid of him.

She had been adamant that he leave her there.

Please, just go, Austin.

Fine. He was gone.

"A cup of coffee would have been nice," Finn groused, but the look he gave Austin before he glanced at Melody climbing into the backseat almost said, *I feel your pain.* Maybe he was softening where Gracie was concerned. Maybe he understood Austin's worries.

They said goodbye to the Kavenaghs. Cash squeezed him hard. "Will you be okay?"

"Yeah. I'm good." Austin had shared the whole story with Cash last night—from the moment he'd caught Gracie trying to rob him to last night's goodbye in downtown Denver.

"I don't like you driving angry."

Cash was right. Austin had to calm down.

With Austin in a marginally better frame of mind, they headed out onto the road, the sun barely warming the land around them.

In the backseat, Melody wrapped a scarf around her shoulders and closed her eyes to nap.

They weren't five miles out of town when Austin spotted a woman trudging along the shoulder of the road.

Gracie.

Why didn't it surprise him? She didn't know how to stay put. Where was she off to without a penny to her name?

Why couldn't she stay in one place long enough to get a real job? He didn't understand.

Not your problem.

"Keep driving, man." Finn's warning tone echoed his thoughts.

He should listen. He didn't. The anger flared again.

Are you brain dead?

Probably. She can at least come to breakfast with us.

"Please. Stop," Melody said from the backseat.

Finn swiveled to look at her. "What? Why?" Austin heard shock in his friend's voice.

"Get her to come back in the car with us."

When Finn would have said more, Melody entreated, "Trust me. I'll explain later."

Austin didn't know or care why Melody wanted Gracie back with them—compassion, he guessed—but he pulled ahead of Gracie and stopped on the shoulder. He needed to help.

With a curse, he was out of the vehicle and striding toward her. Today, he wasn't taking *no* for an answer, because fear fueled his anger. The woman had slept out in an alley, for God's sake.

"If you're walking from here to Timbuktu, at

least do it on a full stomach. Have you eaten any-thing today?"

He didn't wait for an answer, but took the knap-sack from her back, maybe a little roughly.

Last night, he'd thought good riddance. Today he couldn't hold on to that.

He took her hand and dragged her to the SUV. "I didn't sleep last night for worrying about you. Get in the car."

SHE DUG IN her heels. "You high-handed son of a b—gun." Old habits died hard. She couldn't even swear properly, not even all these years later as a grown woman. Besides, she really didn't want to swear at Austin. He was high-handed, he wanted things his own way, but he cared. And it had been so long since anyone had cared. Oh, wait. Not *one* of the people who *should* have cared ever had. No wonder she found him so seductive.

"Stop worrying about me." She tugged on her hand, but he wouldn't let go. "I'm not your respon-sibility. I never was."

"You know that old saying, right? That if you save a person's life, they belong to you for the rest of yours?"

"You didn't save my life. You fed me. I wasn't dying."

"No, but you were desperate enough to lift a wallet." He hovered over her, angry and righteous and not the least bit like the calm Austin she knew.

"Thank God it was from me and not someone more dangerous. You could have been killed."

He'd raised his voice.

"Fine. I was lucky it was you," she conceded. "I appreciate every speck you did for me, I truly do, but I don't belong to you. Besides, I think you got that saving a life thing backward."

"Gracie?"

They both turned at the sound of Melody's voice. The back door was open and she was leaning across the seat to get Gracie's attention. "Get in the car. I have a proposition for you."

A proposition? Yeah, she knew exactly what kind of proposition a *reporter* would have. Gracie shook her head the second the sentence was out of the woman's mouth. She knew what it was. She'd heard it many times in the past, always from someone who wanted to make money off her.

As far back as she could remember, her life had been about people profiting from her labor. No more. Never again. In the future, the *only* person making money would be her.

"No," she countered, her tone as unequivocal as the word.

Melody made a tsk of frustration. "You don't even know what it is."

"Trust me, I know."

"Gracie." Austin moved to stand in front of her. "I don't know what Melody wants, and I don't care. What *I* want is to get you off this highway and take you somewhere safe. At least for breakfast. Get in the car. Please." He'd softened his tone and his stance.

She swayed toward him because she was tired of life being hard, of being alone.

There were some people who didn't need anyone else, who cherished solitude. She didn't think she was one of those. She thought her natural inclination was toward people, but her experience had taught her to hold herself aloof.

If her childhood had been different, who would she be now?

There you go with the "ifs" again, Gracie. Stop it.

A car approached, the crunch of gravel under the tires ominous. Both she and Austin turned to watch a sheriff's vehicle pull onto the shoulder behind them.

Oh, crap.

AUSTIN SWORE UNDER his breath and took her hand to prevent her from leaving. It only needed this. As if the situation weren't frustrating enough.

A cop got out, hitching up his pants over his belly and adjusting his belt. A thick, walrus moustache obscured his mouth. "What's the problem here, folks?"

"Nothing, Officer." Austin eased himself in front of Gracie.

"Why are you pulled over?"

"My girlfriend and I are having a discussion." Austin squeezed her hand, willing her not to argue. She didn't. Nice of the woman to cooperate for a change.

After one look at Gracie's tight jaw, the officer said, "Looks more like an argument to me."

Austin nodded. "Yeah. It is." He smiled ruefully, hoping to get the cop's sympathy. *Women.* He shrugged. *What can you do?*

"You think you can have your argument somewhere other than on the side of the road?"

Austin glared at Gracie. "I've been trying to convince her that would be a good idea."

She refused to look at either him or the officer. She also remained mute, damn her, instead of confirming his story.

"Sir, I'm going to have to ask for your license."

Austin took his wallet out of his back pocket and made a show of getting it out, sending a message to Gracie. *See this wallet, the one you stole from me? Remember that I didn't report you to the police? A little cooperation on your part wouldn't hurt.*

A blush warmed her cheeks. She bit her lip.

The officer left with Austin's ID, but returned quickly. "You shoulda told me you were a deputy."

"I don't like to use it to influence officers of the law."

"'Preciate that." He turned to Gracie who'd been leaning against the car, still with that mulish expression. "Ma'am, I gotta ask. Is this guy forcing you to go somewhere you don't want to go or is he telling the truth? Are you his girlfriend?"

After all he'd done for her, if she didn't agree he'd bust a gut.

After a prolonged silence, she sighed. "Yes. He's my boyfriend. We're fighting."

Austin released the breath he'd been holding.

"Think you could do it somewhere safe?" The officer's voice was surprisingly gentle when he spoke to Gracie. Maybe it was the obvious misery under her defiance. "I can't leave you here like this."

"Okay, I'll get into the car." She climbed in, her back ramrod straight. She wasn't happy, but at least she was in his vehicle.

The cop returned to his vehicle muttering something about young love. Ha! If this was love, then Austin was *never* giving it a whirl, 'cause it felt like crap.

AUSTIN STOPPED AT a drive-through and got breakfast sandwiches, hash browns and coffee, ordering for Gracie even when she said she didn't want anything. Finn paid for everything. When Austin ordered the works for her, she was secretly glad because eating nothing while everyone else scarfed down grease-laden eggs and potatoes would have been murder on her. Her stomach had been grumbling since dawn.

Austin drove them to a rest stop they'd passed a mile back down the road.

Once settled at a picnic table, they ate in silence. Great. Just great. First, she owed Austin all kinds of money, and now she owed Finn for her breakfast. Bad enough that she had to owe a man she respected, but Finn? Crap on a broomstick.

When they'd finished eating, Melody looked at Gracie. "Do you want to tell them or should I?"

"Tell us what?" Austin tensed beside Gracie, a cop's awareness vibrating through him, as if asking *What's happening here?*

Gracie's life was about to crumble, that's what was happening.

"Why do I have to tell anyone anything?"

"This is huge, Gracie. You can't just leave it."

"I can and I have for six years. Why does that have to change now?"

"Because of me. Because I'm a reporter who believes that the world deserves the truth."

"Not about *me*. Why shouldn't I have *my* privacy? Why would *I* owe the world anything? The world deserves nothing from me."

"I'll tell the story with or without you, but I'd rather have your cooperation. I'd like to tell your version of the truth."

"The truth. That's a laugh." The bitterness in Gracie's voice tasted of bile. "This isn't about exposing corrupt politicians or delivering the latest medical or scientific breakthrough. This is gossip. This isn't about lofty ideals like truth. This is about fame and money. I know all about you crappy reporters."

"Hey!" Finn said, half rising from the bench. "Take that back."

"No. Reporters are the scum of the earth. They think they're owed everything when they deserve—" she glared back at Melody "—nothing."

"You'll regret not cooperating with me." For a

small woman with a delicate voice, Melody packed a lot of menace into that one statement.

"Who do you think you are to barge into another person's life as though you own it? As though you deserve to know all there is to know about me? I owe you nothing. You make your living ruining other people's lives. You make your living on other people's heartache. My story isn't yours to tell." She stood. "Got it?"

"Even so, I will tell it." Tiny voice. Big threat.

"Why?"

"Because it's the biggest story I've ever come across. You can tell it to me, or I can make it up. Your choice."

Reasoned arguments, civilized feelings, good manners—everything Gracie had been taught unraveled and the animal deep inside of her sprang out. The years of running, the years of doing everything right and getting nothing back for it but heartache and loneliness, the absurdity of her younger life, blazed up in her. The frustration mounted until it erupted.

"You—" Gracie flew at her, fingers curled to scratch out her eyes. Austin caught her around the waist before she made contact. She fought him, but he was strong.

She grasped his fingers. He wouldn't let go. She scratched his wrists. He held on.

Nobody had the right to her life.

Finn came around the table.

Austin planted his palm against Finn's chest.

"Whatever you're thinking of doing to Gracie, don't. Friend or no, I won't let you hurt her."

"She tried to attack Melody."

"You will not hurt her." Austin's implacable tone left no doubt whose side he was on. "I don't know what the hell is going on here, but I have a feeling Melody deserves some of what Gracie here is dying to dish out."

"Who deserves that?" Finn's face twisted until there was no sign of the good-looking guy women flocked to. Good. Let him feel a fraction of what Gracie was going through. "Melody did nothing to her."

"No?" Austin eased his grip on Gracie, but her legs were shaking and wouldn't stop. He kept his arm around her waist. Thank goodness, or her knees would crumple.

"Sit down, Finn." Austin's cop voice, calm and authoritative despite the tremor she felt running through him, impressed Gracie. What was he feeling so intensely? Anger? Disgust? Well, too bad.

She'd taken too much grief in her life. She was fighting back.

Finn hadn't relaxed his stance.

"Sit!" Austin ordered. He turned to Gracie. "You, too."

"Why?"

"We're getting to the bottom of this. What's going on between you two that has you at each other's throats? You don't even know each other!"

"That witch—" Gracie pointed at Melody, not

caring a whit that she was being crass, because being nice all her life had just about destroyed her "—wants to publish my story. She wants to make money off me, off something that's none of her business."

Gracie leaned forward and hissed, "Parasite."

Melody flinched then rallied. "Your story is part of the public domain. If you hadn't wanted the world to know about you, you shouldn't have done everything you could to get into the spotlight."

"Spotlight?" Austin echoed.

"*I* did everything I could? I was a kid. A *child*. I had no choice."

"Then tell that to the world."

"Why? So you can make your big bucks? So you can get your big break? No."

"Why did you change your looks? Why don't you go out into the world as yourself? Why this hiding, this homelessness? Why not just be honest?"

"I am myself. *Now*. You want a story? You want honesty? Write about yourself. Phony."

Melody's glance shied away, and she looked uncomfortable. Good.

Reporters like her had no idea the kind of damage they did, all for the sake of a buck. "Let's turn the tables here and see how you feel."

Melody shook her head, but Gracie forged ahead. She should know how it felt to have her life dissected, to have all of her secrets laid bare.

"Let's see how you like exposure." Before anyone could guess her intention, she reached across the table, grasped Melody's hair and tugged hard. A wig came off in her hand.

Gracie had known from the second she'd met the woman her hair was fake. She'd seen enough wigs in her life to recognize even an expensive one. She'd wondered what Melody was hiding, but would never have intruded on her privacy under normal circumstances. Unfortunately, this was war.

The gloves were off.

Melody's hands flew to her head, where shorter, thinner hair grew in a dull brown, rather than the lush, rich chestnut of the long wig. "How could you be so cruel?"

"I'm cruel? Take a good look at yourself, then tell me why you or anyone else deserves to know *my* secrets. *Mine."*

Melody started to cry, but Gracie felt nothing for her. She deserved it. She had wanted to expose Gracie while keeping herself intact. The heck with that. "This is what it feels like to be exposed. Do you like it? Does it feel good, Melody, to be forced to tell the world every little detail about yourself? Even when you don't *want* to?"

Gracie leaned across the table and shouted, "How does it *feel?*"

Melody didn't answer.

Gracie left the picnic table, calling Melody a pungent name first, a word she'd never used before, but this woman had become the target of everything Gracie had held in for too many years.

She strode down the road, away from these people and their crappy needs.

FINN DIDN'T KNOW where to look. He sensed Austin leaving to follow Gracie, but his concern was for Melody.

After that one brief glimpse of her real hair, he couldn't look again, pretty certain Melody wouldn't want him to see her until she'd finished putting her wig back on.

All that dark, gorgeous hair he'd admired wasn't real.

Her real hair looked different. Not rich. Not dark and shiny. Not thick. Just…average.

"What—"

"Don't say anything, please." Melody hiccupped then continued to sob quietly beside him.

He wanted to comfort her, he really did, but he didn't have a clue what to say. He thought he should hold her, but was having trouble doing that. Truth was, her real hair freaked him out a bit. He knew there had to be scars underneath.

"It was the fire," she said.

Of course. How could her scalp have healed so well that her hair had grown back in lush and gorgeous?

He should have known better.

When his dad had pulled her out of the car, he'd

had to put out the fire in her hair with his hands. He'd had bandages for days.

Melody's bandages had still been on weeks later when she disappeared. He had no idea how badly her scalp had been burned.

"How long did it take your scalp to heal?"

"Close to a year. I had skin grafts and hair implants. It looks okay, but not nice like this." She pointed to the wig.

It was slightly askew. Slowly, so he wouldn't frighten her after being assaulted by that woman, he reached up and straightened it.

"Want me to go beat up Gracie?"

Melody shook her head.

"How about I go find a dragon, slay it and cook it for dinner? Would that make you feel better?"

A wet laugh escaped.

Melody wouldn't look at him. She stared at his chest, at the table, at the grass beside the picnic bench, evidently as embarrassed as he was.

"Melody," he said, catching her attention.

She glanced up and then quickly away.

"Look at me," he said. It was hard. He was scared. He'd never had to deal with this kind of thing before.

It bothered him that Melody was hurting. His inner little boy wanted to run away, but God, he was thirty-two years old. He should be able to handle this.

When Melody finally met his gaze, he said, "You're beautiful. Don't let that woman make you feel bad about yourself."

"I won't."

"I don't believe you. You're pale. Your hands are cold."

"No one has ever done anything like that to me before." She clenched her jaw.

Because she had started to shake, he pulled her into his arms. She was tiny against his chest. He liked her delicacy.

"That felt violent. Just that. No wonder my mom ran away from my dad. He did things a lot worse than what Gracie just did to me." She curled against him. "I deserved it."

"No, you didn't," Finn whispered fiercely. "She was wrong to come at you and she was wrong to yell at you." In spite of how weird he felt about her wearing a wig, he said, "And she was wrong to expose you. That should have been your choice, not hers."

"I believe she was making the same point about herself," Melody said, tone dry.

He didn't care. Melody was a good, good person. Gracie was a homeless bum. She had no right to treat Melody like shit.

He didn't even care what it was Gracie was hiding or how Melody knew about it. Nothing excused her behavior toward Melody.

"You be proud of who you are. Journalism is a noble profession. We need the press to expose all of the evil of the world. If you don't, who will?"

"Gracie isn't evil."

"Don't be too sure about that. Do you know how we met her?"

Melody shook her head.

"She stole Austin's wallet."

Melody's eyes widened. "Really?" She pulled a notebook out of her purse and rummaged until she found a pen. "I need this story."

"Why?"

"I have a lot riding on being a successful journalist. I want to show my 'family'—" she used air quotes "—the man who abused my mom, and his parents who never protected her, that Mom and I did just fine without them. I *have* to show them we not only got by, but we succeeded in life. As hard as they tried, they didn't break us."

"But—"

"Success is the best revenge. Don't judge me, Finn. That bit of violence from Gracie has left me spitting mad. I understand the point she was making, but nobody abuses me and gets away with it. You have no idea how much I need to write an amazing story and then rub my father's face in my success."

If he lives that long, Finn thought. Melody wasn't thinking this all the way through, and her rationale wasn't completely kosher, but who was Finn to make her give up her goals?

"Gracie's secret is an amazing story? Really?"

"You bet. Tell me everything." She held her pen over her notebook, ready to write.

He liked her pluckiness, her spirit. Even after Gracie had humiliated her, she bounced back. Good.

"Here's the story." He told about Gracie stealing Austin's wallet. "Austin caught her and then fed her. I've been trying to get him to leave her alone ever since." He told the rest, including every unfavorable impression he had of the woman.

When he finished, Melody put her pen down. "I need to figure out how to handle this. There has to be a way for me to do this well, without violating Gracie. Despite what she thinks, I'm not insensitive."

She rested her head on his shoulder and it felt good.

"That felt so violent." She cried quietly.

AUSTIN CAUGHT UP to Gracie. She heard him before she felt his hand on her arm, his touch surprisingly gentle. Certainly not angry. "Hey, hey." He spoke as though soothing an animal. "What's going on?"

She spun around. Her expression must have been fierce because he held his hands palms out to defuse all her negative energy. A crease formed between his eyebrows and concern darkened the blue of his eyes.

A little lost, like a man who didn't know how to handle an angry woman, he shrugged, raising his eyebrows as though to ask, *What should I do?* If she weren't mired in a swamp of hurt, she would laugh at how awkward he seemed.

The big, capable cop had no idea how to deal with this.

She couldn't tell him what was wrong. She had left her old life so she would never have to face this again. She had avoided the circus for six years. Until now. Somehow it had found her. By fluke.

Not true. Not quite by chance. She'd brought this

on herself by trying to rob this decent guy. Maybe she deserved this.

Austin placed his hand on her shoulder, his palm warm and reassuring. Did he have to keep tempting her with his strong, confident touch?

If she were a different woman, she would lean into it, lean on him, but she'd spent too many years fighting for her independence, and had lived six years having no choice but to depend on herself.

She couldn't give in now.

"Talk to me," he urged, the words an order, but his tone sympathetic. "Tell me what this is all about."

"It isn't easy."

"I can see that."

"This isn't how my life is supposed to go. I was supposed to—"

"To what?"

She might as well tell him. Her pie-in-the-sky dreams were a bust now anyway. "I was going to get my money and buy a small house in the country somewhere. I was going to use a part of my money, my…" *Oh, go ahead and say it. The cat's out of the bag, anyway. You think Melody is going to keep your secret now? She'll expose you the second she gets anywhere near Wi-Fi. She has a story to sell. And she's right. It's a big one. Huge. The public will eat it up.* "My trust fund was supposed to have millions in it, but there was nothing left. I was going to buy a new identity, find a simple job somewhere and live a quiet, private life."

"Who stole the money?"

She noticed he didn't mention the *millions* part of her confession. Cripes, the man was too good to be true. "My parents were the only ones who had access."

"Your parents wouldn't do that to you, would they? Maybe the account was hacked."

"If you knew my parents, you wouldn't even ask. They are capable of this."

"Not very good parents if they stole from you."

"Not good at all."

"Come back and sit down. Let's work this out. You need help."

"I need to be alone. I need my privacy."

"Okay, this is going to sound real paternalistic, but I think the last thing you need right now is to be alone."

She smiled, grimly, because it did sound paternalistic. Problem was, he was right. She'd been alone for too long.

And Melody was a real challenge. What to do about Melody?

"Whatever your big secret is," he went on, "Melody knows it and isn't about to let it go." He touched her jaw with one finger. "If this is the reaction you have when only one person knows it, you're going to need help when others find out."

Yeah, she would, but accepting that rankled. "I'm not fragile."

Austin laughed. "Lady, you're the toughest woman I've come across in a long time. Fragile? No. But you do need help. I have a sixth sense about these things."

"Why?"

He retreated. "You don't want to know."

She did. She really did. But she remained silent because, when all was said and done, she didn't like exposing others. He had a right to his privacy.

She followed him back to the picnic table, where Finn glared at her. Too bad. She might have begun to admire him more than she had at the beginning, but at the moment she disliked him again.

Melody cried on his shoulder, weeping pretty, silent tears.

"Oh, for God's sake, grow a set," Gracie said, impatient with her. The woman did want to ruin Gracie's life, after all. "If you want to be the big, bad reporter, then learn how it feels to be a target. What you do in your quest to quench the public's thirst for dirt is rotten."

"I'm not like that. I don't write for tabloids."

"Fine then, in your belief that the public has a right to know. Why do they? My business is my business. Not yours or anyone else's. Why does the public need to know what happened to me? It's prurient interest. Nothing more."

Melody didn't respond.

"What is it, Gracie?" Austin asked. "What's this big secret that Melody knows? I want to help."

Gracie covered her face, breathing hard into her hands. She'd held on to this for so long, how could she just blurt it out? How could she compromise the anonymity, the privacy she'd fought for, that she'd run away for? That she'd given up *everything* for?

Her breath thundered into her cupped hands until

dots danced against her closed eyelids. Austin rubbed her back. She was getting too used to his touch. She would have to stop him. Soon.

"Gracie?" he said.

The time had come.

She dropped her hands, leaving her exposed. The sunlight hurt her eyelids. "I'm Little Gracie Stacey."

The name exploded like an incendiary device in the quiet of the clearing, where the only sound, of a bird whistling to its mate, warbled in light-hearted contrast to the darkness of her mood. There. Done. The name was out and couldn't be taken back.

For better or worse, she had turned a corner.

She opened her eyes. Austin sat still beside her. Melody avoided Gracie's searching gaze asking *are you satisfied?,* face miserable, as though she'd killed a baby. She had. With her recklessness, her ambition, she'd killed Gracie's very last, tiniest trace of hope.

Finn's jaw dropped. "You? America's Little Darling? No way. You're too damned ugly."

Gracie gasped, Melody admonished, "That's mean," and Austin cold-cocked him.

CHAPTER EIGHT

"ENOUGH!" GRACIE SHOUTED. "Whoa. Everyone calm down."

Austin stood beside her rubbing his knuckles, his expression a mix of anger and chagrin.

Finn had gone down for only a couple of seconds, but had bounced back full of rage, ready to do Austin damage.

Gracie pushed her hands against their chests, arms straight and locked at the elbows to keep them apart. Melody tugged on Finn's hand.

"This situation is out of control." Where minutes before Austin had been trying to ease her anger, now Gracie attempted to calm him.

"You two are supposed to be best friends, but you're acting like worst enemies," she castigated. "Enough already. Both of you start behaving like men instead of a pair of immature little boys."

She should have never gotten between Austin and Finn.

"Austin, you should have let me keep walking this morning. And, Finn—" she waited until he made eye contact "—that statement was unworthy of you. I don't like the way you treat me, but you're a decent guy to everyone else. I assume you don't go around saying hurtful things like that often."

He shook his head, one short, sharp, embarrassed response.

"Okay," she said, her breath coming in short bursts until she managed to control it. "Everyone sit."

They did.

Her arms shook from holding them apart.

Finn rubbed his chin and glared at Austin.

Austin scrubbed his hands over his face. "Sorry, Finn."

"Yeah."

Melody elbowed Finn in the ribs.

"I'm sorry, too." He glanced at Gracie, expression definitely sheepish. "I shouldn't have said that. You're right. It was immature and, no, I don't normally say things like that."

"Why do it with me? I know we started off on the wrong foot, but I've done nothing to you personally."

Finn's glance shot to Austin and then to Gracie. "His mom."

His mom? What was wrong with Austin's mother? Was she a thief? A felon?

"Finn." Austin's warning tone piqued Gracie's curiosity.

"Okay," he mumbled. "Gracie, I really am sorry. It was a rotten thing to say and not true. I take it back. Honest."

Finn finally sounded sincere, so Gracie nodded and accepted his apology.

"We've all behaved badly today. We need to stop

fighting and find a way out of this mess. Let's start over." She soaked a tissue with cold water from a plastic bottle and wiped blood from a crack on Austin's middle knuckle. "Melody, I'm sorry I said those things to you about reporters, but with my experience, I'm sure you can understand."

"Yes. Everyone take a deep breath." Melody took the bottle Gracie handed her. She screwed on the top and held it against Finn's chin. "There will be bruising, but the bottle's cold. We might be able to avoid swelling."

Finn tried to shrug her off, but Melody forced him to keep the bottle where it was.

"Pardon my ignorance," Austin said, "but who was America's Little Darling?"

They stared at him. Gracie gaped. There was someone on the planet who didn't know her?

"You don't know who Little Gracie Stacey was?" Gracie asked. "I don't believe it."

"I never watched TV when I was a kid. My mom monopolized our set. We didn't have cable so she only got a couple of stations anyway."

There seemed to be more to it than that, but Gracie let it go. When Austin was ready to share, she would be ready to listen.

"Gracie was the most popular child star since Shirley Temple," Melody said. "She captured the hearts of both children and their parents."

"You don't look like her." Finn nursed his jaw. "She was blonde and blue-eyed and pretty. Sorry."

"The blond hair was fake. As for the blue eyes, as

you can see, mine are pale, not that bright blue, so I wore contacts to make them more blue. They dyed my hair and eyebrows blond. As for being pretty, I was. I've lived a hard six years. It shows. I know that. There's nothing I can do about it."

"The bone structure's there," Melody said. "A couple of weeks out of the sun, using good cleansers and the right moisturizers, plus good nutrition, and you'd be back in spades."

"Tell me everything," Austin demanded.

Gracie twisted the wrapper from her egg sandwich, and then twisted it some more. "My parents decided I was cute and precocious enough to be a model. They learned I was a good mimic and that I could act. I didn't understand that what they were asking me to do would lead to the pandemonium that followed."

She dropped the paper onto the picnic table. "I was only three when this all started, when I was spotted by a television producer, who made a pilot about this idyllic family. You know, wise father, caring mother, funny older brother and sister, precocious little sister. That was me. It was wildly successful. Life was never the same after that. My parents were ecstatic. Once it all started, it didn't stop, like a train racing downhill out of control."

"And it lasted for years," Melody said.

"It lasted for too many years," Gracie conceded. "When I was a teenager, they changed the show to reflect some aspects of life in America for real teens, but it was still whitewashed. When we dealt with issues like drugs or anorexia or bullying, it was always solved in half an hour.

"It was shallow, light-hearted stuff like me mooning over a boy until I got him. Old-fashioned in concept, but the public ate it up."

"Maybe that was the appeal," Melody said. "It was a throwback to earlier times, you know, like Nancy Drew and the Bobbsey Twins."

"The irrelevancy of the show embarrassed me."

"It was extremely popular," Melody said. "You were the best part of the show. A real star."

Gracie shrugged. She didn't take pride in the job she'd done back then. She'd only been following directions. "When I turned eighteen, I put my foot down and stopped acting. I left the show. The studio didn't like it, but I'd been doing it for fifteen years. I was tired. No, I was exhausted. Worn out. An old woman at eighteen."

Which was another reason she'd been ripe for the picking when Jay showed up. He made her feel alive again. Alive and loved. No wonder she'd fallen so hard.

She didn't realize she'd gone silent until she caught everyone staring at her.

She shook herself out of those old uncomfortable memories.

These people didn't need to know about Jay.

Melody was probably already writing the book in

her mind, putting her own spin on every sentence, and how the heck could Gracie stop her?

She stopped talking because she really didn't owe them any more than what she had already given, and it made her sad to rehash it all.

Austin stood up from the picnic table and took her hand.

"Let's walk."

He led her out into the sunlit field. When they were a fair distance from Finn and Melody, when there was no chance of them overhearing the conversation, he asked, "Would it be so bad if people found out who you were?"

"Yes. My God, yes." Even in the heat of this day, she shivered just thinking about it. "The crowds, the paparazzi, everyone wanting a piece of me. It was relentless. They suffocated me. I couldn't eat, couldn't play, couldn't do a thing that wasn't public. I couldn't sneeze without someone reporting on it."

She wrapped her arms across her stomach.

"I had to be perfect. It was drilled into me that I couldn't step a foot wrong or the press would eat me alive. I was America's Little Darling and was expected to be exceptional. Even when I got older, when other teenagers rebelled and experimented, I still lived under the microscope. I was so good. I never drank, never smoked, never did drugs, never swore."

She rounded on Austin. "You heard that name I called Melody?"

"Yeah, it was pretty ripe."

"I've never used that word before in my life. I've never called a person that or anything else."

She rubbed her arms, cold despite the blazing sunlight.

"I can't go back to that. I did everything right. I *was* perfect. When I wasn't, it was by accident. It was my stepping on a landmine I hadn't known existed."

Austin listened without comment or judgment. She liked that about him, the stillness he cultivated.

"All that striving was never enough."

"What do you mean?" he asked.

She couldn't talk about her parents, about love withheld. Even years later, it was still too raw, so she bypassed that issue. "Do you know the press likes nothing better than for you to screw up? They love child stars who become drug-addicted. It's juicier copy than those who stay little goody-two-shoes like I did. So, they constantly search for dirt. They dig and dig. They are relentless."

She tilted her head and listened to the same bird still calling to his mate, his chirps a sweet counter-point to the pain she was dredging up.

"These six years away, on the road and on the run, have been my escape, instead of drugs or alco-hol. This has been my delayed teenaged rebellion."

Austin tucked a strand of hair behind her ear. His tenderness had her yearning for what-ifs again. "I get it now," he said. "Why you're on the road. Sort of. I'm guessing there's still more to the story."

She nodded. "Imagine what they would do if they found out Little Gracie Stacey, the child star who's supposed to be worth millions, has been living the homeless life by choice, only to find out now she truly is homeless and dead broke? I would be hounded to death."

She leaned her hand against a tree, just to feel the scrape of the bark, hard and real against her palm.

"I can't do it again. I can't go back to that. It would kill me."

Austin stepped forward. "No, it wouldn't."

He didn't get it at all. He thought he did, but nothing in his life would compare to her experience. "I'm not being hysterical. I'm not exaggerating. You don't know what it was like. Unrelenting. You're a quiet man. Imagine them doing that to you."

"I can't. But I didn't mean it wouldn't be as bad as you say. I meant it wouldn't kill you because you're strong."

"No, I'm not," she moaned. "I'm really not. I can't go through it again."

He touched her face. "You would survive because you're tough. You made one simple, wrenching decision to give up a life of luxury, to live on the road. Come on, Gracie, you think everyone could have done that? No. Few would and few could. You're exceptional."

She didn't feel exceptional. What she felt was debilitating fear. "Confronted with reporters, with that situation again, I'll explode, Austin, like a great big volcano."

He nodded.

"I'm like an iceberg. This little bit of anger you see here? What you witnessed with Melody?" She pointed to her face, to her scowl. "This is only ten percent of what I feel. The other ninety percent is below the surface."

"You're mixing metaphors. Volcanoes and icebergs." Austin's smile turned mischievous. She was hurting and he was smiling? What the heck?

"You know what they call pieces of icebergs that break away from larger icebergs?"

What did this have to do with anything? She crossed her arms and waited.

"Calves." He imitated her stance, but with a smile instead of her frown. "That means the mother icebergs must be cows."

Had he just called her a cow? She punched his arm and he laughed. She knew what he was doing—dispersing the tension. The dark cloud hanging over her head burst and she laughed with him.

This wasn't over, not by a mile, but she felt better after getting some of it off her chest. It was out in the open and her life would blow apart soon like a watermelon shot through with buckshot. And it would be ugly.

At the moment, she was too tired to fight anymore. She needed time to gather her defenses.

He said, "Let me help."

Maybe she should take his help for another day. Or two.

She followed him back to the others, to the woman

who had seen too much and the guy she didn't particularly like, but was coming to understand. Finn was protecting Austin. Gracie had come to know, a little, the source of his fear.

Austin's mom.

She gathered up her garbage, wondering how she would deal with Melody. She didn't have an answer yet.

She also didn't know what to do about Austin and the surge of feelings she had for him.

Crap on a broomstick, Austin was handsome, decent, generous, kind. And intelligent. Did he also have to be funny? The guy had to have his faults. Oh, yeah, he did have a few. He had to have his own way all the time. He needed her to be how *he* needed her to be.

She wasn't done finding her balance between who she'd been as a child and adolescent, and breaking through the tough shell she'd had to build on her travels.

Then she would happily be who *she* needed to be.

ONCE THEY WERE back in the car, Austin asked. "Did you have a plan? Where were you headed?"

"The only plan I had was to stop in a small town south of here called Accord. There's something I want to do there."

"You've been there before?"

"Yes." And here she was retracing her steps. So much for moving forward, and for starting a new life. Bitterness raged through Gracie. Good thing she was no longer in touch with her parents. She'd been ugly with Melody. She wasn't sure what would she do if she had to face her parents now.

Austin spoke to Finn. "You mind if we drop her off in town while we go fishing? Get out the map. I think the spot we were going to is close to Accord."

"Yeah." Finn seemed chastened, less inclined to surliness, which eased her tension. A bit.

Despite having given Melody a taste of her own medicine, Gracie still didn't trust her. And she'd need to deal with that.

They stopped in a small town to use a public washroom. Gracie stayed in the car. Melody left her purse on the backseat. Big mistake. She shouldn't trust Gracie right now. While the others were gone, she took Melody's wallet out of her purse and checked out all of her ID, including her driver's license with her date of birth. Those could be useful.

Oh, my God, eureka. She found Melody's birth certificate and the name listed wasn't Chase, but Messina.

This was why Gracie took her knapsack with her everywhere. She didn't trust a soul. For a reporter, Melody was far too naive.

Gracie had never invaded a person's privacy like this before, but she was desperate.

The more she knew about her enemy, the more she had to use against her.

Everyone returned to the car, but by then Gracie had returned everything to Melody's purse.

Ten minutes later, Finn said, "Look! Pull over."

A deer had gotten caught on a fence, trying to jump from a field to the road. Its front legs hung over the fence and its hind legs kicked out, but none of them touched the ground. No traction.

Finn turned to Melody and Gracie in the backseat and said, "Stay in the car. That animal will be panicking. Once we get her over the fence, she'll be unstable and scared before she gets her bearings. I don't want you two hurt."

You two. He was including Gracie in that, the heat of the moment making him human and compassionate.

"Come on," he said to Austin, but the other man was already getting out of the car.

"Whoa, easy," Finn murmured until he reached the animal. He put one hand on top of the fence and vaulted over in one swift movement.

Austin held the animal steady, taking some of her weight from the fence.

Avoiding flailing hooves, Finn managed to grab her around the torso and push up. Between the two of them, they got the deer over the fence.

A car sped toward them from the other direction so they held on to the flailing animal until it passed.

For his efforts, Finn got a hoof in his forearm.

The second the animal's hooves hit the shoulder of the road, it bounded across and into the woods on the other side.

Finn shook his arm and swore but with a big grin. He and Austin slapped each other on the back, jubilant. In their willingness to do what was right, and in their affection for animals, Gracie saw the roots of their friendship.

Back in the car, Finn said, "Good thing that was a wooden fence. If it had been barbed wire, that doe would have been torn to shreds."

Gracie sat back and listened to their quiet conversation, relieved that at least one aspect of their relationship had returned to normal.

In Accord, Austin followed Gracie's directions to a long-term care facility on the edge of town.

"You want to visit an old-age home?" Finn stared at the large, detached brick building.

"It's a long-term care facility. There's a difference."

"Yeah? What's the average age of the residents?"

Old, but she didn't say that.

When she climbed out of the vehicle with her backpack, so did Melody.

"Where do you think you're going?"

"With you."

"No, you aren't."

"Yes, I am."

Gracie stared her down, but Melody didn't budge. She hated this woman. Seriously hated her.

She strode into the building letting the door slam in Melody's face.

At the front counter, she asked for Callie MacKintosh. When the owner came out of her office, a smile lit her pixie face.

"Hey, I remember you," she extended her hand to shake. "Gracie, right?"

"That's right. Can I help out again? I really enjoyed it last time."

"You can help out anytime you want. My residents talked about your visit here for a long time after you left."

She looked past Gracie. "Who's your friend?"

Gracie came within a hair's-breadth of asking Callie to kick Melody out, but instead said, "This is Melody Chase," without further explanation.

They shook hands.

"I'm just going to sit in the corner and work while Gracie does her thing, if you don't mind."

Gracie does her thing. Melody didn't have a clue why Gracie was here. And *work?* Right. Probably writing an article about Gracie. Or more likely a book. She would make more money from a book about America's Little Darling. All those royalties coming in for years.

Melody stood to make a fortune exposing Gracie. She could be the worst writer in the universe, but she would make money hand over fist by being the first on this story.

Why was it so important to her? Was it just the money? Gracie had to dig into her background.

"I don't mind at all." Callie turned to Gracie. "Do you want to set up in the solarium again?"

"Yes, please. It's a beautiful room."

When they entered the warm sunlit room, Grace waved to a couple of the women who seemed to recognize her.

"You're back," one cried. "Does Callie still have

any of that hot-pink Vegas Nights left? I want that on my nails today."

"I'll check." Gracie washed her hands at a sink in the corner and then sat at a table beside the window where the lighting was good.

Callie brought her a large makeup chest and Gracie opened it. Inside was everything she needed to give pedicures and manicures. She did both well, two more of the talents she'd picked up by watching how it was done to her a million-gazillion times throughout her career.

She remembered the first woman in line. "Mrs. Pearson, hi. How's your nephew?"

Apparently, Dr. Pearson would be a perfect match for Gracie and could rescue her from her nomadic lifestyle, Mrs. Pearson had confided.

Nope. There was no such thing in this world as rescue. The only life Gracie would ever have was the one she carved out for herself. Too bad all the rules had changed yesterday and she had to start over.

"Are you having a manicure today?"

Mrs. Pearson nodded.

"Okay. Choose your color. Do you want a pedicure, too?"

Again the woman nodded.

Callie returned with a tub of water she placed on the floor. Gracie squatted in front of Mrs. Pearson and removed her shoes and socks then placed her feet in the water.

Gran, I miss you.

Gran had been loving, gentle and kind with Gracie, but visits with her had been so few and far between that Gracie had still felt herself starving for affection as a child. Those brief visits with Gran, though, lived on in her memory.

She used to do this very thing for her grandmother, the only one in her life who had treated her as a person rather than a commodity. Was it any wonder Gracie gravitated toward older people?

While Mrs. Pearson's feet soaked, Grace trimmed and painted her fingernails.

Then she patted a clean towel over the old, veined feet, cut the toenails and painted them.

In the corner sink, she emptied and rinsed the bucket, cleaning it and the tools with disinfectant Callie had provided.

She repeated this for all of the women who wanted attention, and most did.

It wasn't only women who gravitated toward her, but also men who wanted their toenails cut. Most of these people couldn't bend over far enough to do it themselves anymore.

The staff had their hands full getting everyone fed and clothed every day. Gracie didn't mind handling this detail.

Maybe this was her future—giving manicures and pedicures. Trouble was, she only wanted to give them to old folks, and she would never charge them. After massive wealth and untold advantages when she was young, was she doomed to poverty?

In this place, where she could feel close to her grandmother, she calmed down.

She would find something to do, and it wouldn't be acting, despite her talent. She was young, healthy and smart. She would find something.

All these people in this home made her feel closer to Gran, even Johanna, Callie's mom, who was a decade or more younger than most of the others, having developed early onset Alzheimer's in her fifties. Even Johanna's fractiousness couldn't bring down Gracie's spirits, leaving her to wonder whether the woman understood what was happening to her.

Johanna caught sight of something over Grace's left shoulder and her face lit up. Gracie turned to check out what she had seen. A man had entered the room with two puppies in his arms. He set them on the floor and they ran from resident to resident, sniffing and catching pats to the head and scrubs on fat bellies.

Callie kissed the man. Must be her significant other.

The puppies looked like huskies. Johanna reached for one of them, but Gracie caught her hand.

"Not yet. Your nail polish is still wet."

Johanna stared at her fingers. "Pretty," she murmured.

Only one thing bothered Gracie.

Melody was taking photographs on her cell phone. When Gracie finished the last manicure of the day, she strode over, snatched the phone out of Melody's hand before the woman realized her intention, dropped it on the floor and crushed it under her heel.

"Oops." Gracie's fake shrug felt good.

"My phone." Melody's jaw dropped. "I can't believe you just did that."

"So sue me." She got into Melody's face, up close and personal so there would be no doubt how serious she was. She had never been a violent person, but she had nothing left to lose. "I will never, ever, let another reporter take advantage of me, railroad me or use me. I'm fighting back. If you don't like it, tough."

She picked up her knapsack and approached Callie. "Is there someplace private I could go for a few minutes where I can check my email? I have my own computer."

"Sure," Callie said, still standing next to the man with the puppies. "Use my office. We have Wi-Fi here."

Once inside Callie's office, Gracie closed the door and locked it. She didn't trust Melody to not barge in. She booted up her computer and the internet, and immediately started a search to find out everything she could about Melody.

She was good at ferreting out details. She'd spent a lot of time in libraries taking shelter from storms, using their computers so she looked like she had a legitimate reason to be there, other than just to get warm. She had probably never fooled a single librarian, but scooting around the internet had given her something to do during those long hours.

Jay had been a techno-geek and had taught her a lot. It took her a while, but the deep search she did on Melody yielded results. That birth certificate information came in handy.

Gracie researched Melody's mother and her origins. Interesting. Texas. Where Melody was going. What was that about?

She had a hunch and checked it out. Bingo. Supposition. No hard evidence, but Gracie thought she was really on to something.

What she found out would suit her purposes very, very well.

Melody, prepare to have the tables turned.

Gracie checked her watch. Austin should be here soon. She didn't take the time to update her blog because she'd used Callie's office long enough. She closed down her computer, stashed it in her backpack and returned to the solarium.

Austin wasn't here yet. She sat beside Mrs. Pearson.

"I remember last time you were here you sang for us." The woman smiled.

Gracie returned that lovely smile. "Yes, I did. Do you want me to sing again?"

"Oh, yes. Elvis, please."

The residents fell silent. Gracie sang "Love Me Tender." Halfway through, several of them joined in. By the time Gracie finished, Mrs. Pearson had tears in her eyes.

"I had such a crush on Elvis. Such a waste that he died so young. His own fault, I know, but a waste. Sing something else for us."

"Sing the Everly Brothers," one man called out.

"Phil died not long ago. Would be nice to hear one of their songs."

Gracie sang "All I Have to Do Is Dream." The man closed his eyes and hummed along. He was off-key, but Gracie didn't mind a bit, just loved that she brought him pleasure.

Melody murmured, "They're back," and Gracie said goodbye to everyone, one by one, loving the kind regard and affection returned to her, and the wishes for her speedy return.

She had been invisible for six years. Here, with these people, she mattered.

She turned to find Austin in the doorway watching her.

Yes, she wanted to say, there are people who like me and who would want to see me again, for myself. Here she was neither a movie star nor a charity case, but just Gracie Travers, the name she'd borrowed from her gran, a woman who treated them well, who helped take care of their bodies and who bolstered their spirits with her songs.

In Austin's eyes, she saw admiration reflected there, too, as though what others thought of her rubbed off on him. But she didn't want that. She wanted him to see who she was on her own, and to like her. Just her.

She left the building and he walked beside her to the car.

"You can really sing. You have an amazing voice."

"Thanks."

Melody joined them. "It was one of the reasons she

was so popular on her TV show. It seems the woman is wasting her talent on this homeless whim of hers."

Gracie rounded on her. "It's not a *whim*. Don't you get it? I have my reasons and they are as valid as anything you have going on in your little life."

Time to get in a few digs, to let Melody know Gracie had researched her. Time to give her another taste of her own medicine. "How's your father, Ms. Chase? Or is it Paloma? Or Messina?"

Melody flinched. So far, so good. Gracie was right that Melody's mother had been on the run and using aliases. She decided to play another hunch. "Or is it *Grady?*"

Melody stopped walking and shook her head, eyes wide and imploring. "How did you find out?"

Oh, bingo. She'd gotten it right. The last had been nothing but a guess based on the fact that Melody's mother's record of employment had stated she'd worked for the Gradys before leaving Texas.

"Research online."

"But how did you know where to look?"

"I'm a woman of many talents." She stepped close to Melody, ignoring that Finn had gotten out of the SUV and was approaching, suspicion rolling from him like toxic gas. "Your father is a prominent, wealthy politician in Texas. I could sell your story to the tabloids. I could expose you as his love-child. Wouldn't that feel good?"

"That's my private business."

"This—" Gracie gestured down her body to indicate her clothing, then waved her arm through the air to include the building where she'd just made forty or so people happy "—is *my* private business."

"But I'm not famous. You are."

"So what? That gives you the right to expose me when I've walked away from that fame? I'm not here as America's Little Darling. They don't know me as Gracie Stacey, but only as Gracie, a woman who cares for them and makes them feel good about themselves despite their illnesses or aches and pains."

Finn had reached them. Gracie sensed Austin step in front of him to halt his approach.

He might have mellowed toward Gracie since this morning's argument, but he was like a mother bear when it came to Melody. The guy had it bad for her.

She kept her focus on Melody, because this woman had the power to hurt her, and Gracie was through being nice. From now on, she was fighting dirty and mean. "You don't own me or anything about me. Got it? I will use this information against you."

MELODY FROZE, all her secrets on the verge of being revealed when she and her mom had worked so hard to keep them hidden for thirty years.

Their past, their present, her mom's whereabouts, could be blown sky-high by Gracie.

Did it matter anymore? She was a grown-up. Her dad was dying. He could no longer hurt her mom even if he could find her. *But,* Melody finally understood Gracie's point. She finally got how destructive curiosity was.

If Melody had still been young, this could have devastated their lives.

Was this how Gracie felt? As though she couldn't run hard, fast or far enough to escape her past?

Exposure hurt, as though someone were stabbing her with pins and needles, with blinding flashes of light.

What did exposure matter? Why would it matter now? She was on her way to see her dad. Having put so much of Melody's story together, though, Gracie would be able to find her mom—and tell her dad and his family.

Again, why would it matter? Her dad had cancer. That would make him too sick or weak to go after her mom. The time for fear had finally passed. All that lingered was the habit of holding secrets.

Secrecy and anonymity had been a pattern for years, just as it had been for Gracie.

What hypocrisy for Melody to threaten to expose Gracie when she had worked so hard in her life for the very things Gracie strove to protect.

Melody would have ruined Gracie's chance at a normal life, the very thing she wanted to pursue after meeting her dad. Such arrogance on her part.

Her need to prove a point to her family was nothing compared to the price Gracie would have paid for Melody's interference. Exposing Gracie would have cost Melody nothing and Gracie everything.

"Well played, Gracie." Melody nodded, thoughtful and as chastened as Finn had been this morning. "I get it. I do. I won't expose you."

Melody took the notepad she carried everywhere out of her bag. She tore out the pages of notes she had made since meeting Gracie, including everything she'd written while observing Gracie with the folks in the care facility.

"Now you get it?" Gracie asked. "You understand how it feels to be laid bare when you have no choice?"

"I understand."

"I lost everything when I walked away," Gracie said. "I will protect my right to privacy with every breath. I'm going to hunt through your past. I'm going to find every secret, every dark corner of your soul. If you expose me, I will expose you."

Melody realized Gracie was outlining an ironclad insurance policy.

"No one, *not one soul,* will be allowed to take advantage of me. I don't care who your friends are—" she directed her piercing gaze toward Finn "—or who you have acting as bodyguard, I will destroy you if you expose me. Got it?"

"Trust me," Melody said. "I understand now. It's not great to have your secrets revealed before you're ready." She adjusted her wig. "Did it look very bad?"

"No. You hair looks fine, just not lush like that wig. You shouldn't wear it. You should just go out into the world as yourself."

"I could say the same to you."

"It's not the same thing at all. You have no idea what that would do to me. I couldn't survive that media circus again."

"It was wrong of me to intrude on your privacy, and to threaten to expose you."

"But—"

She handed her notes to Gracie, who took them and put them into her knapsack.

"It won't happen again. There won't be a story. I promise."

"Thank you," Gracie said quietly, not looking like she was ready to give up her distrust entirely.

Melody hoped the woman would believe her. She was telling the truth.

GRACIE ALLOWED HERSELF forty-eight hours to get over the shock of her parents' betrayal. Traveling became an easy road trip, with all of them easing into just enjoying the passing scenery and the towns they stopped in.

Soon, Gracie would have to figure out what to do with her life, but she needed this break. Maybe she would stay with Austin, Finn and Melody a little longer. Yesterday and this morning had been truly pleasant, peaceful after the emotional blowout of the day before. No sniping. No sarcasm. No recriminations. They had behaved badly and it was time to do better.

Gracie and Melody eased into a friendship that developed with the lurching steps of a toddler learning to walk.

Having both lived on the run, they had something in common.

It seemed that Melody had taken Gracie's lesson

to heart and was trying to make up for the pain she had caused.

The tally in Gracie's book of what she owed Austin grew and grew. It made her heartsick and nervous. She ate the meals he bought her and slept in her own double bed in the hotel room he rented and shared with her.

Austin and Finn were fishing again.

Gracie and Melody occupied the top of a sunny green slope that fell gently into a rushing river.

Austin and Finn stood out in the middle of the river tossing lures on the ends of long, arcing lines into the water, their low, murmuring voices scuttling across the surface of the water.

Gracie lay back on the grass and closed her eyes. The sun warmed her lids.

"Wow," Melody whispered. "Look at them."

Gracie sat up so quickly, dots danced before her eyes. "What is it?"

"They're beautiful. I don't know if I believe in God, but someone did an amazing job when making those two men."

Gracie followed Melody's line of vision to Austin and Finn. "Yeah. They are mighty fine specimens."

They glanced at each other and smiled. Then Gracie noticed something strange. Melody had shredded the sandwich she'd bought earlier.

Gracie pointed to it. "That's a waste of food."

Melody looked a little bewildered. "I did that?"

"Yeah."

"I'm sorry. I should have given it to you."

"I'll eat it the way it is." Even though Gracie knew she was gaining weight, thank goodness, she still struggled to fill a hole that never felt sated.

Melody handed the food to her.

Gracie took a bite, chewed and swallowed. "What's wrong?"

"What do you mean? Nothing's wrong. I'm fine."

Melody had to know how nervous she sounded. "You're going all the way to Texas?" Gracie asked. "Is it to visit your family?"

"If you can call the Gradys that."

"What do you mean?"

"I mean that technically they *are* my family, but I've never met them."

Gracie stopped chewing. "You've never met your family?" Gracie thought back to the research she'd done. "Wait. You mean your father? You've never met your dad?"

"That's right."

"Why not? Why did you have so many surnames?"

"We were running."

"I figured as much. From what? Abuse?"

"Yes. My dad abused my mom when I was an infant, so she took me and ran. We ran for my entire childhood."

Sharing this with Gracie was a huge concession on Melody's part. What it signified, Gracie assumed, was that she trusted Gracie to not use it against her. "How do you know Finn?"

"I was a preteen and my mom and I were on the run again. She had a car accident just outside of Ordinary. A deer jumped out at us and hit the car. We crashed into a tree and the car burst into flames. Mom was thrown, but I was stuck in the back. I panicked and couldn't get my seat belt undone. Finn's dad rescued me."

"Wow. That's amazing. How badly were you hurt?"

"My hair was on fire. I've had skin and hair grafts."

"For what it's worth, I'm sorry I pulled off your wig." Gracie tilted her head and studied Melody. "You do know that your natural hair doesn't look bad, right? There's more than enough of it to cover whatever scars you have."

"Thanks. That's what my mom says, but I'm still self-conscious." She tore apart a thick blade of grass. "Finn's mom made him visit me in the hospital and we got to know each other pretty well. I developed such a crush on the guy. Then my father showed up and we ran yet again."

Gracie grinned. "Do you still have a crush on Finn?"

Melody returned her smile. "Oh, yes. It's still there, as strong as ever. I know you two don't get along, but there's more to Finn than meets the eye. We've been corresponding for ten years. He's a good man."

"I'll have to take your word for it. Anyway, it doesn't matter. I'll be leaving soon."

"Going where?"

The million-dollar question. Gracie shrugged.

Now that Gracie knew Melody's whole story, she was sorry she'd threatened to sell the information to a tabloid. *Gordon Grady Shocker: Love Child Revealed.* No, maybe not. It had given Melody an understanding of what reporters do to their subjects, and of how it could really hurt.

Gracie watched Austin walk to the shore with a fish he'd caught, sunlight sparkling from his dirty-blond hair. The happiness in his eyes, his long, confident stride and his boyish smile coalesced into an attractive whole that stole Gracie's breath.

"Come here," he said and, in that moment, she would have followed him anywhere.

"Finn's going to take a break. You can borrow his hip waders. I'm going to teach you how to fish."

She climbed into the oversize boots and made her way out into the water, slipping and sliding over rocks.

Austin steadied her with a hand on her elbow, his grip strong and gentle at the same time.

They stopped in the middle of the stream and Austin taught her how to cast and send the line out with its brightly colored fly into the water, arcing in the sunlight like a thread of gold.

Austin stood behind her, his bulk solid and comforting against her back, his arms holding her as though she were rare and fragile, his hand on her wrist warm and firm, and Gracie crossed a line, over-the-moon for a man who wanted more from her than she could give.

She couldn't do this anymore. She couldn't spend time with this man who was stealing her heart one molecule at a time. In another few days, she would be hopelessly in love, with no way to save herself. Leaving him would be painful, but they had no future.

CHAPTER NINE

THAT EVENING, Gracie and Austin fought.

"Austin, you still don't get how hard it is for me to keep taking from you. I'm becoming a broken record."

She couldn't possibly tell him she was falling in love with him, so she fell back on the issue of finances, which was still valid.

"You don't have to be like this. I can provide for you, so what are you so worried about? It's not a hardship for me."

"That's not the point."

"Then what is? This?" His arm swept the alleyway in the town in which they'd stopped for the night, taking in the pungent odor of garbage. They were in Taos, New Mexico.

"I've gone far enough with you." More than far enough. Too far. She cared for this man to a depth she'd never felt before. She hardly knew him and yet, by comparison to her feelings for Austin, the crush she'd had on her husband, Jay, seemed shallow. Insubstantial.

Austin was the real deal, a man who could be trusted.

"This is where you think you should be?" His voice dripped with sarcasm.

No, but until she figured out an alternative, this was where she would stay. "I can't let you pay for more hotel rooms and more meals. Can't you see what this does to me?"

The likelihood of ever being able to pay him back for the food he bought her every day was slim. She couldn't think about adding the significant cost of accommodations.

No. She wouldn't stay with him.

Who are you kidding? It's becoming less and less about money, and more and more about not being able to share a room with him.

They hadn't had to share a bed since that first night, but the intimacy of being in the same room with him the past two nights, taking turns using the shower, behaving like a real couple, had torn her apart.

Daydreams ran rampant. What if this could be real? What if Austin returned the attraction?

How could he? She was eaten alive by thoughts of the girlfriends he must have had in his hometown, women with respectable homes and jobs. Women who were a lot more attractive than she was, even though with regular meals she didn't look as much like a scrawny, plucked chicken.

Clean hair helped, as did the clean clothes. The moisturizer Austin had bought for her that first day freshened her skin.

Frustration with herself set in when she thought

this way. She knew too well how superficial physical attraction was, and how little looks truly meant in a relationship. Far better to be a good, generous person than to be the hollow little celebrity she used to be, the puppet without a thought of her own.

She had not only grown up since then, she had grown. Period.

She might not be as pretty now, but she was real.

The daydreams crashed to a halt when she remembered what her past could do to Austin if they were involved. He wasn't the kind of man who would appreciate the media frenzy if, in some strange alternate universe, he chose her to be his significant other. If he chose her on a whim, he would hate his future with her.

This forced intimacy with Austin made her dream, and she knew how dangerous dreams were.

She'd known the highest highs of *having* and now she knew the lowest lows of being without. The responsibility for pulling herself out of this was hers alone.

Austin just didn't want to accept that. For some reason, the guy needed to give and give.

She made up her spot behind a Dumpster, settling in to sleep, wrapping her sweatshirt around her and cupping her shoulders with her palms. They didn't feel as bony as they used to.

"Go!" she ordered, desperate to get him away from her so she wouldn't give in to temptation. "Get the hell out of my life."

Austin made a sound of frustration. She was pretty

sure he wanted to go caveman on her and force her out of the alley, but didn't. Instead, he walked away.

Goodbye. At last.

Oh, damn.

She rested her forehead on her knees. She might have burned her bridges. It saddened her to no end.

That was her last thought before she drifted off to sleep. She startled awake, with a palm mashing her lips against her teeth and her hands pinned in a beefy fist.

She screamed in her throat.

"Shut up, bitch!"

The man on top of her was strong, and he'd been drinking.

Crap. They were always stronger when they were drunk.

She kept her cool. She'd been through this before and had learned a thing or two about self-defense.

She bucked, she bit, and kicked out with her feet.

The guy held on.

She aimed for sensitive parts.

He didn't budge.

Panic set in. She knew what made a man this strong. A drug of some kind. Meth, maybe?

She heard a zipper open. Dear Lord, in all of her travels she had avoided rape. She felt her blouse rip. Damp air washed her chest.

Tears leaked from the corners of her eyes.

No! It wouldn't happen now.

When he straddled her, she heaved up hard with her hips, knocking him off-balance.

He tried to catch himself and his hand fell away from her mouth.

She screamed for all she was worth.

A second later, the guy was off her and flying through the air. The sound of flesh on flesh and the crunch of bone echoed violently in the darkness.

The guy rolled on the ground, clutching his nose. "What'd ya do that for, man?"

Austin stood above her like an avenging angel. He had his phone to his ear, and she could hear him calling the local cops.

When he ended the call, he crouched in front of Gracie.

"Are you okay?" She didn't recognize this man, hard as the granite face of a mountain, furious and itching for blood.

This Austin frightened her. Gone was gentle Mr. Decency. *This* man made one hell of a formidable adversary. Vikings and berserkers came to mind.

"Okay?" he asked again.

No, she wasn't, but she wouldn't tell him that, not after she'd fought so hard to sleep here tonight. "I'm good." Her shaky voice betrayed her. True danger had come too close in this dark, dank alley.

How long could she continue to live like this? She ran trembling fingers through her hair.

Every particle of her body vibrated.

"You are not good," Austin said. "You're shaking."

"I'll be fine in a minute, as soon as the cops get here and take him away." Then it hit her. Cops. If they found her sleeping here, they could haul her in for vagrancy.

She scrambled to her feet, lost her footing and leaned against the wall. Her head spun. She'd almost— That guy had nearly—

She rested her forehead against the brick, just for a moment and then rallied.

"I have to go. The cops can't find me here."

"I'll explain you're coming back to the hotel with me. There won't be charges."

"I can't go with you."

"Goddammit," Austin shouted. "God-freaking-dammit. Can you stop being independent for just one damn minute?" He spun away from her and rammed his hands into his back pockets. She heard him hissing air into his lungs.

Her attacker struggled to his feet. "Bitch." He lurched toward her.

Austin grabbed the guy's shirt and punched him in the jaw. The man fell back to the ground.

"Gracie, please." There was desperation in Austin's voice. "Stop. Okay? Can you do that for me?"

"Stop what?" Gracie panted, the air too thin and her ribs too tight.

He took her by the arms, shaking her, but with a tight leash on the violence she sensed coursing through him. No comparison between him and the drunken brute who had assaulted her. If there was one thing she knew about Austin, it was that he cared.

"Stop being so damn tough." He enunciated the words as though each carried the weight of his fury.

"I can't." Her voice broke, but she couldn't give in. "I really can't."

"Why not?"

"Because I can't go back to being vulnerable. People hurt me. I have to be strong."

Austin opened his mouth to argue. They heard a siren and watched a cruiser pull up at the road end of the alley.

"Please, please," Austin said. "Let me get you out of this."

He leaned his forehead on hers. "Please, let me help."

In his plea, she heard real pain. It hurt him to see her get hurt, to see her in danger. No one had ever cared this much about her. She couldn't turn him down, not when doing so would hurt *him*.

She nodded.

Two cops entered the alleyway and approached.

"You the folks that called in an assault?"

"I did, Officer." He gestured toward the man on the ground with his flaccid penis hanging out of his fly. "I caught this guy trying to rape this woman."

"That right, ma'am?"

Gracie held her torn blouse closed. She started to say that he'd awakened her with his hand over her mouth, when Austin cut in.

"Apparently, he dragged her into the alley. I came along and heard her screaming."

The cop sensed something fishy. He glanced between the two of them.

"I'm going to reach into my pocket and get out

my ID." Austin held his hands away from his body, manner non-threatening. "That okay with you, Officers? I'm a sheriff's deputy in Montana."

Austin produced his badge and his driver's license. They read it before returning it.

"You want to tell us what really happened here?" the second cop asked.

Austin sighed. "My girlfriend and I were fighting. She walked out of the hotel and said she'd find her own place to sleep. I was worried and went out looking for her."

The guy on the ground shouted an obscenity.

"He's high as a kite," Gracie said.

"I heard Gracie scream and came running. He was on top of her holding her down, with his penis out. It was erect at the time."

They all stared at the pitiful flaccid penis. It looked pretty harmless now.

"I want to take her back to the hotel if she'll just stop being *stubborn*."

"I'm not—"

He shot her a warning glare and she subsided. She didn't want to have more to do with the police than she had to.

"I'll go back to the hotel," she conceded.

"Are you okay doing that, ma'am?"

"Yes. I am. I'm going with Austin willingly."

"Great." Austin heaved out a breath and shared a look with the cops. *Women,* his wry expression said, *can be so unreasonable.*

Ooooh, when they got to his room she was going to give him a piece of her mind.

"Does Gracie have to go to the police station or can we just go on home? She looks beat."

She was beat. "I don't want to press charges." Showing up in court to testify was exposure she didn't need. "I just want him off the street so he can't hurt another woman tonight. I want to crawl into a safe bed."

"No problem, ma'am. We can charge him for being stoned in public." Both cops grasped him under his arms and lifted him. One of the officers jerked his head aside. "And for being drunk. This guy reeks of booze."

They dumped him unceremoniously into the back of the cruiser and drove off.

Austin reached for her elbow, his touch commanding, not tender and solicitous as it normally was. The calm act he'd put on for the police was over.

Gracie's senses went on high alert.

She picked up her bag and walked with him to the hotel. His hand still gripped her elbow as though he thought she might take off.

"You okay? That had to be scary." His words were innocuous enough, but there was still that leashed violence in him. He held himself in check, but too carefully.

"Yeah. Austin, thanks." In a rare burst of dependence, she leaned close because the incident had left her chilled. He remained rigid, with none of the easiness she had come to expect from him. "I've had to face that kind of stuff before, but—"

"What?"

She rushed on. "I've always been able to fight them off. I have a little knife. I even cut a guy once so he would know I was serious."

Austin's breathing became heavy and harsh. They walked under a streetlamp and it cast harsh light onto a jawline that could probably cut diamonds.

"I always won," she hurried to reassure him. "Really. I learned a lot about self-defense over the years, but tonight, the guy was really hopped up on something. I was worried."

As hard as it was for her to admit the truth, she needed to. "I was glad you were there."

His expression softened, barely. "Me, too." They turned into the hotel and took the elevator upstairs.

In his room, Austin said, "I like you, Gracie. A lot. It's that simple. You know that independent streak of yours I'm always complaining about?"

She nodded, unable to speak because he was standing too close to her, his clean, soapy scent messing with her brain waves.

"I admire it. It reminds me of me when I was—" He slammed the brakes on whatever he was about to say.

"Of what?" she asked, but he didn't answer, closing the door on whatever he was about to reveal.

"Never mind. I like how feisty you are, but holy shit, if you ever scare me like that again, I'll tan your hide. Understood?"

"Yes, sir." She saluted like a soldier, to cajole him out of his anger, but he was having none of it.

"This isn't a joke. Rape is awful. Horrible. In my line of work, I've seen what it can do to a woman. It lives on for years inside of its victims, eating away at them."

He grasped her arms, his grip too tight, but his sentiments right on. "I don't *ever* want to see that happen to you."

"Me, neither."

"Do you know what I want for you?"

She shook her head, mute, because the way he was looking at her lit a fuse inside her she didn't even know still existed. She'd thought desire long dead, beaten out of her by lies and betrayal. But Austin was real and angry for her and worried about her and, if her dormant powers of attraction were accurate, wanted her.

She hadn't seen that particular light in a man's eyes for too many years, and doubted what she remembered of Jay's attraction to her. But Austin... well, as she knew, he was real.

He leaned close.

"What are you doing?" she whispered.

"I'm about to kiss you."

"Why?"

"Because I have to do something or I'll yell this place down. You frustrate me, woman."

"Woman? You sound like a caveman. I have a name. It's—"

"Quiet. You talk too much."

Before she could protest, his lips were on hers, firm and demanding.

Gracie felt his kiss to her toes, felt it everywhere, as though bubbles were dancing in her stomach and diminutive fairies were jumping for joy in her brain.

More, they shouted. Give us more. They danced jigs. They threw fairy dust into her bloodstream.

When he pulled back, she said, "I don't talk too much."

"You do." He kissed her again. Just what she'd wanted.

The fairies whooped and danced some more. The fairy dust in her blood floated and twirled. The fairies sang love songs. "A kiss is just a kiss," she told herself.

But no.

Not this one. This was *the* kiss, the one that would go down in every history written from this point on, in the annals of romance, as the best kiss ever.

Austin drew away and Gracie sighed. He knew his away around a woman's lips. "You've been practicing."

He picked up his shaving kit and dropped it into his bag then walked toward the door.

What—? Where—?

"What are you doing?"

"Going to get a room of my own."

It shouldn't hurt. It did.

"Okay," she said, unsure what she was agreeing to. "Can you tell me why?"

"I can't stay with you tonight."

His rejection stunned her. "But—"

He left, closing the door behind him.

Fine. She didn't want sex with him, anyway. Truly. She didn't want to confuse what she owed him with what she had, or didn't have, in her power to pay.

Better to keep the relationship clean and pure, right?

The fairies disagreed. They pouted, railing against the unfairness of life that they should be left excited and eager and wanting, while Austin had apparently felt nothing. They crossed their little arms and stomped their tiny feet.

Gracie crawled into bed and turned her back on Austin's empty bed, facing the streetlamp seeping in around the edges of the curtain.

Holy Hannah, how was she supposed to sleep tonight?

Frustrated sexually, and knowing she wouldn't sleep, Gracie took a hard look at her future and knew she had only one option.

There was only one reasonable thing for her to do next. She had to visit her parents. She had to find out whether there was any money left and she had to wring it out of them.

Sure, she had been furious with them, but now that the edge was off her anger, she could face them without ripping them to shreds.

Then she would threaten to sue them for her money.

She could be as tough as she needed to be, and as

ruthless as they were. And, she smiled serenely, she could act. She had honed her skills for years.

She could fool her parents. No problem.

AUSTIN DIDN'T SLEEP. In the morning, he stepped into the elevator with his bag, ready to check out, still full of worry and anger.

Gracie had nearly gotten seriously hurt last night. How far would that guy have gone? He'd been about to rape her. Would he also have killed her?

Chilled, Austin jabbed the button for the ground floor.

Gracie didn't know it, and would probably be furious if she did, but Austin hadn't gone back to the hotel when she had told him to. Instead, he had sat on a bench on Main Street. He'd nodded off. Her scream had awakened him.

His blood had turned to ice and then to lava. He was surprised he hadn't killed her attacker instead of just breaking his nose.

Didn't she understand how dangerous her lifestyle was? One of these days he wasn't going to be there. What then? Who would protect her then?

How could one woman be so stubborn?

He wanted to wring her neck.

After he'd kissed her last night, he'd had to leave the room because he'd wanted to make love to her badly, but not like that.

The first time he and Gracie made love—*and they would*—it wouldn't be with him full of anger.

It wouldn't be while he was ready to burst with frustration because of how much she pissed him off.

It would be because of how much he liked her, just honest to God liked her and her spirit, her honesty and her generosity.

That day when he'd seen her singing with the senior citizens, he had seen an angel in action. All the old women sitting around her had bright pink or red nails. The owner had told him that Gracie had done that. And their toenails, too. She'd even cut the men's toenails. Who did that kind of thing unless it was part of their job? Who did it voluntarily? A saint. A woman who cared.

When he left the elevator and entered the foyer, he found her sitting in one of the chairs, looking less confident than usual. Maybe last night had frightened some sense into her.

"Hi," she said.

"Hi. What are you doing today? Coming with me or staying here?"

"I've been thinking. Can I have a lift to a bus station? I shouldn't go any farther south. I'll take off on my own from here."

He nodded, but his gut clenched. "Where are you going?"

"Can you sit for a minute?" Gracie asked. "I need to say some things to you and you're giving me a pain in my neck looming over me."

"Not the first time a woman has told me I'm a pain in the neck."

She smiled but soon turned serious. "Thank you

for last night. I don't know whether I would have gotten away from that man or not. I honestly can't thank you enough for helping me."

She leaned forward, whatever she had to say clearly important to her.

"I appreciate last night, but I won't depend on you forever. I've been on my own for a long time."

Too long, as far as he could tell.

"I lay in bed all night thinking instead of sleeping. It's time for me to leave you, but living on the road and sleeping in alleys no longer works."

"Thank God. Glad to hear it." Good that she didn't want to sleep in alleyways. Not good that she was leaving him. That was the last thing he wanted.

"I know I needed help last night, but in general, I don't need to be taken care of. I don't believe in it. I think we are all responsible for ourselves. I've never been rescued by anyone in my life. I've had odd moments when some people gave me bits of their time and seconds of sympathy, but my life has been…" She sat back and put her fingers to her lips. "This is hard for me to admit. My life has been empty and friendless for hours, days, weeks, years on end. I learned a long time ago that I'm on my own. There is no rescue."

"And yet you've been rescued by me a number of times," Austin said.

"There is that, but this is temporary. An aberration. My life is my own to direct and make happen. I'm just not doing a very good job of it at the moment. That needs to change, and it will change because I will find a way to make my life work the way I need it to work."

He admired her backbone. Her willpower awed him. "But you're in a rotten place right now and need help. And as you've admitted, I've had to rescue you more than once."

"That's because you keep making me accept being rescued," she shouted.

Austin smiled. "You have any idea how strange that sounds?" He sobered. "Don't you ever get tired of being alone?"

"Always." Her honesty floored him.

"Don't you get tired of being responsible every second of every day in your life?"

"Every second."

"Don't you ever want a helping hand?"

"Yes, and I've been taking one since we met, but not for always. Not for forever, Austin. It ends today."

"Okay." Austin smiled but it felt hollow. "One last breakfast?"

She returned his smile, but it looked sad, sad, sad. "I'd like that.

"SING FOR US?" he asked.

They'd stopped and picked up fast food for breakfast and were sitting in a park at the edge of the city. Gracie was glad they took these opportunities to eat outside. Meals were cheaper this way.

Every time she took her notebook out of her bag and added in another meal, Austin frowned.

"Sing for us?" he asked again.

Gracie blushed. "I don't do that in public anymore."

"What I don't understand was why you haven't been making money by singing. What you did for those seniors was amazing. Did you see how happy you made them? How much did you make that day?"

"Nothing. Those mani-pedis were volunteer work."

"That's what I thought. So why couldn't you have been making money all along by singing in bars and hotels? Your voice is incredible."

"It's also distinctive," Melody chimed in. "Right, Gracie?"

"That's right. I would have been recognized once enough people started to hear me. I know I look different now, but sometimes it doesn't take much to change the way a person looks at you."

She turned to Austin. "Do you remember when I had to go to the washroom at the Kavenaghs and you thought it was because I'd eaten my burger too quickly?"

"Yeah. It wasn't?"

"No. Jessica and I were sharing a joke and I winked at her. She recognized me. I was going to leave then because I thought she would blurt out who I was. She promised to keep my secret, though. That's why I stayed."

"A wink? She recognized you because you winked?" Austin asked.

"It was her signature," Melody said.

"How's that?"

Gracie answered Austin. "Every show, no matter

what the plot had been, or who in the TV family the show had centered on that week, ended with a close up of me winking."

"It was cute," Melody finished off her hash browns and loaded everyone's garbage into a bag. "The public ate it up."

"Who would have thought people would remember so much from such an old show?" Austin's skepticism showed his ignorance of how prevalent these things were these days.

"Old shows are all over the internet," Melody said. "There are constant resurges of interest in retro material."

"Jessica had been watching a lot of my old shows lately. She saw that wink and she knew."

"Wow. I'm surprised." His brows lifted as though a thought had struck him. "Shouldn't you be getting some kind of royalties every time those reruns air?"

"Yes, but it would all have gone into the trust fund or conservatorship or whatever it was that my parents set up when I was young."

"So it doesn't do you any good, does it?"

"Nope." Gracie explained to Melody what had happened in Denver, including what all her original plans had been once she turned thirty.

"You could have disappeared somewhere into middle America," Melody mused, "and we would have never seen nor heard from you again."

"That was the plan."

Melody's considering nod looked appreciative.

"I'm impressed. It would have worked. Too bad your parents turned out to be so dishonest."

Austin swore, directing it at her parents.

His phone rang and he checked the number. His expression turned to stone.

"Hi, Mom." He listened and listened. He stood and paced.

Gracie glanced at Finn, his expression as hard-edged as Austin's.

"That hardly qualifies as an emergency," Austin said. "No, I'm not coming back. I have another week of vacation."

He listened some more, then set his jaw. "You know what, Mom. I'm not doing this anymore. Call Deputy Turner. He would be glad to hire someone to come in and fix the washer for you."

Finn snorted. "Some emergency," he mumbled.

"Goodbye, Mom. I'll see you next week."

He approached the park bench.

"Good on ya, man," Finn said. "Nicely done."

Austin nodded and in his eye was a glimmer of triumph. Maybe he gave in to his mother too often. "We need to hit the road."

He picked up Gracie's knapsack before she could stop him.

"Why is this so heavy?" On the flip of a dime, he was in cop mode again.

CHAPTER TEN

CRAP. SHE WOULD have to tell him about the computer.

"Melody, Finn, can I have a minute alone with Austin?"

They left and Gracie took her bag from Austin.

"Sit," she said. "You're looming again."

He settled onto the grass beside her, but with a distance between them that was more than physical.

She pulled the laptop out of her knapsack.

Austin didn't say anything for a moment, but Gracie could sense the volcano about to blow.

"You could have sold that for food." Instead of the swearing and ranting Gracie had become accustomed to with Jay, Austin held it leashed, as he had last night. The anger was there, though. Boy, was it there.

"You stole my wallet instead of selling this?"

"Austin, look at it."

He glanced at it too briefly. "Yeah, so?"

"Did you notice how old it is? I could get maybe thirty dollars, tops. If that."

"Are you sure?"

"Yes, Austin. My ex-husband was a computer guy. I learned a lot from him."

"You were married? Where the hell is he now?"

Gracie ran her hand across her forehead. "I keep forgetting that you know nothing about Gracie Stacey. Melody would know all about this."

"I'm not Melody. Explain."

She didn't want to go through the whole story about Jay, but figured Austin deserved an explanation. "I met Jay when I was eighteen. He was charming and happy-go-lucky, and he brightened my days by giving me endless attention."

"You didn't already get that as a television star?"

Gracie smiled because she heard jealousy in his voice, simply because she'd been attracted to a man a dozen years ago. She couldn't remember any man ever being jealous on her behalf. It warmed her.

"Not in the way you think. To the public, it looks like attention, but it isn't the kind that children need. You're constantly fussed over. Your hair, nails, teeth, makeup all have to be perfect, but there's no one reading to you or playing with you. No one can take you to the playground or the park, because doing so would cause pandemonium. The press would follow and ruin any chance you might have to just play like a normal kid."

Austin stretched out on the grass and rested his head on one hand. With the other he played with her fingers. She wasn't used to casual touch, but she liked it from him.

"And your parents? Where did they fit in? They weren't playing with you or reading to you?"

"Reading? Yes. Scripts. Not children's books."

A gentle breeze lifted Austin's hair and she reached out to fix it then stopped herself and dropped her hand into her lap. He caught her hand.

"Why did you do that?"

"Do what?"

"You were going to touch me, but you didn't. Why?"

Gracie played with a blade of grass and shrugged. "I'm not used to touching people spontaneously. I wasn't hugged or held a lot when I was a kid. That's why Jay appealed to me so much. He's a hugger. He wasn't afraid to touch me like others were. People don't treat famous people normally. Jay seemed to."

Austin gently pulled her hand toward him and kissed her fingers, one by one. "I like to touch, too. I also like to be touched. You can touch me whenever you want."

"I'll just bet you would let me touch you anytime and anywhere. Right?"

His answering grin was boyish and mischievous. She liked this playful side of him.

"Tell me more. What happened with this guy who touched you too much?"

Gracie laughed. "He didn't touch me too much, but he touched me a lot, and gave me attention and I really liked it. A year later, we got married."

Austin played with her fingers some more, distracting her and sending chills skittering up her arm.

"Why aren't you still married to him?" He sat

up suddenly. "You *aren't* still married to the guy, are you?"

"No. Six years ago, I found out he'd had an affair."

Austin grimaced. "I'm sorry."

"It got worse. I found out he'd been unfaithful throughout our marriage. He hadn't ever loved me, only my money and my fame. I'd fallen into the classic danger for a rich woman. Jay hadn't wanted me for me."

Austin still held her fingers and tugged on her arm until she fell forward onto his chest. His strong arms came around her like steel bands across her back and he kissed her.

The fairies in her brain did somersaults and sprinkled more fairy dust into her blood. It beat like thunder in her ears. Pounded like hammers on anvils in her pulse.

When Austin finally pulled back, Gracie stared into the brilliance of his blue eyes and lost the last resistant piece of her heart.

She scooted away. "Don't. I can't do this."

"Why not?"

"I don't trust. I don't have a future. I don't have a life."

"You could share my life."

Gracie didn't want to mistake what he was saying. "What do you mean?"

"You could be part of my life. We can continue traveling to Texas and see how our relationship develops."

Oh. He wasn't offering her forever.

"I need my own life, Austin. I need to find a way to make a living. What would happen if I hooked my star to your wagon and then a year from now, we realized our relationship wasn't enough for a lifetime? I would be in the same place I am now."

"I wouldn't leave you in poverty like that guy and your parents did."

"But I would still have to find a life for myself, a career, a way to support myself. I have to do that now, Austin, before I can ever be with someone else again."

She didn't want to talk about this anymore. She packed the computer back into her bag.

"One more question."

She stopped what she was doing and waited. "What?"

"Why didn't you take any of your money when you left? Weren't you old enough to have access to it?"

"Jay and I got an allowance from my parents. The day I left, I cleaned out our bank accounts, but it wasn't enough to last six years. Any money I wanted from my parents after that came with too many strings. They, and the studio, wanted me back for a reality show, or another sitcom. They wanted me working in that industry again, and I wouldn't do it. So…" Gracie shrugged. "They wouldn't send money."

"Wow, you were born to a real pair of losers."

It hurt to hear him talk about her parents like that.

She knew it was true, but she didn't like hearing it from someone else. What could she say to Austin, though? How could she defend indefensible behavior?

"They weren't losers, though, were they?" she asked. "They got away with everything in the end."

"One more question. Last one, I promise." He ran a finger under her eye. "You look tired."

"Talking about the past does that to me. I don't like it. What's your question?"

"Why is the computer so important to you that you wouldn't sell it for even thirty bucks?"

"If that. I have a rich imagination. Sometimes I think I should have been writing scripts for our shows. When I got older, I would give the writers suggestions that they would use."

"What does this have to do with the computer?"

"I write."

"Really? Anything you can sell?"

"Not in the way you think. I write a blog." She told him her alter ego's name. "Check it out someday." No one else knew about her alter ego. It felt strange to admit to being so screwed up and so unhappy with the way her life had turned out that she had to pretend to be someone else.

"I'd like to read it someday. Another question."

She waited patiently.

"Why write as someone else?"

"I have to."

"Why?"

"Why? I've explained to you what my life was like. I don't want that media scrutiny again."

"But this is online. You could have still been yourself, but no one would be able to find you."

She rested her elbows on her knees. "Oh, Austin, that's so naive. No offense, but Jay could hack anything."

"The guy sounds like a real prince."

"No, he wasn't, but he knew his way around computers. If I'd used my real name and people wanted to find me, it would have taken a good hacker a matter of minutes to find out where I was posting from, follow the pattern for a few days and then find me on the road. I would have had reporters all over me."

"I still find that hard to believe." Austin chewed on a blade of grass.

"I know you do. Paparazzi make big, big money on those photos you see in the tabloids. It's a lucrative business. Look at Melody. She seems like a decent person, but she was ready to make money from my story by writing it and selling it to the highest bidder. Ask her."

"So don't let anyone else write it. Do it yourself."

"Me?"

He pointed to the computer. "If you've got the writing chops."

"I like to write, but I can't stand the thought of doing an exposé. My parents weren't the best, but they're the only parents I have. How could I write about them?"

"I would think it would be easy if they were so rotten to you."

"Look at it this way. I know you had a good childhood, but would you write about your parents if they'd been bad? Wouldn't you feel some kind of loyalty to them? We only get one set of parents. Why bash them to the masses?"

Austin stood abruptly. She had hit a nerve. His mother sounded terrible and she had no idea what had happened to his father. Early on, she had made an assumption that his childhood had been idyllic. Obviously, she'd been wrong.

"Last night in bed," she said, standing, too. "I made a huge decision. I'm going to see my parents."

"Really? Where?"

"Las Vegas. They love it there. Doesn't that say a lot about them, that they would choose someplace as shallow and full of glitz as Vegas?"

"What do you hope to accomplish?"

"Closure, I guess, but mainly I want to see whether there's any money left. I need to confront them. I need to know if I have anything before I decide where to go from here." She'd tossed and turned before finally realizing she had no alternative but to see her parents before moving on. "This is a great big unfinished thing in my life, isn't it?"

"Yeah. Huge." He gazed off into the distance.

"I want some of my money, Austin. I want to be equal to you and Melody and Finn. You all have something. I've been nothing but a parasite on this trip."

"No, you haven't."

She stopped him with a hand on his arm, his skin sun-warmed beneath her fingers. "We both know I have. I've paid lip service to not wanting to take, but that's all I've done. If I can get money from my parents, even a little, I can change my ID. Jessica said I should go Goth to really change my looks. I know I could pull that off."

"And then what? When that money runs out do you head out on the road again?" His voice took on a harsh edge.

"Maybe I wouldn't be able to buy a house as I had wanted, but I could go back to school and get a career. I need to do something, to be someone other than this homeless drifter. This wasn't supposed to last forever."

She smiled. "Maybe I could become a nurse and work with senior citizens. I just love them, Austin."

After a prolonged silence, he said, "I hate to admit it, but this is the right decision for you."

"I know. It won't be easy, but it feels right."

When they walked back to the picnic table to join Finn and Melody, he held her hand.

"I need to take money from you one last time— for bus fare. I will pay you back. Will you drop me off at the bus stop?"

"Of course. Do me a favor? Take my phone number. Please."

She wrote it in her notebook, below her tally of everything she owed him.

Once there, Finn and Austin entered the men's washroom while Melody and Gracie used the women's.

As they washed their hands, Gracie asked, "Has Finn ever talked to you about Austin's childhood?"

"No, why?"

"I'm curious. Whenever I say anything about it, Austin gets strange. He's hiding something."

"Aren't we all? You and I had pretty bizarre childhoods. Finn's was strange, too."

"How?"

"He didn't meet his dad until he was almost twelve. His mom had grown up in Ordinary but moved away after she got pregnant with Finn. Just before his birthday, his mom moved back here with him. Finn didn't even know who his father was. He lived in Ordinary for months before he found out that Remington Caldwell was his dad. His parents had lied to him through the sin of omission, and Finn had to figure out who he was by himself. It screwed him up for a while. Things worked out in the end, though, when his parents finally got married and they became a really close family."

"So that's why he's so screwed up." She softened it with a smile.

"Hey. I resent that." Melody swatted her arm playfully.

Gracie giggled. "I thought you would. That's why I said it." She sobered. "But you know nothing about Austin?"

Melody shook her head.

Gracie thought of something else. "Melody, why didn't you and I share hotel rooms instead of me bunking with Austin?"

"I asked Austin that once. He said he liked things the way they were."

Gracie smiled to herself. He'd liked having her near and yet had never made an untoward pass.

Beside the bus, Austin handed her the ticket he'd purchased. They said goodbye before Gracie boarded, a direct route to Las Vegas.

She hugged Melody hard, because the friendship of a woman was a rarity in her life.

"Will you keep in touch? I want to know how everything goes with your father."

"How can I get hold of you?"

"Contact me through my blog." She gave her the name, a sign of how much she had come to trust Melody. Melody's eyebrows rose, but she nodded.

Gracie turned to shake hands with Finn, but he did the oddest thing. He brushed her hand aside and hugged her. What was that about? But she hugged him back.

"Sorry," he whispered. "I was an ass."

Yes, he had been, but she smiled. No point in rubbing it in.

And then there was only Austin, and she didn't know how to say goodbye. How could she let go when she'd never thought to feel this way about a man, with this depth?

She would miss Austin down to the soles of her feet. She would miss him with every breath.

For a week, she had known a brief respite from unrelenting loneliness. Now that the moment of goodbye was here, she sensed the same emotions roiling through him as through her. A phone number in case she got into trouble would not be enough. She *had* to see this man again.

How did she possibly go back to being alone?

He hugged her, lifted her into his arms and off her feet, and squeezed the breath out of her. She hung on for dear life.

When he set her on her feet, she whispered, "You're the best man I've ever met. I know where you live." She leaned close and held his dear face in her hands, her voice so fierce her throat hurt. "I'll come to you. One day, the town of Ordinary will see me walk in. I will find you. I will be whole and strong and no longer needy and I will come as an equal. Watch for me."

Just as fiercely, eyes bright, Austin said, "If you don't show up, I'll come searching for you. Take that as a promise or a threat, but *you* watch for *me*."

She spun away, mounting the stairs to the bus blindly, because her vision had misted.

She took a seat on the far side of the bus so she wouldn't see him as she drove away.

That would be too, too painful.

THEY DROVE INTO Dallas at noon and Melody became a bundle of nerves.

"What first?" Austin asked. "Stop to see Melody's father or go see cattle?"

Finn turned in his seat to look at her. "What do you want?"

Her knuckles hurt from clutching her purse strap. Austin had parked the car in Trinity River Greenbelt Park and watched her in the rearview mirror. Melody felt the weight of his and Finn's concern.

She didn't like to be the center of attention. She left that to others and reported on their stories.

Melody stared out the window. The compact Dallas skyline rose in the distance, with modern glass towers reflecting sunlight and cumulus clouds.

More than a million people called this city home. In Texas, all roads led to Dallas. Four of the major interstate highways, at any rate.

One quarter of Texas residents lived in the Dallas-Fort Worth Metroplex and somewhere amid this bustle was her family.

They had money and had made a name here. In one of those office buildings, her father ran a business. Or he had. He was in a care facility now.

She didn't want to see him sick. Whenever she had imagined seeing him at all, it had never been like this.

She had become a coward. How ironic that she'd pushed Gracie to reveal her identity to the world, but when it came time for Melody to expose herself to her family, she wanted to turn tail and run.

"Can we go see the cattle first? I—I need time."

Finn reached into the backseat to take her hand and massage her fingers. "Calm down. You'll be okay."

Melody nearly lashed out at him, telling him it was easy for him to be calm, he didn't have to meet his father for the first time, but that would have been unkind. Finn was doing exactly what she had asked him to do—support her in a time of emotional need.

Melody had to respect that.

What she didn't respect was this sudden lack of backbone in herself. She hadn't expected it. She'd thought she would come down here with guns blazing to give her father a piece of her mind, but now she was here and didn't know what to feel, couldn't sort out these emotions that roared through her like waterfalls. How lowering.

Where in this bustling city did her family live?

Her grandmother was still alive. What kind of woman raised an abuser? Had Melody's grandfather been abusive, too?

In her research, Melody had learned it was behavior that could be passed on in families. Maybe her dad hadn't been born ugly. Maybe he had merely imitated his father.

Had her grandmother ever tried to protect her mother from the abuse, or had she been a victim, too? Should Melody resent her or feel sorry for her?

"Let's just go," she blurted. "I can come back later by myself."

Finn glared at her. "I told you I'd come with you. You're not doing this alone, Melody."

Yes, he had said he'd come with her, but she didn't want him to see her like this, so uncertain. She'd hated that he'd seen her without her wig. The way he'd looked at her still sent chills through her. He'd been green around the gills, as though looking at her had made him sick. How could she expose herself even more to him?

Hell, this was the boy she'd had a crush on for twenty years. She still had that crush, but now it was on the grown man. He'd stood up for her against Gracie, even though Melody had been at fault.

He squeezed her hand, then turned back to face the front. His knee jiggled. She'd never met anyone with as much nervous energy as Finn.

He had organized this trip for her, merely because she had asked him for help. True, she had been better at their correspondence over the past ten years than he had been, but the second she had asked for help, his email response had been short, but perfect.

When and where?

How could a woman not love a man like that?

Austin followed Finn's directions to the vet's ranch on the far side of the city, anxious to check out what might become his first head of cattle.

On a beautiful flat piece of Texas, they got out and stretched their legs.

A lanky, prematurely balding man about Finn's age and with mischief in his eyes came out of the house.

"Finn," he called. "How've ya been?"

They man-hugged with plenty of backslapping.

Finn made introductions then said, "Let's have a look at the cattle."

They followed Jason around the house to a white fence that stretched for miles. On the other side, about fifty cattle wandered the field and Austin had to admit Finn had been right. They were prime. Even without Finn checking them out, Austin would buy them.

"I want them."

Finn grinned. "Told you. Careful, buddy. You shouldn't sound enthusiastic in front of the seller."

Jason clapped Austin on the back. He might be wiry but he was strong.

"Finn, come into the field with me and check them out. I'll give you a rundown on any problems."

Austin's dream was about to come true, but there was a hole the size of Texas inside him and her name was Gracie. How did he get past that?

He and Jason talked and they settled on a fair deal for both of them, yet still that emptiness dogged him. How was she? Had she found her parents? Was she safe?

Would he ever see her again? His future, his dreams, were finally coming true after years of struggle and all he could think about was Gracie.

GRACIE ARRIVED IN Vegas and made her way to the Bellagio. It used to be her parents' favorite hotel. She was counting on that still being true.

When she'd married Jay, Mom and Dad had taken a permanent suite at the hotel. Guess who'd paid for it? Gracie.

At the front desk, she asked for them and was stunned to find they'd moved on. She traveled the strip, asking at the Mandalay, the Venetian and the

Mirage, as well as at Caesar's and the MGM Grand, all while being accosted by bright lights and noise.

They had to be somewhere nearby. Vegas was their favorite city.

She hated it. It represented everything that had been wrong in her life.

Even before she'd been married and had lived here with her parents, she'd never understood the appeal. No wonder when she'd left Jay, she'd gone in search of the real America. In her short life to that point, she'd never seen it.

Now, with her senses assaulted and overwhelmed, all she wanted was to be with Austin. No one here could match his straightforward decency.

At a small hotel on the edge of town, she found a couple registered as Mike and Chantelle Stacey. As if Gran would *ever* have named a daughter of hers *Chantelle*. Mom had been christened Susan. What would her current friends think to find out she was plain, ordinary Sue and not the exotic Chantelle?

Gracie had never forgiven her parents for giving her a rhyming name. Gracie Stacey. Maybe her mother had always thought her child would be famous and had predetermined this as a good stage name. Her mom was stunningly beautiful and her dad handsome. Maybe they had hoped their kid would be a model. When it had turned out that Gracie was not only pretty, but also talented, they must have thought they'd won the lottery. A name like Gracie Stacey was too cute to be anything but a stage name. Unfortunately for Gracie, it was all too real.

Susan had distanced herself from her past with more than a new name. Their visits to Gran had been stingy and handed out to Gracie as rewards for doing what her parents wanted. They had manipulated her in the worst possible way. Even so, those few, short visits had been the highlights of Gracie's childhood.

At the front desk, Gracie got their room number and rode to the top floor. Her parents might no longer be able to afford the best, but they still got the penthouse suite. Dated and sad, the hotel had seen better days. Oh, how the mighty had fallen. What had they done with her millions? What had happened to her money?

She knocked and waited, heart drumming to the beat of a rock band on psychedelic drugs. She hadn't seen her parents in six years.

The door opened…and there was her dad, still handsome, still dapper…and scared to death when he saw her.

Bingo. Guilty as sin.

He didn't move, stood as stiff and unwelcoming as a corpse.

"Glad to see you, too, Dad."

He shook himself out of his shock and smiled. "Sweetheart, wonderful to see you!"

His voice was too bluff and hearty. She hadn't inherited her acting skills from him. *Oh, Daddy, can't you be real with me? Your own daughter?*

"Where have you been? We've been worried sick about you. We tried to find you."

"I know. The last private detective you hired was

a mean bastard. He took his work seriously. He hurt me."

"God! We would never have wanted that." The calculating edge in his eyes put the lie to that. They might not have wanted her hurt, but they had wanted their meal ticket back at any cost.

He reached for her, but his hug was as false as his welcome. "Come in. Your mother will be glad to see you."

Her mother.

Her parents were a team, a perfect match for each other. Gracie should celebrate that they had a good marriage, but found it nearly impossible to do when, in the mansion of their love, there had never been a room made available for their daughter.

"Chantelle's in the living room. Come."

Probably listening and already calculating what she can get from me. Was Gracie being unfair? These people weren't evil, they weren't serial killers, they didn't torture people. *But they didn't offer much in the way of love to their child, did they?*

No, they had certainly never done that.

She stepped into the suite as though entering enemy territory, wary and expectant. All she wanted was her money. She had given up expecting affection from Mike and Chantelle years ago.

Even only a bit of money would do, just enough to go back to school, to get a career and earn enough to buy that little house in the country somewhere.

Susan/Chantelle stood up. She might have been surprised to see Gracie, or even shocked. It was hard to tell. She'd had too much work done. A frozen face watched her enter the room, brows drawn up to her hairline, mouth pulled wide, lips filled with enough collagen to float a ship.

Gracie took a second look at her dad. Yep, he'd been tucked and filled, along with buffing and scrubbing, preserved like a well-manicured lawn. Artificial turf, perfect and everlasting.

Gracie preferred her men real.

"Gracie, what are you doing here?" Gracie wondered if Chantelle realized how hostile she sounded. She must have, because she followed it up with, "We've missed you. Where have you been?"

"Here and there. Were you worried about me?"

"Of *course* we were."

Gracie had the good sense, and the experience, to take that with a grain of salt.

"Michael, make some tea."

Dad went to a corner where a small kitchenette had been set up with a coffeepot, microwave and two-burner hotplate.

He put on an electric kettle to boil.

"Sit," Chantelle ordered. This version of her mother looked so grotesque, so unlike the woman she used to be, that Gracie couldn't think of her as Mom.

Oh, Lord. They had become caricatures of themselves. They'd lived too long in Hollywood and Las Vegas, the lands of make-believe.

Gracie sat, wondering what to say to these people, who were, for all intents and purposes, strangers. More so than Austin and Finn and Melody, who were real to their cores.

She missed them.

Aw, what the heck. She couldn't make small talk. She might as well get to the point.

"Where's my money?"

Chantelle dropped to the sofa, one hand scrabbling for the arm for support and the other coming to rest on her too-firm chest. "Money? What do you mean?"

"I turned thirty."

"Thirty? Impossible." Chantelle brushed her fingers along her unnaturally taut jawline. That would make her fifty-five.

"Yes. It is possible. I stopped at a bank in Denver. Guess what I found out when I tried to access my money?"

Gazes slid to the floor and to the view outside the windows, to the barren landscape beyond the neon of the strip. Neither her father nor Chantelle would look at her, a clear sign of guilt.

"There's nothing in my trust fund. Nada. *Rien.* Dick all."

"Gracie," Chantelle admonished. "We don't swear in this family."

"We do now, especially when *I* worked so hard for that money."

"You worked hard?" Her dad unplugged the kettle and crossed his arms over his chest. "What about how hard your mother and I worked on your contracts to make sure you were paid fairly? To keep

you safe from the paparazzi? To keep a level head on your shoulders?"

"You were paid well as my agents," Gracie countered. "You lived a sweet life because of it. You enjoyed the best of everything, traveled, lived and ate first class. While you were doing all of that, the person doing the bulk of the hard work was me."

Agitated, she stood. "Where is the money that was put into trust for me by the studio? I know you were the caretakers of that trust. You weren't supposed to be living on it. You do know that's fraud, right? Where is it?"

Chantelle looked to Mike to handle this. "We can get it for you," he said.

"Why wasn't it in my account?"

"We invested it. It wasn't making enough of a return in the trust. Hell, we did a lot better on our own elsewhere."

"I want all of it. Every cent."

"We can't liquidate overnight. Tomorrow, we can get you enough to be comfortable for a while until we can access the rest."

Chantelle looked her over. "You can buy clothes, makeup, get a manicure, spruce yourself up. Look more like your old self."

"It's late now. Tomorrow I'll go to the bank and get you ten thousand." Dad spread his arms in a gesture of helplessness. "Sorry, sweetie, that's the best I can do on short notice."

She stared at them. Should she believe them? They might be strangers, but they were still her parents.

"We'll get you a room here," Dad said. "I'll pay for it."

Just for fun, to see them squirm, she said, all innocence, "You mean I can't stay here with you, Mom and Dad?"

"No. I mean we don't have room for you, other than on the love seat. You would be uncomfortable." Exactly the sort of thing she'd expected her father to say. He directed her toward the door, herding her like a recalcitrant lamb. "Let's go down to the front desk and get you into a room. Chantelle, I'll be back in a few minutes."

They left, Gracie acutely aware that her mother hadn't even hugged her. Lost little-girl sadness rode to the lobby in the elevator with her.

Her dad got her a small room on the third floor. At the door, he air-kissed her cheeks then entered the elevator to return to his suite.

Imagine air-kissing your daughter. If she ever had children, she was going to hug and kiss the daylights out of them every single day. Real hugs, real kisses.

Before going to bed, she got out her notebook and added the cost of the bus fare to the tally she owed Austin. She ran her finger across his phone number, holding herself back from calling him. Just to talk. Just to hear his voice.

She slept fitfully, because she knew. She knew her parents. Along the way in her travels across America, she had grown up.

This side trip to Vegas had merely been a last-ditch

effort to connect with them, to make sure there was nothing here for her.

Sure enough, when she went to their suite the next day, there was no answer. She returned and knocked throughout the day. Still no answer. When she asked at the front desk, she was told they had checked out and had no intention of returning.

Worse, they hadn't paid for her room and she didn't have a dime. Last night, Dad had told the front desk to add her room to his monthly bill. What kind of fast-talking had he done this morning to get out of it? Had he lied and told them Gracie wanted to pay for it herself? Had they lived here for so long that management had taken him at his word? Or had he slipped the desk clerk a bribe?

Screwed again, she returned to her room, sat on the bed, and reviewed her options, which were… non-existent.

Her parents hadn't even left her crumbs, and she was once again a Charles Dickens foundling.

Please, sir, I want some more.

After all of her talk of finding herself, of getting strong so she could come back to Austin as an equal, she was flat-broke and out of options.

For a long, long time, gutted, she sat on her bed staring out the window that faced the desert surrounding Vegas. Metaphors lined up left, right and center. On the far side of the hotel, the flash and greed of the Strip mocked her childhood and all that she'd turned her back on.

The poorer quarters, those of the workers who supported the lifestyles of the rich and famous, the cleaners, housekeepers, waiters and desk clerks who kept the casinos running, echoed the meager living she'd been trying to make, without exposing her identity.

The desert in the far distance that butted up against the Spring Mountains to the west represented her heart. She had grown up since leaving her husband and parents, but she hadn't made a true lasting life for herself.

Not only her life, but also her emotions, her soul, were a barren wasteland.

She'd thought she'd hit rock bottom when she'd robbed Austin. Not even close. This, here, now, trapped in a hotel room for which she couldn't pay, losing her father for the last time, was the worst, because now she was going to have to take yet again from Austin Trumball.

She had no one else to whom she could turn.

She picked up the receiver of the phone on the bedside table and touched it to her forehead, delaying the call until she could draw strength from, of all absurd things, her desperation. She could do this. She could reach out even while it killed her to do so. She placed it against her ear. The dial tone, dead and mechanical, buzzed too loudly. She needed to hear a human voice, the sound of someone who cared. Her fingers hovered above the number pad.

Despair won out over pride.

Hollow and dry-eyed, she dialed long-distance and made a collect call.

When Austin answered, she uttered her three most difficult words.

"I need help."

CHAPTER ELEVEN

"WHAT DO YOU say to a father you're meeting for the first time as a grown woman?" Melody sat in the rental car beside Finn. Austin had left that morning to drive to Las Vegas to help Gracie.

Finn squeezed Melody's hand. "I'm glad I came with you, Mel. I'm glad you're letting me help you with this."

They left the car and entered the palliative-care facility where her father would reside until he....

Her mind refused to go there.

Too soon, they stood outside her father's door.

Finn held her hand, his grip crushing her fingers, seeming as nervous as she felt.

"Just be yourself, Melody."

She pressed her hand against her stomach where butterflies didn't just flutter, they danced jigs and reels.

"I can't do this." She turned to leave.

Finn urged her back beside him. "If you don't, you'll never forgive yourself. For the rest of your life, you'll wonder about him."

True.

"There won't be a second chance, Mel. The guy's dying."

Melody flinched. "Do you have to be so blunt?"

"Yes."

Finn was right. Her father was dying and she had to see this through.

Strengthening her resolve, she opened the door and stepped inside.

A man lay on the bed staring out of the window, thin, hair white, skin sallow.

He'd been so handsome in the photos she'd found online.

Cancer ate away at a person literally. There wasn't much left of her father.

When he heard the door open, he cast her a disinterested glance, did a double-take and then stared.

His face lit up. "Melody?" He sounded as if he was afraid to believe it was truly her.

"Yes," she said, then stopped and stared, unable to come up with words that made sense.

This man was her father. She was finally meeting her dad.

Tears welled up, stinging her eyes, because she wouldn't let them fall. She wasn't sad or regretful that she'd missed a life with her father. No, not at all. She was angry. Truly. This was the man who had hurt her mother.

What should she say to a man who'd forced her mother to run away with her to keep them both safe?

She stepped closer, remembering all the times

she'd imagined this event, and all the things she would say to this terrible man.

Nothing came out, because the man lying in the bed was pitiful, small and fragile. He had no defenses, but he had her eyes. Even if she wanted to deny a connection, she couldn't.

"Melody," he whispered again, his voice as ravaged by illness as his body. Cancer, and the efforts to cure it, did awful things. "I've waited a long time to meet you."

They'd missed so much, everything, birthdays, all the firsts...words, steps, dates. He should have been around vetting boyfriends.

"You could've been in my life all along if you hadn't hurt my mom." Her voice, carrying with it the acid of anger, burned its way out of her throat.

A ragged sigh escaped her father's dry lips. "You'd better sit down. I have a lot to tell you."

Finn snagged a chair for her from the corner of the room. She ignored him.

"This should be interesting. I've always enjoyed a good story." Melody didn't bother to hide her skepticism.

"I never abused your mother."

"Yeah, right. Isn't that what all abusers say?"

"I don't know what anyone else says. I only know my own truth. I didn't hurt your mother." His voice took on strength. "If you want the truth, sit and listen." A father's command.

She sat, but didn't relax into the seat.

Finn retrieved a chair from the hallway and placed

it close to hers. He sat and laid his arm across the back of her chair, taking her hand in his other hand and holding tightly. She took comfort from his presence.

"The problem wasn't me. It was my parents. Your mother was young. She worked for us as a maid. I fell for her hard."

He smiled, adding wrinkles to his thin face, but erasing the creases of illness and fatigue. "She was so pretty. Almost as pretty as you are."

She couldn't let him believe things that weren't real. She reached up and took off her wig.

He startled. "Was that from the car accident?"

"Yes."

His gaze sharpened. "You think your natural hair looks so bad you should cover it?"

"I know so."

"It doesn't." His attention turned to Finn. "What do you think? That she should wear a wig?"

Finn blustered, but said nothing more than, "Well…"

"You don't deserve my daughter." He gestured toward her. "Bring that chair closer."

She scooted right up beside the bed. Her father took her hand out of Finn's. "That's better. You are quite beautiful. You have your mother's delicacy. I loved her with all my heart."

"Then why didn't you marry her? Why didn't you make the relationship legal?"

"She ran away long before I found out about you."

"I don't get it."

"Your mother had nothing. She was poor. An orphan. My family was wealthy and had a world of resources. When my parents found out she was pregnant, they wanted you, but not her. They tried to pay her off. She ran."

"Where were you?"

"Away at college. I knew nothing about this. When I found out what had happened, that Elizabeth had been pregnant and my parents were working to get sole custody of you, I joined the search, but not to take you away from her. I wanted to marry your mother, but she was always one step ahead of me."

Melody didn't believe it. "My mom wouldn't have lied to me all those years. She said she ran because you hurt her."

"No one would have helped her if she'd said she was running from her boyfriend's parents, who wanted to keep her child. Most people don't understand that mothers can lose their children to those with money and powerful contacts. Abuse, though? That they can relate to. I regret what your mother did, but I don't blame her. My parents were ruthless. My mother still is. She's one of the least likeable, most ambitious people I know. Don't blame your mother for running or for her lies. She knew my parents wouldn't stop until they won."

"But…what about at the hospital? You were violent."

"I had reached the end of my rope. I had despaired of ever finding Elizabeth and had married someone else by then. Unfortunately, Diana and I couldn't have children. I love her, but you were my only child.

I wanted to know you. Do you have any idea how many times I missed you? Apparently, you were in the hospital when I arrived and the pair of you managed to sneak out. You were so close and yet I couldn't see you. I lost my temper and behaved like an idiot, but I was hurting."

Melody couldn't wrap her head around this. "It's all so different from what my mom told me."

"Don't blame Elizabeth. My parents were formidable adversaries. Maybe when she heard I was searching, too, she thought I would use my wealth and contacts to get sole custody. It wasn't like that, but how would she know?" He paused to catch his breath and she grew alarmed.

"You should rest."

"Not yet…I want to tell…everything. The closest I came before then was when you were recovering from your open-heart surgery. Did your mother tell you that?"

Melody shook her head.

"Did she tell you that I paid for the operation after the fact? Otherwise, your mother would still be paying for it. It would have been like carrying a mortgage. Those operations are expensive."

"I often wondered how Mom covered the bill."

"I'm glad she had it done so you could live a more normal life, apart from the running, that is." He smiled sadly.

"One question. Did you take advantage of my mom?"

"No. We were both young and passionate, but

there was more to it. I'd like to believe she loved me as much as I loved her."

"She loved you, but she ran away from you."

"She ran away from my parents. She loved you more than she loved me, as was right."

This man was too reasonable, so different from the picture her mother had painted of him.

The hard clacking of heels echoed in the hallway and a woman walked into the room, tall and energetic for a seventy-something senior citizen.

Her father's mouth thinned. "What are you doing here, Mom? I can't have a moment alone with my daughter?"

The woman turned her avid gaze on Melody and asked, "Is this really her?" She nodded. "Yes, I can see that it is. She has your eyes and your father's mouth."

Melody hated this woman on sight. "And my mother's backbone. Stop looking at me like I'm an expensive meal. You caused my mother a world of heartache. I hate you."

Her grandmother reared away from her. "I did what I thought was best for you."

Melody was no naive kid. She understood a lot about what happened thirty-one years ago. "No. You did what was best for *you*." Blindly, she turned back to her father, desperate to get away before the tears that were blinding her vision actually fell. "I will come back to see you again."

To Finn, she whispered, "Get me out of here."

In the hallway, she bent over and put her hands on

her knees, drawing in oxygen with gasps, as though her lungs had stopped working. Maybe they had. Her heart, too.

Everything she had known about her life had been false.

"I need to call my mother. Let's get back to the hotel so I can do it privately."

"Melody, I can see you're in shock. You're mad at that woman, but I think you're angry with your mom, too. You should wait until you calm down."

She rounded on him. "Finn, I know you mean well, but shut up. I'm going to get to the truth if it kills me."

In her hotel room, with Finn listening, she spoke to her mom. "Why did you lie?"

After a protracted silence, her mom asked, "Where are you?"

"In Dallas." She heard the sharp inhalation on the other end of the phone.

"You've seen him?"

"Yes. He told quite the story."

"How...how is he?"

"Not good. He's dying."

"Don't leave. I'm coming down. I'll get the next flight out and see you tomorrow. Where are you? Where is he?"

Melody shared everything then hung up and stared at the floor, unseeing.

Finn sat beside her. "You okay?"

"I don't know." Her voice broke. "I've always thought my mom was the best, strongest, most courageous woman on earth. How could I have been so wrong about her?"

"Maybe you weren't. Don't judge her until you talk to her. Okay?"

"It's hard not to."

"Yeah."

She leaned toward him and he wrapped his arms around her. She wanted him.

"Finn, I need you."

He kissed her and she returned the kiss, turning up the heat in her desire to escape this disaster.

Finn was right there with her, returning the urgency with which she kissed him.

They fell back onto the bed and Melody reached for the buttons of his shirt, running her hands over his chest. For such a long time, she had wanted this man. Now, he was here with her, matching her passion with fingers as experienced as hers were fumbling.

Her blouse was open and his hands were on her breasts before she thought to warn him.

He stopped kissing her and pulled back to look at her, but the lust in his gaze quickly turned to horror.

"Is this from the open-heart surgery your dad mentioned?" Finn asked, pointing to the vertical scar on her chest that looked like a puckered ladder of skin. "I—I never knew you had that."

He moved away from her, physically. His spirit recoiled, too. His lust deflated like a popped balloon.

Melody drew the two sides of her blouse together and sat up. So did he, buttoning his shirt.

"It's an old scar."

"I can see that. Why did you need surgery?"

"I was born with a hole in my heart. I was a child, but I will always have this scar."

"A hole in the heart is a big deal."

"Yes, Finn, it was." When he didn't say anything, she continued, "And it's a big deal right now, isn't it? Between us? You don't find me attractive, do you?"

"I do. It's just that...."

"That what?"

He started to sweat, remembering the roots of his queasiness, the first time his dad had taken him on a vet call more serious than most, to a ranch where a cow was having trouble giving birth.

Finn loved animals. He wanted to go on all his dad's visits, but his dad, thinking he was too young, had hesitated with the more difficult cases. Finn had hounded him until finally this time he said, "*Okay*. Jump in the car and let's go. Hurry."

Finn had gone off ready for the greatest of adventures. It had certainly been an adventure. Not a great one, though. A nightmare.

As it turned out, his father had helped the cow to deliver. The calves, though, as in two of them, had been conjoined, sharing one back leg, both with a second withered hind leg. Seriously grotesque.

To say that Finn had been grossed out put it mildly. He'd been appalled, terrified, freaked out.

His dad had made him stand outside the barn

while he and the rancher had put down both the calves and the poor cow who'd given birth to them. She was dying.

He remembered the gunshots. One. The remaining calf had bawled pitifully. Two. The mother had protested, her moo plaintive and painful to hear. Three. Thundering silence. He had flinched with each one.

Later, he'd asked why his father hadn't just put them to sleep, but his dad hadn't had enough medication with him to do all three. Hence, those bloody, echoing shots that lingered in Finn's mind for years.

His father had talked him through it and, to Finn's credit, he'd gone on to become a vet, but sometimes he still had trouble with anything out of the ordinary.

His squeamishness was his shame. There were times when he still felt like that little boy, when he should be a man.

"Melody, I'm sorry. This kind of thing—" He pointed to her chest and then her head. "The burned scalp. The scar. This kind of stuff sometimes bothers me."

"Your girlfriends have all been perfect, have they?" Bitterness.

He had the grace to blush. "Yeah. They have been." She turned away from him.

"Don't be angry, Melody," he pleaded. "This is a lot to take in. To get used to."

"I'm not angry, Finn."

"You're not?"

"No. I'm disappointed."

He rubbed his chest, where shame burned. Her

disappointment was worse than anger. Anger he could rail against. Disappointment just made him feel small. He *was* small and immature, but he'd never been able to rise above his issues other than to save an animal's life.

Making love to Melody? It wasn't going to happen tonight.

He left the room because she asked him to.

"I need to be alone," she said at the door, her voice full of a hurt he wished he could fix. "Think about this after you go... How do you grow from this?"

Hours later, tramping the streets of Dallas, he still searched for the answer to her question. How *did* he grow from this? How did he become a better person?

His life had been too easy, not like Melody's. She'd had a lot of hard years to accumulate wisdom, while he had been out having a good time.

Once his parents had reconciled and gotten married, Finn's life had been great. Maybe too great. Things had come to him easily. Maybe too easily. He'd grown into adolescence with his dad's good looks. He'd missed the gawky stage that most boys went through, and the girls had flocked to him.

Girls. Sex. His first experience, instead of being awkward, had been awesome. The best. Women had fallen all over him in college. He'd grown used to it, used to sex being fun and easy. Now he had to wonder, had he shortchanged women? Had he given enough?

They'd always come back for more, and he'd always been the one to end the relationships.

Friends had fallen into his lap. Good grades had been a piece of cake.

He was clever. Maybe too clever. Another *maybe*. Too many of them.

Skip maybe, boy. Go straight to definitely. You've had it too easy. You haven't had to work for anything in years.

How did he fix this? How did he get over the squeamishness? He didn't have a clue.

He returned to the hotel and knocked on Melody's door.

When she opened it, he didn't beat around the bush. Melody was a great person.

"You deserve better than me," he said. "You deserve the best. I'm not it."

She nodded. "Yeah, I agree. I deserve more."

She didn't have to agree with him so readily. He tried not to feel insulted.

"You used to be a great guy, but somewhere along the way you lost your humility, Finn. You're easygoing and fun because you don't want to deal with the tough things. That's fine. Go on and live the rest of your life that way, if you want, but it isn't enough for me."

Despite the changed dynamic, the lost affection, he wouldn't abandon her.

"Will you let me stay to help you until your dad… you know?"

She nodded, but she'd lost her spark. "I would appreciate that."

"Contact me when your mom gets in tomorrow? I don't want you seeing her alone."

"I will."

She closed the door, but not before Finn caught another glimpse of her disappointment. Man, it hurt to be on the receiving end of it. It hurt even more to realize it didn't begin to match the disappointment he felt in himself.

MELODY AWOKE EARLY after a miserable night.

Hadn't she worried about Finn's reaction to her body? In the past ten years, she hadn't wanted him to see her because of her physical flaws. Yet in her need for comfort yesterday, she had forgotten to be cautious. To warn him first before letting him see how imperfect her body was.

She'd told him she was only disappointed with him, that she wasn't angry.

Wrong.

This morning she was very angry. Part of loving a person was accepting their flaws and differences. She loved Finn and accepted him. He should have accepted her. But then, he obviously didn't love her.

She shouldn't have expected him to. They hadn't seen each other in so many years. He had defended her so vociferously against Gracie, Melody had accepted it as true and deep caring. Maybe it was, but it wasn't the love Melody wanted and deserved despite having a less than perfect body.

After her shower, she came out of the bathroom to find a message on her machine.

Her mom was in Dallas and on her way to the care facility.

Melody dressed and left her room. At Finn's door, she hesitated before knocking, building her defenses. The man had rejected her body. She wouldn't soon forget that.

She needed a friend. She had to think of him as no more than that.

When she felt strong enough, she knocked. He answered, his smile sheepish. She hated this. This wasn't how she wanted their relationship to go, even as friends.

"Finn," she said. "Last night things didn't work out between us. Can we go back to being friends?"

He exhaled loudly. "Yeah. I want that. I thought you would turn me away today. Melody, I…know I didn't behave well yesterday, but I need you to understand how much I respect you."

Respect. Not love. Message received loud and clear. It would have to do.

"I understand, Finn. I really need a friend right now. Mom's in town."

"I'm here." He grabbed his baseball cap and left his room.

At the care facility, Melody saw her mother waiting in the lobby.

Her mother raced to her and pulled her into a hard embrace. "I'm so sorry," she whispered. It sounded like she'd been crying.

Melody spotted Randy, Mom's husband and the nurse who had helped them to escape from the hospital outside Ordinary all of those years ago. He hovered behind Mom like a guardian angel.

"Liz," he said, easing her away from Melody. "Give the rest of us a chance." He wrapped Melody in a bear hug. Randy was a great guy. She'd been happy that her mom had found him. After all those lies, though, did her mother deserve him? "How are you doing, sweetheart?"

"I'm confused, Randy." When she looked into his eyes, she saw awareness. He knew everything. "When did she tell you?"

"A while ago. Just after you said you'd been in touch with your father. She needed someone to know the truth."

"So, I was the only one in the dark."

"She had her reasons." Randy's deep voice held a caution, and maybe a reprimand.

Melody didn't care. Her life had been a lie.

"How could you?" She turned on the woman who had raised her, who now watched her with such dismay and sorrow.

So what? Heedless, Melody charged on.

"How could you lie to me? Not only lie, but a lie of this magnitude? You kept a decent man away from his daughter and let me think he was a monster."

"You don't understand. His parents would have taken you. I couldn't lose you, so I ran." Her mom reached for her, but Melody skittered away.

"Why make up such a heinous lie about my dad?"

Anger flared on her mom's face. "It's easy for you to criticize me, but imagine my situation, Melody. I had no money, no family, no friends. I had been orphaned years before and had grown up in foster care and group homes. I was alone in the world and dirt poor. I was only eighteen and finally had my own family, *you,* and you're damn right I was going to fight to keep you."

Her mouth twisted with bitterness. "The one sure way for me to get support was to tell people I was running from an abusive relationship. Do you honestly think people would have helped me if I'd said, oh, my baby's grandparents want to steal her? They would have thought I was crazy. They would have said that kind of thing doesn't happen these days. Well, guess what? It does when you have money and power. Gord's parents had both. They were one of the most powerful couples in Texas. They had the governor, the local sheriff, lawyers, all in their back pockets. I had *nothing.*"

"But—"

Liz ran over Melody's objection with the righteousness of a preacher on speed. In the fire in her mom's eyes, Melody saw the woman who was capable of doing anything to save her daughter. "I had nothing but my wits. You're damned right I lied. I did whatever I had to do to keep *my* child with *me.* I was your mother and had every right to keep you." She pointed at Melody. "You go ahead and hate me." She turned to include everyone circling her, because some woman Melody didn't recognize stood behind Finn, beside the woman who'd come into Gord's room yesterday, Melody's grandmother.

"You," Liz spat, pointing to Melody's grand-mother. "You were evil. You had no right to my daughter." She turned back to Melody. "Don't you dare judge me until you walk in my shoes. I was poor and did what I had to do. I'm sorry I hurt Gord, but I was only eighteen and had no way of knowing whose side he would be on. He'd been raised to respect his parents and to follow his father into politics. How was I to know if he would accept an illegitimate child? I couldn't imagine he would marry me." She gestured with her chin toward Gord's mother. "*She* told me he would *never* agree to marry me."

Melody's gaze flew to her grandmother. The haughty expression on the woman's face didn't change and Melody saw what her mom had faced down as a teenager. Implacable arrogance and an overblown sense of entitlement.

Well, she didn't deserve Melody.

Liz choked and scrambled in her purse for a tissue. Randy handed her a handkerchief from his pocket. Liz wiped her eyes. "I am truly sorry I hurt Gord and separated you two," she said, her attention solely on Melody now. She lifted her chin, the defiant gesture familiar from all of those times they'd run away. "But that's *all* I'm sorry about. If I had to do it again, I would. You belonged with me."

The balloon of Melody's indignation deflated. In the same situation, would she have done anything differently? Given everything she'd just heard, she didn't think so.

As far as her grandmother was concerned, after learning the facts, Melody didn't trust her one bit.

She reached for her mom and held her, rubbing her back to still the shakes. "You did the right thing, Mom. I love you. You did an amazing job of protecting me."

"Thank you," her mom whispered. She straightened and said, "I want to see Gord."

Her attention shifted to someone past Melody's right shoulder, the woman who stood beside Gord's mother. "Are you his wife?"

"Yes. I'm Diana." She came forward and shook Liz's hand. "Gordon never meant to take Melody away from you. He just wanted to meet her and get to know her."

"How could I have guessed that?"

"Given his mother's attitude, how could you have, indeed?"

The old woman gasped. "Diana, how can you say such a thing?"

Calmly, Diana said, "It's true, Ida. You ran roughshod over your son. He's dying now. It's time for every speck of truth to come out. I know you aren't an evil woman—"

Melody snorted and Diana's eyes glinted with humor. "Okay, that's a matter of opinion, but you think you deserve more than you actually do. What would you have done if someone had tried to take Gordon away from you when he was a baby?"

"If I were poor, I would have considered what was best for Gordon."

"Bullshit."

Ida gasped at Diana's crudity.

"Knowing you," Diana went on, "you would have fought tooth and nail to keep him."

Melody suspected Diana didn't swear often. She liked her, this woman who was wealthy and looked like a conservative church-going woman, but who had a down-to-earth sensibility that appealed.

"Can we stop arguing?" Melody walked to the elevators. "I want to see my dad. I'm going to stay here in Dallas until— As long as—"

Finn touched her shoulder. Dear Finn. He might not be able to accept her body, but he would support her.

"You will all stay with me while you're here." Diana joined them at the elevator.

"How can you accept us so easily?" Liz asked. "We're disrupting your life."

"I have an ulterior motive," the elegant woman confessed. "When Gordon goes, I will have nothing but memories and an empty house. I love him. I would like to get to know the piece of him that is left behind. His daughter."

The piece of him that is left behind. *Me.*

I have this opportunity to get to know my dad before he dies. I'll make the most of it.

As it turned out, they had only three days together before he died, but they were stellar days.

FROM THE CORNER of his eye, Finn watched Melody stand between the grandmother she disliked and

Gord's wife. An endless stream of visitors came through the doors of the funeral chapel during visitation hours. Melody handled it like a trooper, even offering support to her grandmother and Diana when they needed it. He was humbled by her strength.

For two days, he had stood ready, on guard, to give Melody anything she needed. In that time, watching her, he'd learned what strength of character really looked like.

And he'd learned that he loved her. Deeply, truly loved her.

If he stood a hope in hell of becoming worthy of her, he had to develop a backbone's worth of strength of character of his own.

During the funeral, he stood beside her at her father's grave. Silent tears skimmed Melody's cheeks and she wiped them away with a handkerchief.

Melody was strong. She had more character in her little finger than Finn had in his entire body. She humbled him.

He had plans, though. He had a situation to fix, one of his own making.

If Melody could show this much strength, then he should do no less.

She leaned on him and he put his arm around her. After the service, while others filed back to limos, he stopped her with a hand on her arm.

"Melody, I've learned," he said quietly.

She frowned. "What do you mean?"

"This past week, I've watched you and discovered what true strength looks like, what courage is.

You faced a challenge more difficult than anything I've ever had to deal with in my life and you did it with grace." He brushed back a lock of hair from her forehead. It was from her wig. He wanted to touch her real hair, not something fake, not something that wasn't truly part of this beautiful woman.

"I'd like to see you get rid of this rug for good."

"Really, Finn? But you—"

"I was wrong. God, Melody, so wrong. I've grown to love you."

Her face lit with hope.

"I want you. I want *you,* exactly as you are. Will you spend tonight with me?"

She smiled and walked away without saying a word, but that smile left him buoyant and effervescent. Aw, Mel.

They had a subdued family dinner at an upscale restaurant, toasting Gordon's memory.

Tonight, he planned to make Melody his, and tomorrow he would take her home with him. When dinner ended, he took her to a hotel instead of to Diana's home, not much caring what anyone thought.

For the things he wanted to say to her, the things he wanted to do with her, he needed privacy.

It was long past time for him to grow up, to put aside childish fears. Melody wasn't a sick cow or a mutant calf. She was a beautiful woman, one he loved more than any woman he had ever known. She deserved a hell of a lot better than him.

Too bad. He wanted her. She was getting him, heart, body and soul for the rest of his life.

His fears sounded childish now. He couldn't believe he had ever let something so…foolish…hold him back.

Tonight, he wanted to change that, to fix what he had done so wrong the first time around. Tonight, he was making love with the woman he loved as the man he wanted to be, a better man, the man she deserved.

It was time to hand over all of himself, including his fears, to a woman he admired and had grown to love in the space of a too-short road trip. Only two weeks. He needed more. He wanted a lifetime.

Then again, his love for her had started when he was twelve and had never quit. He realized now how much her reaching out to him ten years ago had meant to him. He had thought it was only in terms of having his little girl buddy back, but no. It had been much more than that.

All the fun, shallow times he'd had with women had just been his marking time until Melody had been ready to come back.

He hadn't understood that he'd needed to grow to be worthy of her. Tonight, he planned to prove to her how much she meant to him. How much he loved her.

He undressed her with care, starting by taking off her wig and hanging it on the arm of a chair.

"Don't wear this anymore," he said.

"But I—"

"You don't need it. You really don't. Your scars don't show. Maybe your hair isn't as thick as the wig, but it's thick enough to cover your scars."

"They don't show, but you can feel them, Finn." She forced his fingers into her hair so he would run them over her scalp, challenging him. He understood what she wasn't saying. She wanted to see whether she repulsed him.

"Sorry, babe," he said. "I've done all of the running I'm going to do. I love you, Melody. All of you."

"Even this?" She spread apart the blouse he'd unbuttoned a moment ago.

Forcing himself to look at her scar, he wondered why he hadn't been able to accept it earlier. These scars were part of the woman he adored. He leaned forward and kissed her, nuzzled his lips between her breasts.

"Even this, Melody." He breathed on her skin and she shivered.

He took his time with her, because she deserved it. He grinned just before he took her nipple into his mouth because he knew that in taking his time, he would build the pleasure for both of them.

In the loving of Melody Messina, Finn found a piece of himself he hadn't even known was missing.

In the moment of climax, he found a peace that renewed him.

In holding her while she slept, he found completion.

MELODY AWOKE TO contentment, to rightness in the world.

"Morning, babe." Finn spooned with her.

She'd had only a couple of boyfriends over the years, but she had never known this sense of rightness.

She kissed the palm of Finn's tanned hand and placed it on her breast. She wanted more of what they had shared last night. Twice.

The first time, Melody had let Finn call the shots, but the second time had been all about what she had wanted, which was to explore his lean, tight body.

They made love again in the warmth of the morning sunlight streaming through the open draperies. When they had finished, replete, Melody asked, "Why is the skin of your back and chest tanned to butterscotch? Do you run around without a shirt all the time? I thought you were a vet," she teased. "Is that how vets work? Shirtless? I have to get myself some animals and have more vets make house calls."

"The only vet making calls to your house, lady, is going to be me."

"Seriously, why are you so tanned?"

"I get acne on my back. The sun keeps it at bay."

"The perfect man isn't so perfect, after all."

"Never said I was." His hands roamed her body, his nervous energy proving to be entertaining in bed. He touched a particularly sensit— "Oh, that's, um, so good."

Finn chuckled and it was altogether too self-satisfied, so she turned the tables on him. His laugh ter turned to deep moans and Melody felt a satisfaction of her own that she could do this to Finn.

Half an hour later, they shared a shower, washing and drying each other.

"Finn?"

"Hmm?" he mumbled, focusing on getting every inch of her dry.

"What now?"

"What do you mean? We'll go to breakfast and then say goodbye to your mom. She flies out today."

"I know." She made him stop playing with her body. "I mean, what comes next for us?"

"Are you tied to living where you live? If so, after we get married, I guess I'll have to research veterinary possibilities in the area."

Oh. Oh, he would do that for her? "Did you just propose to me?"

"Yeah, marry me. Please."

She had wanted this for years, but had never truly hoped it could be real. "Yes, Finn. Yes."

He smiled and rested his forehead against hers.

"If you don't mind moving, would you come back to Ordinary with me?"

She threw herself into his arms. "Yes! Yes, yes."

Finn's great, big bellyfuls of laughter bounced off the walls and tiles of the bathroom.

"Melody, my love, let's go home. Today. As soon as we can get packed and book a flight."

"Home to Ordinary. I like the sound of that, Finn."

CHAPTER TWELVE

AUSTIN DROVE GRACIE home to Ordinary, stopping only for food and rest stops on the way. After he said the town would help her heal, Gracie went willingly. She hoped he was right, because she sure as heck didn't know where else to go from here.

Her first view charmed her, Main Street an odd mix of modern and traditional, with a large restaurant named Chester's Bar and Grill anchoring one end and an old hardware store putting an exclamation point to the other. "This place is beautiful."

Austin smiled. "It's far from perfect, but I'm glad I live here. I like the people."

Townspeople waved to Austin as he drove down Main. They glanced at Gracie with curiosity.

"They're wondering who I am."

"I left town with my buddy and I'm returning with a woman. Of course they're curious." Austin laughed, clearly happy to be home and why not? Apparently, today he was taking possession of his ranch. She would be happy, too, if she were moving into her own little house right now.

"What a great downtown. Look!" She pointed to

the diner and wondered whether it had changed at all since the fifties. Not by the looks of it.

Austin smiled, obviously enjoying her excitement. She liked how quiet his smile was, how understated. She, on the other hand, was more than excited. This was Austin's town. She hadn't had a personal connection to any of the cities or towns she'd passed through over the past six years.

Now she did. She wanted to shout out her open window, *the man I love lives here.* But of course, she wouldn't, because that kind of exhibitionism, that kind of impulse to draw attention to herself wasn't in her nature, and it never had been.

Plus, while she knew Austin wanted her, she didn't think he loved her.

They parked in front of a store called Sweet Talk.

"I want you to meet my friend C.J.'s wife. This is the best candy story for miles around."

Gracie stepped inside, then stopped, delighted. "Oh, my," she breathed.

"A lot of people have that reaction."

"It's amazing."

Chocolate animals decorated with icing lined the shelves, bunnies in pajamas and robes, carrying candles and books, preparing for a cozy read before bed; lambs in colorful jackets and pink booties; deer in jeweled harnesses, as though ready to pull a sleigh at a moment's notice. All were wrapped in polka-dotted cellophane and tied with big pastel bows.

One wall was lined with candy cases, full to bursting with sweets to buy in bulk. Tiny paw prints scattered across the floor led to wrought-iron tables and chairs nestled in the window.

"Janey sells the best hot chocolate in town."

Austin asked the clerk whether Janey was in. The clerk called her from the back. When she entered the room, Janey squealed, "Austin, you're home!" and threw herself into his arms. He hugged her back hard.

"How's my favorite girl?"

Gracie didn't like it. Not one bit. Who was this woman and why did she think she had the right to hug Austin so tightly, as though she owned him?

The woman pulled out of Austin's embrace, altering Gracie's assumptions. She had to be in her mid-forties, her gaze on Austin motherly, not sexual. What appealed to Gracie the most, though, was the woman's appearance—middle-aged Goth in a small-town charm bracelet of a candy store.

Spiky jet-black hair framed a heart-shaped face.

Gracie counted six piercings around her face, hung up on the tiny skulls lining the woman's ears.

Janey turned her large dark eyes on Gracie and said, "Introduce me to your friend, Austin."

Austin reached for Gracie with a gentle insistent touch on her arm that made her feel special. "This is Gracie."

The way he said it, with tenderness and pride, made her heart soar.

She shook Janey's hand and found the woman's grip strong.

"Are you heading straight home?" Janey asked Austin. "I can give you chocolate for your mom."

"No." Tension increased in the hand on Gracie's arm. "I'm picking up Sadie and stopping by the ranch first. Chocolate would probably melt in the car."

Whatever Janey saw in Austin's expression had her nodding in understanding. "Okay." She started back toward the door leading to a workroom and said, "If you see C.J., tell him I'll be home early tonight." She spoke her husband's name with affection. "Welcome home. Nice to meet you, Gracie."

They left the store and started toward the SUV when a man called, "Austin."

Austin stopped walking and turned slowly toward the pharmacist standing in his lab coat in the doorway of a drug store.

Registering the weird vibe between them, Gracie glanced from one man to the other.

"Can we talk?" The man looked hopeful.

"Same answer as last time. Nope." Austin climbed into the driver's seat. "Get in the car, Gracie," he ordered.

She did and Austin took off with a squeal of tires before she even had her seat belt on. Considering what a stickler for safety he'd been throughout the trip, it caught her off guard.

"Who was that?"

Austin's jaw flexed as if he was grinding his teeth. "I can't talk about him."

They drove right through the rest of town and out into the country.

"Where are we going?"

"I need to pick up my dog."

They pulled into the driveway of a pretty ranch and parked beside the house.

Austin got out of the car, leaving her to wonder whether she should do the same. It had been a long drive and her legs needed to stretch, so she did, but Austin's behavior was decidedly strange. For a man whose manners were spot-on, his behavior had been off ever since they'd come close to town.

When she stood beside the car, her uncertainty must have shown, because he reached out his hand. "Come on." His voice, harsh since seeing the man in town, softened.

Slipping her fingers into his as naturally as putting on a glove, she followed him to the stables. They stepped out of the sunlight into a spick-and-span building, where dust motes played hide-and-seek with bars of sunlight streaming through high windows.

A form leaped out of the shadows and launched itself at Austin, startling Gracie, jumping not just against him, but actually *into* his arms. A dog.

Austin laughed. The dog barked, crazy with joy.

"Sadie, girl, I missed you." He nuzzled her neck, scratched her ears and endured her licking his face, all while his laugh rang through the old farm building, wonderful after the darkness with that man in town.

"Wow, I hope I get the same welcome the next time I go off somewhere."

He stopped petting Sadie to glare at Gracie. "You aren't ever going anywhere again."

Gracie didn't respond because she knew how things could change so quickly and easily you were left breathless. She knew that even the best-laid plans could go awry.

She changed the subject. "She's an Aussie." Australian shepherds were her favorite breed. How fitting that Austin owned one.

Austin put Sadie down on the concrete floor. She spun in circles around him. "Sit. Stay." She did. He entered a stall where a horse nickered and sniffed his face.

He scrubbed her neck. "Hey, girl. My horse Shadow," he told Gracie.

"I don't know much about horses."

"Come over slowly."

She did and got to know the horse who nuzzled at her breast, startling a laugh out of her. "What's she doing?"

"Usually when I come, I bring carrots in my shirt pocket. She thinks you might have some."

"Sorry, girl. Next time." She planned to keep that promise.

"Let's find C.J.," Austin said, closing the stall door. "I want you to meet him."

They left the barn with Sadie jumping around Austin so much she almost tripped him. It didn't seem to bother him. Why wasn't Gracie surprised that he inspired so much devotion? Mr. Decency likely treated his pets like gold.

A man in his early fifties stepped out onto the back

porch. "Heard Sadie going nuts and knew it had to be either you or a squirrel."

"Ha-ha. Nice to know she gets this excited for squirrels as well as me."

C.J. grinned and shook Austin's hand. "Welcome back."

When Austin introduced them, Gracie liked C.J.'s firm grip and direct gaze. He had a sexy, aging-well Marlboro Man vibe going on.

"C.J.'s the reason I decided I wanted to own a ranch."

"He was twelve when he first came to stay with us," C.J. told Gracie. "He only stayed for…what?… three, four months?"

Austin nodded. "About that."

Why had he stayed here when he was twelve? For a few months. Would he tell her if she asked? She was beginning to think the man had nearly as many secrets as she'd did, only he hadn't shared his with her as she had done with him. The look he slid her way didn't invite questions, but C.J. kept talking as though he didn't notice the tension behind Austin's smile.

"He sure got the bug quickly. He followed my kids everywhere, became a shadow to me. Wanted to learn every last detail about ranching."

"Those were some great times." Austin directed this at Gracie, obviously trying to concentrate on the good and set aside whatever bad memories shadowed his eyes. "I'd never been out of town before and the fresh air, the exercise, were all a revelation to me."

C.J. smiled, turning his tanned face into a network of lines. "I guess Cash inspired him to be a cop, and I taught him how to be a rancher."

He turned his attention to Austin. "Now you've bought the Olsen ranch, you can do both."

"Yeah. I'm going to bring in some of the adolescents hanging around town once I get set up. Keep them out of trouble. Teach them a thing or two about ranching."

"Catch them before they get into real trouble. Good thinking. Good luck with it."

They left C.J. to his work, drove down the road with Sadie in the front seat between them, and turned into another driveway. The white house with blue shutters they parked in front of was smaller than C.J.'s and Janey's, but spotless. Lace curtains fluttered in an open window.

"Mrs. Olsen left the curtains." Austin stepped onto the porch. "Good of her. She would know I wouldn't have any."

They entered the house, their footsteps ringing hollow. Only a few pieces of old furniture dotted the first floor.

"The Olsens moved out while I was gone, but Greg was supposed to have stayed on until I got here today. Let's go find him."

They located him in the barn, wiping down tools and straightening an already clean tool bench.

"There you are." An old man with stooped shoulders and a ready smile approached.

"Hi, Greg. Thanks for how well you left the house. Thank Ada for the curtains she left."

"No problem. There's a few things I'll show you before I go. The furnace can cut out sometimes, but I got a trick for getting her started again. You'll get another few years out of her. The herd's out in the north pasture. When do your fifty arrive?"

"Soon."

Gracie sat on the front porch steps while Greg showed Austin around and talked about things like fuse boxes and sump pumps and septic systems. "You ever have questions about anything, you give me a call." He handed Austin a small sheet of paper, presumably with his phone number on it.

"Good luck, young fella." Outside, he stopped and stared at the fields. "These old bones will appreciate the break from the work, but I'm going to miss this view."

No wonder. Golden waves of wheat shimmered in the sun to blue-gray low hills in the distance.

"I'll take care of the place. Come back and visit anytime. I mean it." Austin shook his hand and Greg left quickly, driving his pickup truck away fast, without a backward glance.

Austin watched him go. "Bet that was hard for him."

"It seemed that way. Can we look around the house?"

"Sure."

Three bedrooms on the second floor were empty. One of them was a good size, large enough to be a master bedroom. The other two rooms would make great kids' rooms.

Gracie imagined she heard the patter of future children running through this house. They returned to the first floor. The appliances and fixtures were old. It didn't matter to Gracie. This was a good, solid house. It had been well-loved over the years.

A horn sounded in the driveway.

"Who's that?" Gracie asked.

"Either furniture or cattle arriving."

They went out onto the porch. Morning glory vines wound up the newel posts. Two old rose bushes acted as parentheses on each side of the house. Gracie could imagine sitting on wicker chairs in the evenings, watching the sun go down.

A couple of men got out of a delivery van.

"Got a bedroom set for you," the one with a clipboard in his hand said.

"Good. Bring it in."

Austin had bought a large sleigh bed, a king to accommodate his size. The men carried up a chest of drawers to match and a small wardrobe. He'd bought good quality. He would probably never have to replace this furniture.

Austin had a future.

What on earth did she have?

While Austin signed the delivery invoice, the other man dropped a bag of linens onto the mattress.

Gracie opened it and went upstairs to make Austin's bed.

After the men left and Austin joined her in the

bedroom, she said, "You should really wash these before using them, but I noticed there's only a wringer washer in that back room downstairs. I didn't see a dryer."

"No. No dryer." He helped her slip the fitted sheet onto the new mattress.

"I like this dark burgundy you chose. It complements the dark wood well."

Austin shrugged. "I like dark colors. Masculine colors."

Once the bed was made, Gracie gravitated toward the amazing view out the window.

"You've done well, Austin," she said quietly. "You're creating a solid future for yourself."

"I hope so. I'm trying to."

"*Trying* to? What does that mean?"

Another horn honked outside and Austin went downstairs, seeming relieved to not have to answer her question. After all she had told him about herself, the man was still an enigma to her.

At Austin's shouted, "My cattle!" Gracie ran downstairs.

Three trucks delivered the cows Austin had purchased. They were unloaded into neatly fenced-off corrals.

"What about food?" Gracie asked. "Will they just eat grass?"

"Tonight I'll feed them stuff I arranged to have delivered while Olsen was still here. Tomorrow, I'll decide which fields I want to put them in."

He spent the next hour sorting out the already

sorted-out barn, not stopping until Gracie finally said, "Is there any food in the fridge? I need lunch."

Austin slapped his forehead. "I'm sorry. Of course you're hungry. It's been a long time since breakfast."

He walked out of the barn and climbed into his vehicle. When she got into the passenger seat, she said, "I guess you need to get some groceries?"

"Yeah, but let's stop at the diner first. Now that you've mentioned food, I'm starving."

They ate burgers and fries in town, with everyone and his uncle coming over for an introduction. Gracie liked Austin's friends, the open, friendly townspeople.

Eventually, though, while they lingered over coffee, Gracie began to wonder why they had been in Ordinary for hours and hadn't yet gone to see his mother. Austin didn't seem in any rush to do so.

What was he avoiding? Why was he slow to take her to his mother's house?

"Are you ashamed of me?"

He gaped at her. "Why would you think that?"

"Because we've been in town for hours and you haven't taken me to meet your mother, who you *live* with."

"I'm not ashamed of you. Trust me on that. I'm proud to know you." His eyes shone in the sunlight streaming through the front window. "You've overcome huge obstacles and come out on top. You never turned to drugs or alcohol. You kept yourself whole. You've got backbone, Gracie Travers, and I admire that."

His words warmed her to the depths of her soul. High praise from a good man.

"So why won't you introduce me to your mother?"

He stood abruptly. "Let's walk."

Outside he took her hand and led her to a park at the end of Main Street. They stepped into a small gazebo.

"Town council built this about five years ago. Sometimes we put on small concerts here. Everyone likes it."

"So do I. It's peaceful." She sat on a bench and patted the seat beside her. "What wouldn't you tell me in the restaurant? What's so important that we needed privacy?"

"I need to tell you about my mom."

"EVERY BOY NEEDS A FATHER." Austin wasn't sure why he started with that when Gracie had asked about his mom. It just seemed to rise to the surface like a bubble that had been sitting inside him for too long. "I had two of them."

"What do you mean?"

He sat beside Gracie and leaned forward, elbows on his thighs, clasping his hands between his knees. He didn't know why he couldn't look at her right now. "My real dad, not my natural father, died when I was six.

"That man we saw on Main Street? He was my natural father. Brad McCloskey."

"Ah," she said. "That's why he seemed familiar. You look alike."

"We do. Mom got pregnant with me when she was in high school. Brad didn't believe I was his kid. My mom hadn't slept with anyone else, but Brad didn't believe her. He'd just been using her, holding out for the girl he really wanted, Mary Lou, who wouldn't sleep with him until marriage, so he used my mom for sex. It really broke her up when he pushed her aside."

"What happened?"

"This other guy, Stan Trumball, married her because he liked her. I grew up thinking he was my real father. He *felt* like my real father. Unfortunately, he died when I was six."

He leaned back and crossed his arms over his chest, tucking his hands into his armpits.

"Mom kind of fell apart." No kind of about it. She'd become the kid that day and Austin became the parent soon after. "She had a hard life growing up and didn't find stability until Stan. She was needy, though, so when he died, she had no anchor. She started to drink."

He felt Gracie watching him, but refused to turn her way. It was hard enough admitting all of this without seeing pity in her eyes.

"She never stopped drinking. When I was twelve, Brad's wife, Mary Lou, noticed the resemblance and put two and two together. She knew it was only a matter of time before everyone else in town would, too. She was spiteful and got my mom hooked on meth."

Gracie gasped, but Austin forged on. "Mom overdosed one day and Cash got her into rehab. That was when I found out that Brad was my real dad, not Stan."

"I imagine that was a shock."

"Understatement. Cash was a rock, though. I stayed with him for a while until he left to go to Denver to ask Shannon to marry him."

Austin grinned. "To ask her forgiveness, more like, 'cause of things he'd done wrong in their relationship."

"Were you angry that he left?"

"No. I told him to go. It was obvious the guy was crazy about her and miserable without her."

"But what happened to you?"

"Cash arranged with the authorities for me to live with C.J. and Janey while Mom finished rehab. It was the best part of my childhood. Amazing. Like the dawn after a long night."

"Did you have to go back to your mom?"

"Yeah. She got clean, so there wasn't any reason for them to leave me at the ranch."

He still remembered the conflicting feelings the day they drove him away from the ranch to go back to the trailer. He remembered that long, long look through the rear window until he could no longer see the ranch. He loved his mom, but he'd wanted that ranch life to be his permanently.

He finally forced himself to look at Gracie. "My mom…"

"Yes?"

"She's still needy. She won't let me go. She's mad at me for buying the ranch."

"So you don't want me to meet her?"

"It's more than that. I don't want you to see where I grew up, especially now that I know how wealthy you were growing up."

"Austin, I hated my life. I've shared my history with you. I want to see where you were raised."

Austin bent forward and jammed his fingers into his hair. "I don't want you to see it."

"I want to."

He sat up. "Okay. Don't say I didn't warn you."

"I won't. I promise."

They walked back to the car.

"You know what happened to Mary Lou? The goody-two-shoes who Brad married instead of mom?"

"What?"

"She became a drug dealer. Manufactured meth on her parents' farm. Ended up burning herself in an explosion and going to jail."

Austin smiled, but it felt grim as hell. "Looked good on Brad."

He drove a few blocks to the cheap end of town, where old trailers sat crowded on small lots.

Austin pulled up in front of his mom's trailer, but didn't get out.

Funny that he had lived here his whole life, but didn't think of it as home. It was Mom's.

He should have pushed to get out of here sooner, but he'd been waiting for the right property to be

MARY SULLIVAN 305

available. Many ranches were too large and he couldn't afford them. The Olsen property was perfect. The second it had gone on the market, he'd scooped it up.

Austin forced himself to take a good long look at the dented tin can he'd grown up in. Most days, he barely glanced at it. There was a limit to how much embarrassment he could stomach. As a respected deputy in Ordinary, he should be able to provide his mother with a better home than this, and he could. He would gladly.

"She won't let me give her more. She won't come to the ranch to live with me." She wanted only this—and for him to stay here and take care of her.

Lord, the place looked sorry. He kept the small patch of lawn weeded and mown. In the spring, he'd planted pots of geraniums for his mom. Last summer, he'd built new steps and a small porch he'd painted a cheery red. He'd added a striped awning over the door.

But the trailer itself? A drunken sailor had more stability. The aging brown-and-white bucket listed to the right, within a hair's-breadth of giving up the ghost. His mom wouldn't let him paint either the walls or the shutters. Said she liked it just the way it was. He'd had to hold her back from tearing down the new awning. Rust ran in rivulets from the windowsills. She *liked* this? *Why?*

He got out of the car. So did Gracie and Sadie. Sadie ran around back to explore. Maybe she thought they were back to stay and she was burrowing into her doghouse. Nope. Austin was never living here again.

"Austin? Why won't she leave?" He heard the disbelief in Gracie's voice.

"She's got this weird thing going. She likes the pity she gets from living here with nothing. Plus, she has this irrational fear of change."

"It sure leaves you in a bind, doesn't it?"

She understood. Some of his tension eased. "She won't let me do more for her, even while she complains about her lot in life. I can't do enough to make her happy." The neighbors had to have heard their fights. How could they not? They lived on top of each other in these trailers.

A man couldn't take a deep breath in this warren of tin cans, couldn't fill his lungs with the oxygen he needed.

Stubborn woman. She could live somewhere else—*anywhere* else—with him, but wouldn't. He pounded his fist on the hood of the car. Pain shot through his arm.

Gracie's soft touch on his arm anchored him. "Easy. You need to take care of yourself now."

She was right. He'd been through this too many times in the past. In buying the ranch and moving out, he was doing the only thing that made sense for him.

His mother had no one else but him. They had only each other. Given that, how could he turn his back on her?

He couldn't abandon her, but he couldn't stay here, either. At his age, he deserved a home of his own.

He walked toward the trailer slowly, because he didn't relish this visit. Mom had been furious with him for taking a vacation, the only one he'd ever taken.

She was beyond furious that he'd bought the ranch and was moving out. The feeling of a noose loosening, of an easing around his neck, had started the second he'd signed the papers and the ranch had become his. For the first time in his life, he felt freedom within his grasp.

So close.

He just had to say goodbye to Mom and get his few belongings.

"I shouldn't have brought you here," he told Gracie.

"Why? This is part of who you are. I want to know about all of you, including your past and the forces that shaped you."

Trouble was, he didn't want Gracie to see those forces.

He fingered the yellow leaves of the red geraniums. Even this one simple task he'd given her, to water the flowers, had been too much.

She was a healthy woman. There was nothing physically wrong with her. She simply liked to have others take care of her.

Sadie ran around from the back of the trailer and jumped on him, whimpering. "Hey, girl, what is it?"

She whined and jumped down, circled, whined again.

"What's wrong, girl?" Austin stepped toward the door of the trailer.

Sadie nearly tripped him. "What's wrong with—"

Gracie grabbed his sleeve. "I smell smoke."

Austin leaped onto the porch and into the trailer. Mom stood in the kitchen beside the stove, where a fire roared in a frying pan.

"I can't put it out," she said, in a voice as detached as though she'd said, "I can't tie my shoelaces."

"Out of the way!" Shoving her aside, he reached under the counter for the fire extinguisher and sprayed the pan until he smothered the fire. Foam residue covered the stove and wall. Soot coated the ceiling.

He tossed the empty can into the sink, while his heart tried to beat right out of his chest. He didn't dare look at his mother, the fear racing through him nothing compared to the rage that burned hotter than the grease fire he'd just put out.

His mom brushed past him to leave the kitchen. Good thing.

The room stank, smoke choked him and he wanted to throttle his mother. He opened the window and a breeze rushed through the room.

Slowly, because he needed to calm down, and carefully, because he knew from his day job that violence was never the answer, he cleaned the mess both the extinguisher and his mother had made.

What the hell had she been cooking? There was

no food out on the counter. So why heat a pan full of grease?

But he knew…and hung his head, swallowing his frustration.

She'd heard him drive up and had seen him get out of the car with a woman. He knew his mom well, knew every manipulative maneuver in her playbook.

She had done something similar just before he'd left for this trip with Finn, pulling another trick to keep him here, as she had done the last three times he'd tried to take a vacation.

She hadn't wanted him to go, didn't want him to live on the ranch, and certainly didn't want to see him with a woman.

This had to stop. Something had to give. She'd manipulated him for thirty-one years. It ended today.

When he thought he might, just *might,* be able to talk to her without wringing her neck, he entered the living room. One of them had to be the adult.

She waited for him where she usually sat in her ancient plaid armchair, shooting daggers at Gracie, who stood just inside the doorway.

His mom's lips were drawn up tightly enough to form a network of lines radiating from her mouth. Didn't bode well. *See?* her expression accused. *I can't take care of myself. You'll have to stay and do it for me.*

"It won't work, Mom." His voice rasped like a file on metal. Her gaze slid to his feet. He stepped in front of her and squatted down so she would have to look at him.

"What won't work?" Still her eyes slid sideways and avoided meeting his.

"This trick to keep me living here."

"It wasn't a trick. The pan caught on fire."

"Stop," he ordered, his voice cutting through all of the years of games. Considering that he hadn't had a father figure in his life in a quarter of a century, he sure knew how to sound like one. "We both know what you're doing."

She picked at a piece of loose thread on the arm of the chair, her limp hair falling across her face, silent.

"I'm moving out," he said. "I took possession of the ranch today." He scrubbed his hands over his face. Lord, this was hard. She'd conditioned a lot of years of guilt into him. "You could come live with me there. It's a great house. There's plenty of room."

"I don't want to move. This is my home."

"I know you don't like change, but you would get used to it in time."

"Why can't you just stay here with me?"

"Look at me, Mom. I'm a grown man. It's time for me to have a life of my own."

"Who is she?"

"Gracie Travers. Gracie, this is my mom, Connie."

"Hi," Gracie said.

"Is she moving in with you?" His mother directed the question at Austin without responding to Gracie.

"She will be staying with me, yes."

"Is she your girlfriend?"

"Yes."

His mom remained mute. She wouldn't like that

one bit. She'd interfered with all of his relationships. He'd never met a woman strong enough to take on his mom.

"I'm moving out," Austin said firmly enough to close the door on any more arguments. "I'm packing my stuff to take with me."

"But—" Trust her to keep trying.

"We both know you can cook without burning down the trailer. The only time anything catches fire is when I try to leave."

He stood. "I'm not moving across the country. I'm not moving to another town. I'll stop in every day I'm at work and I can stock the fridge regularly for you. You'll only need to replenish basics like bread and milk."

She didn't thank him. Why had he expected her to? Her neediness ran so deeply she never thought of niceties.

"I can keep taking you to AA meetings and your therapist." Janey had taken care of those drives while Austin had been away, so Mom wouldn't miss any meetings. "You want anything extra, just call."

As long as it isn't alcohol or drugs.

That last was unfair. Mom had only once ever flirted with drugs—methamphetamines—that one time and rehab has straightened her out.

Alcohol had been an on-again, off-again problem. Mom needed some kind of crutch. Usually that was him. With him gone, though? Maybe she would return to the bottle.

Don't. I can't be your whole life anymore.

Sometimes the weight of her needs sat like glue on the wings he'd wanted to spread for years. Mucilage on his fuselage. That sounded so close to something Finn would say, Austin barked a short, bitter laugh.

In these moments, it was hard to remember that Austin loved his mother.

But he did.

Life would be a hell of a lot easier if he didn't.

She sipped from the mug at her elbow. He wasn't sure what was in it. Always this terrible suspicion. Was life like this for all children of alcoholics?

I need out. I need to get away from you.

He stood and kissed her on the forehead.

"I love you, Mom. Trust me. You'll be fine."

He strode to his bedroom, impatient to leave and afraid she might break down, might beg him to stay. He needed to be strong.

PRUNED MOUTH. TIGHT JAW. Narrowed eyes. Gracie knew that look of jealousy and had dealt with it many times during her career.

Connie wanted Austin all to her herself. Gracie didn't take it personally. Austin's mom would dislike any woman Austin brought home. Gracie knew it in her bones.

She could deal with her. Compared to some of the stage mothers of rival actors that she'd had to deal with as a child, this woman was an amateur.

Gracie had fought in the trenches and had won. This would be a walk in the park.

"He won't keep you for long, you know," Connie said. "He's never had the same girlfriend for more than a few months, so don't get too cozy on his ranch. Don't think it's going to be your own private love shack."

Love shack? What decade was this?

"I have no expectations of permanence with Austin. He's a good, kind man who is giving me a place to stay for a while. That's all."

"Are you sleeping with him? Buying his affection with sex?"

"That's none of your business." Connie was a real piece of work.

You poor woman. Unless you learn to give an inch, you're going to be the sorriest, loneliest woman on the planet. Let your son go.

Gracie had come here expecting to like anyone who had raised a great man like Austin, then had realized how well he'd done in spite of his mother, and had prepared herself to do battle with a jealous woman...but now felt only pity.

This woman, this vulnerable soul, didn't have a clue how to make her life better.

There was no way for Gracie to break through her tough shell, especially not as a rival for her son's affection.

As she'd had to do so many times once she'd grown up enough to understand the difference between what happened on TV shows and what happened in the rest of the world, she had to accept that this was real. This wasn't saccharine make-believe. There were great towns full of great people, but there were also all the heartbreaking stories of those who couldn't make their world right. Lost souls haunted every place she'd ever been.

Ordinary, Montana, while exceptional in many ways, was full of real people, not the celluloid masses that Hollywood would have the public believe are real.

Poor Austin. How had he come out of this intact, so whole and good and decent?

An even deeper question was why he'd helped Gracie. He should have run screaming for the hills. He shouldn't have been helping another woman when he'd managed to leave his dependent mom behind.

Staring at Connie, Gracie finally understood Finn's antipathy toward her. He must have thought her a younger version of Connie. He must have wondered why Austin was taking on another burden.

Finn had probably warned Austin against taking on Gracie as a project.

The next time she saw Finn, if she ever did, she would tell him she knew he'd only been trying to help his friend.

Austin walked from the back of the trailer where Gracie assumed his bedroom was, with a duffel bag in his hand, tall, masculine and rock solid in his convictions. Gracie fell even harder.

"Come on," he said, ushering her toward the door. "Bye, Mom. I'm back at work the day after tomorrow. I'll stop in on you then."

Gracie stepped out of the trailer ahead of him,

but wasn't so far out that she didn't hear Connie stop Austin.

Please, let him go.

At his mother's quiet, "Austin," Gracie sensed him stiffening, but he turned back around in the doorway.

"Yeah?"

Gracie watched Connie. Her mouth worked, her lips tightening even more, but it didn't look like anger. Her chin trembled.

"Stay safe."

"I will." His voice broke and he rushed outside, shutting the front door behind him.

Talk about tough. His mother wasn't completely evil after all, but in a funny way, she'd just made Austin's leaving even more difficult.

Austin stood outside the tin can he'd grown up in and leaned close to Gracie. "This is why I bought my ranch. I want sheets that don't smell sour and clothes that aren't stiff with dirt."

"Why are you whispering?" With the doors and windows closed, his mother wouldn't be able to hear him.

"Because these tin cans sit one on top of another. Because my mom and I couldn't say two words to each other without the neighbors knowing about it. Because I can't breathe here." He rubbed his temples. "Because I suffocate here."

Hence his ranch, his wide-open spaces and fresh air.

"I admire you, Austin. You're making your life happen."

He smiled ruefully. "It's taken me a long time."

"You had a lot of resistance from your mom."

"Yeah. This is only scraping the surface of my childhood, Gracie. You want to know who I am? Come on."

He whistled for Sadie. She came around the trailer and settled into the front seat between Austin and Gracie.

Austin parked on Main then dragged Gracie down a short laneway on the far side of Chester's Bar and Grill, and around to an alley running behind the businesses on the north side of the street.

She'd slept in many like it. This one was pretty clean.

A Dumpster sat tucked against the wall behind Chester's. Austin smacked his hand against it so hard his palm had to sting.

"This was my restaurant. I never had the money to go through the front door of the diner or Chester's or Sweet Talk. I dove into Dumpsters and ate rotting food. I ate trash, Gracie, not because I decided to run away from an old life I didn't like, but because I *had* to. I was starving."

He spread his arms wide. "This back alley was my kitchen. If Cash hadn't caught me one day and become my Big Brother, I would have stayed lost, invisible, no part of any system that offered any help. I would have gotten involved in drugs and alcohol, because that was the only example I had before Cash. I started smoking when I was ten."

A breeze kicked up, lifting the scent of grilling meat from the bar.

"So, yeah, I became a cop and I try to help others, because I don't want what I went through to be part of anyone else's life."

He slumped against the wall.

"You want to know the worst thing, Gracie?"

"What?"

"I still want to save her."

She stepped close and wrapped her arms around him. "Of course you do. She's your mother."

"Despite it all, I still love her."

"Yeah." She kissed him, softly and sweetly on the lips. He needed support. For once, Gracie had something to offer him.

"Talk to me," she said. They stood in the alley with Austin leaning against the brick wall while Gracie held him. She listened while he told her the story of his life, shattering all the assumptions she had made about his childhood.

She commiserated and supported him, and for the first time with Austin, she felt necessary and needed.

In time, they walked back to the car and got inside. Sadie, who'd been sleeping in the breeze through the open window, perked up, tongue wagging.

Austin scratched her head. "You're going to love living on the ranch, girl."

He seemed more light-hearted and younger than when they'd arrived in town. Who had he shared all of this with in the past? Cash, certainly, but he'd left town.

Finn? She would bet so. But Finn wouldn't have held Austin, wouldn't have kissed him when the telling became hard.

As they drove down Main Street on their way out of town, they passed a group of teenagers. Austin called out, "Hey, are you heading to the park to shoot hoops?"

"Yeah," one called back while dribbling a basketball on the sidewalk. "Wanna come?"

Gracie saw longing in Austin's glance and said, "Go, if you want to."

"You sure you won't mind?"

"Nope. I'd like to watch."

Austin pulled a U-turn. "Don't tell the cops. That was illegal."

She smiled, happy to see him loose and carefree.

He parked in front of the park then led her to a basketball court off to the side. "Do you play?"

"No. I wasn't allowed to be involved in sports in case I got myself injured. A broken bone could screw up production for weeks."

He squeezed her hand. "Too bad. I'm a big believer in getting and keeping our youth active."

"It's a great idea."

"We need another skin," one of the kids said.

"Okay." Austin reached for the tail of his T-shirt and pulled it over his head. Gracie's breath caught. She never got used to how beautiful he was. She had no idea what he did to stay in shape, but Lordy, Lordy, it worked.

He had a fine chest, broad shoulders and mmm-mmm-mmm great biceps.

She heard girls giggling and followed them to a small set of bleachers beside the court. One of the girls ran onto the court to play.

"Jenny," a tall, skinny boy said. "You wanna be a skin?" His eyebrows did a Groucho Marx, dirty-old-man wiggle.

"In your dreams, Justin."

Gracie sat to watch the game on the ground level of the seating, while the young girls sat in the second and top levels.

She listened to them gossip and talk about clothes, makeup and homework. She'd never been as carefree as they sounded, had never had the chance to just hang out. Her days had often been ten and twelve hours long. There had also been school lessons with tutors.

When she fell into bed at night, she didn't even have the energy to dream. Maybe that's why she was a rabid daydreamer now, when she had the freedom to be, when she had so many down hours as a homeless person.

Austin played until sweat ran down his body his face alight with joy. Thinking back over their time together, she realized he did too little of that. He was too serious, always thinking too much of others and too little of himself. She would have to see whether she could change that.

Yeah? When?

You know you can't stay here. This is just a visit.

Austin hasn't said anything about making it perma-nent and you still haven't sorted out your life.

"He's so good-looking," one of the girls behind her said. "I really like when he wears his uniform."

Who were the girls talking about? Was one of the boys a football player or something?

"For an old guy, he's a real hottie."

Old guy? They were talking about Austin. Ap-parently, he was a hottie—oh, yeaaaaah, they got that right—but also, apparently, thirty-one was old. These girls made Gracie feel ancient.

When Austin finished his game, they strolled back to the car holding hands.

She had never done this kind of thing as a teen-ager. Hand-holding, getting to know boys, going to school with them—all had been foreign to her.

This felt good. Amazing.

They stepped into the grocery store and bought supplies, just like a normal couple.

Back at the ranch, they put everything away. While Austin showered, she made a simple dinner.

Afterward, they wandered upstairs. She knew what came next. There was only one bed. She didn't know what her future would hold, but for now, she was going to make love to Austin.

In his house, with his arm around her shoulder and his lips nuzzling her neck, how could she deny this any longer?

She unpacked the toiletries Austin had bought for her that first day and set them up in his bathroom next to his shaving cream and soap. It felt good, like playing house. If only this were real.

None of those thoughts, Gracie. Tonight, enjoy this man and your time together. For just these few hours, set worries about the future aside.

Austin retrieved condoms from his shaving kit.

In the bedroom, they undressed each other, Gracie with her hands all over the chest she'd admired earlier while he'd played ball.

On the bed, naked together, Austin took over, loving her with a thoroughness that left her breathless.

When she reached for him, he stopped her.

"Let me love you," he whispered.

"I want to give to you, too."

"Let me do this. Let me love you."

She let him, because his tender touch robbed her of speech and thought, and she'd craved touch for too long. Like everything else he did, Austin took lovemaking seriously.

He was thorough, had her arching off the bed wanting more and more. Dear sweetness, she'd thought he was amazing in every way, but Austin did this to perfection, most especially in dedication… to…detail. Oh, that was good.

"Do that again," she panted, and he did. She stopped thinking, might have even stopped breathing, and rode a wave of sensation and desire to a thundering completion. His lovemaking was beautiful, stimulating and exciting.

And all wrong.

When her heart rate returned to normal, she sat

up on the edge of the bed, her soul howling with the injustice of having to reject Austin, a man who could give and give and give, but not take.

What good was loving someone when she couldn't begin to provide as much as she'd received, when she wasn't *allowed* to offer, let alone bestow? Their life from the start had been unequal, with Austin doing all of the giving and her the taking.

In the end, there was no satisfaction for her in only receiving. She wanted to share.

"That was unacceptable," she said.

Austin stopped the delicious kisses he'd been lazily trailing down her spine and rose above her, a frown creasing his strong brow. "You didn't like it?" A shadow of insecurity colored his tone.

"Like it? I loved it. You played me like Pinchas Zukerman plays the violin."

"Who?"

"Never mind."

"Then why was it unacceptable?"

"Because I want to give." Frustrated by his stubbornness, she raised her voice. "Why is that so hard for you to understand?"

"I…I don't know. I like taking care of you."

"I don't want to be taken care of. I want to be equal. I *am* equal. Homeless or not, rich or poor, I'm a worthy person. I deserve to be treated as an equal."

"I do treat you as an equal. I don't understand." He stood abruptly, every line of his body taut, tense and beautiful. If she didn't stand her ground, she would be back in bed with him, and that would be a mistake. Whatever happened here would color their future together.

"I've never had a woman complain about my love-making before."

"Why would they? It's awesome."

"*Awesome?* Then why are you complaining?"

"Because I'm not *a* woman. Not every other woman. I'm me. An individual. I'm not a generic person who will take anything you dish out. I have my own desires, my own need to contribute to our relationship. I have a big heart. As much as you need to take care of others, I also want to take care of you."

"Like you took care of your parents and everyone around you, and got nothing for yourself for years?" She didn't appreciate his sarcasm.

"No, not like that," she snapped.

"Then what? I still don't get it. If you enjoyed the sex, why complain?"

"Imagine if things were reversed. Imagine if I said to you that you couldn't move a muscle while I made love to you. That you weren't allowed to touch me or to taste me, or to *do* anything."

One corner of his mouth kicked up. "I'd like that."

"You *think* you would, but I'd be willing to bet you'd hate it. You would have so much trouble giving over control it would be painful for you."

"No, I wouldn't."

She gritted her teeth. She wasn't getting through to him.

She'd met his mother today. Everything about Austin made sense. She'd wondered how he had come out of that relationship unharmed, but now she saw where the damage had been done.

Austin didn't know how to let go of control.

"No," Gracie said, pulling on her clothes. "You don't get to have all the control."

"I don't want control."

"You sure do. You *need* it, so your world will feel sane. So it will make sense. Because what you fear most in life is chaos. You need order. You need everyone around you to be a certain way. You need life to make sense. Well, guess what?"

"What?"

"You don't get to control the whole world and everyone in it so it will make perfect, logical sense. So nothing will ever sink into chaos."

"I don't want—"

She talked right over him. "All the charitable things you do, the kids you take care of, your mom—it's all admirable. But you take it too far. Your mother made you so neurotic you have to fit everyone and everything into boxes."

"That's not what I do."

"Consider this… According to you, the last thing you wanted when you left here for your trip was to have someone to take care of. You said you'd fought tooth and nail to get away from your mom."

"I did."

"Right, and instead of having me arrested when I stole your wallet, you insisted on feeding me."

"I understood you. I knew where you were coming from and what it was like to be so hungry you did a desperate thing."

"True. I get that. But you wouldn't *stop* taking care of me. You couldn't just let me go."

"I wanted to help you."

"I know, and I appreciate that, but you also wanted to control the situation, to put me where I would be safe. Where nothing could ever hurt me." She went over to him and placed her fingers on her cheek. "And I know why. Every time you looked at me, you saw yourself as a child, and that hurt too much. You can't change what happened to you. You can't erase your past. You can't live everyone else's life so yours makes sense. People *will* get hurt. People *will* go hungry. Make your great plans and follow through on them, because what you're doing is awesome. Help the young people of Ordinary, but don't control them. You can't make their lives happen the way you want them to. You can't drive their futures."

She stood to leave. "You can't drive my future. We're back to the same old thing, Austin. I need to find my own way in the world."

"Where are you going?"

Gracie wasn't sure what was feeding the panic in Austin's voice.

"What will you do? How will you support yourself?"

"I'm not your problem, Austin."

"Yes, you are."

She put her hands on the shoulders that carried too

much responsibility already and that, even as broad as they were, shouldn't take on more.

She could live with him, she could start a family with him, but it would always be an unequal affair, and that would hurt. She would always feel like his pet project. She would eventually wither and cease to exist.

"See? That's what I'm talking about. I don't want to be your *problem*. It comes back to the same inequality we've had since the moment we met. I want to come to you as an equal." She was beginning to sound like a broken record. She had to take action instead of just talking.

"You are now."

"No, I'm not. I'm someone for you to take care of. But I don't want to *be* taken care of. I want there to be give and take in our relationship. I'm not sure how you can learn to take. And I'm not in any position to give."

"When will you be? How will you be?" He stepped into his jeans angrily. His zipper rasped in the quiet of the night. "If I'm always making more than you as a deputy, does that mean we can never be a couple? Are we in a competition here to see who can make a better living?"

"Of course not, but I want to be viable. I want to do more than clean your house and wash your clothes. I want to come to you as a woman who can stand on her own two feet and support herself. I need to change the dynamic of how we met and how things have been between us."

He exhaled heavily. "I'm afraid if I let you go, I'll never see you again."

"We both know it's more than that, Austin. You think that if I don't need you, you have no value."

His hand shot to his chest. Bingo. She'd hit the nail on the head.

"You're right," he conceded, crestfallen. "Why would you possibly want me if you don't need my help? What do you see in me other than that?"

"Oh, baby." She got into his space, rested her head against his big, solid chest, wrapped her arms around his waist and hung on like a barnacle. "I see an amazing man. Strong, dependable, ethical, moral. All the things that were missing in the people around me when I was growing up. If I'd known someone like you, if I'd *married* you instead of Jay, I would have never left you."

His heartbeat raced under her ear, galloped at the same pace as her pulse, the two of them so in sync they might as well have been conjoined. And she had to tear them apart.

"Okay." He sounded as if he was breathing heavily, as though he were trying to keep control of himself. "I want to negotiate this leaving with you."

"Negotiate? What do you mean? There's nothing to talk about. You're staying here to run your life on the ranch. I'm leaving to find my way in the world."

"I know. I accept that, Gracie."

"You do?"

"I have no choice, do I?"

"No," she answered softly. "I guess you don't."

"At least let me give you money so you won't be on the road broke again." He took her face between his palms and kissed her forehead. "Let me at least know that you have that."

"Okay, I'll borrow some money from you."

"Where will you go?"

"Hollywood."

Austin winced, frowned and opened his mouth to object.

"Let it go, Austin. Let me go." She kissed his lips. "Just as you asked your mom to let you go, now I'm asking you for the same thing."

He closed his eyes and nodded. "Let me hold you until then."

They lay down on the bed and spooned until the sun rose, not speaking, just holding, Gracie committing these feelings, these moments, to memory. Everything necessary had been said.

At dawn, Austin got up and made her breakfast.

Gracie ate it and then, without looking back, without goodbye, slipped out into the world again, with the seed of a plan that, come hell or high water, she was going to make happen.

CHAPTER THIRTEEN

GRACIE WOULD HAVE to do the unthinkable. Sooner or later, if she lived a real life under her real name, if she got a job using her own Social Security number, as was looking more and more inevitable, she would be found out. Reporters would come knocking and she wouldn't be able to persuade them to back off as she'd done with Melody.

Her privacy would be shattered.

The only way to deal with it was to control it, and to do it on her terms.

That started today, just as soon as she landed in Los Angeles.

She swallowed her apprehension, screwed up her nerve and used her real ID to fly to California. The man at the ticket counter did a double-take when he saw the name on her passport, looked at her dark hair and shrugged, perhaps not believing she could possibly be *that* Gracie Stacey.

Four years ago, she had had to renew her passport, using the address her parents had still had at the time, not the cheaper hotel where they'd stranded her a week ago. By then, she had already gone back to her own natural dark hair color. The photographer hadn't batted an eye when he'd taken her picture.

A woman would have known who she was, especially anyone who read the gossip rags.

On the plane, she buried her head in a romance novel she had picked up at the airport, but had trouble concentrating on the story.

When the engines wound up and thrust the plane into the air, she murmured, "Hollywood, here I come."

The young guy sitting beside her on the plane grooved to the music in his earphones. She might as well not have existed. Good. She had another few hours of anonymity, and savored them.

After she landed in L.A., she took a cab to Hollywood. In all of her years of traveling, she had never returned here. Rather, she had deliberately avoided southern California.

No offense, you pretty state. I just don't like what some parts of you represent.

There was only one option left. When she thought about it, Gracie wondered why she hadn't just given in and done it sooner. Then she wouldn't have turned to crime, picking Austin's pocket.

"But then I wouldn't have met Austin."

"Pardon, ma'am?" the cabbie asked.

"Nothing." She smiled. "Just talking to myself."

They drove down Hollywood Boulevard, Gracie as ill at ease here as she'd been on the Strip in Vegas.

Couldn't be helped. This was where all of the

wheeling and dealing was done. Gracie had a bunch of her own wheeling and dealing to do.

The cab pulled up to the address she'd given the driver.

She paid—*Thank you, Austin*—and then entered the modern glass-and-steel office tower in which she knew the production company that had made *Picture Perfect Family,* her TV show, still resided.

On the eighteenth floor, she exited the elevator into a quiet hall, her steps hushed by plush carpeting. Old movie and television posters lined the taupe walls.

At the end of the hallway, she entered a glass-walled office, where a stunning young woman sat at a reception desk protecting an intimidating oak wall and door. Were all the women in Hollywood beautiful, with perfect hair, nails and teeth? Even if they didn't start perfect, they sure ended up that way after cosmetic surgery, enhancements, veneers and procedures.

Gracie marched right up to the desk. "I'd like to see Marcus Elliot."

The woman looked her up and down, not the least bit subtle about it. "Do you have an appointment?"

"Nope, but he'll see me."

"I don't think so. No one gets in without an appointment."

"I will. Tell him Gracie Stacey is here."

Gracie had the satisfaction of watching the arrogant young woman's jaw drop before she did another quick survey of Gracie's shortcomings.

The woman stood and entered the office, closing the door behind her.

Gracie heard the woman's low murmur, followed by a shouted, "Get her the hell in here!"

The woman must have been too slow, because Marcus yelled again, "Move! Where is she?"

He stepped into the reception room, overpowering both in his physique and in his personality. He hadn't changed much, other than traces of gray at his temples, no doubt left there strategically. Knowing Marcus, he would dye his hair to look younger, but leave that bit of gray to look smarter. Here in Hollywood, image was everything.

When he saw Gracie, he stopped and stared. The receptionist ran into his back. She apologized, but there was intimacy in her tone.

Marcus hadn't changed. He still liked his women young and beautiful. He had come on to Gracie the second she'd turned eighteen, but she'd shot him down.

"I see you've got a few more gray hairs than you used to." Gracie grinned, because while he might have been a player for whom the bottom line was everything, he had treated her well, even after she had rebuffed his advances.

"It *is* you."

He spread his arms. "Come here, kid." She stepped into his embrace and he wrapped her in a huge hug that didn't quit, his affection real. "Where the hell have you been?"

Gracie wasn't sure whether the severity she heard in his voice was mocking or real.

"Let's go into your office," she said, aware of listening ears, both the girl's and of those who'd poked their heads out of nearby offices at Marcus's shout.

As he ushered her into the office ahead of him, he asked, "Coffee?"

"I'd love one. With everything in it."

"Candace, bring coffee." Marcus closed the door in the poor girl's face.

He sat behind his massive desk while Gracie settled across from him in a plush leather armchair she could probably sleep in comfortably. She'd forgotten how the wealthy lived in this town.

The gap between the rich and the poor just kept getting wider. The rich, insular and isolated, didn't believe it, but Gracie had seen the evidence personally on her journey into the nooks and crannies of America.

With a little luck, she wouldn't add to Marcus's coffers, but rather to her own. She wasn't here for sentiment, but for cold, hard reality. And money.

"I need your help," she said, but stopped speaking because Candace had entered with a tray of coffee cups, cream and sugar.

After she set it down, she straightened and stared at Gracie, mouth open.

"I know," Gracie said. "I don't look much like the old me, do I?"

"Nonsense," Marcus said. "You look fine."

"I don't at all, Marcus. I'm not the least bit Hollywood anymore and never will be again."

"Nonsense," Marcus repeated. "A week at a spa, a month with a trainer, a session with a good hairdresser and we'll have you back in Hollywood shape."

Before Gracie could protest, Candace blurted, "I loved your shows!" friendly now that she knew this raggedy woman was *somebody*.

"That will be all, Candace."

"Just a second, Marcus," Gracie said before turning to Candace. "Thank you. I appreciate your saying so."

The woman might have irritated her at the start, but Gracie had always responded to her fans with civility. Every single fan had contributed to Gracie's paycheck back then, and had allowed her to live a pampered lifestyle.

Candace backed out of the room as though Gracie were royalty. Gracie was long past the point of thinking she deserved it. She'd come to abhor the idiocy of idolizing movie stars for having good looks or acting talent, while the people who did the important work in life were ignored.

She doctored her coffee and drank. Excellent, of course. Only when she had finished the full cup did Marcus speak.

"You look like you need a few good meals."

Gracie laughed. "You should have seen me a couple of weeks ago." *Before Austin started feeding me.* She was still thin, but the hollows of her body were filling out and she'd noticed this morning that her eyes were no longer haunted by desperation.

"Are you here for work? Are you considering that reality show we offered? It was five years ago, but I could get investors interested again. I could get it off the ground."

"If anyone could, it would be you. But no, Marcus, I won't be acting again. Ever."

He ran his fingers through his short, curly hair. That wasn't the answer he'd hoped for. "You said you need help? If it's money, I keep only a couple of thousand in the office, but I can get you more."

Gracie held up her hand. "It's about money, but not in the way you think."

She explained about the trust fund being emptied, about her parents and all of the money being gone. About them ditching her in Vegas.

Marcus swore. "I wanted the company to set up and run the trust fund for you, separate from your parents, because I knew what they were like. You know—your dad's gambling."

"Gambling?" She hadn't suspected a problem. She'd thought it was greed. "So that's where the money went."

Marcus set down his coffee cup and leaned back in his chair. "You didn't know? He's had it bad for years. Of course, they wouldn't hear of it when I suggested an account that the studio would run."

"No, I guess they wouldn't have liked that."

"You'll sue, of course, but it will be hard to get money that's already gone."

"No. There's no point in suing. I saw them in Vegas a week ago. There's nothing left."

"If you don't want money from me, what do you want?"

"I want you to open doors for me."

"What kind of doors?"

"I need to get in to see a publisher. I'm going to write my story."

Marcus startled and Gracie moved forward to grasp one of his hands. "Yes, it will be a tell-all, but I will be kind to you. You always treated me well."

"About that time at your eighteenth birthday party...." He flushed. Gracie couldn't remember ever seeing Marcus chagrined. "I'd had too much to drink. You were the cutest little thing and then all of a sudden, you were grown up and beautiful. I had a terrible crush on you."

Gracie smiled. She wasn't here to expose anyone. "That won't be in the book."

"I can hook you up with a publisher. Anyone will buy your story. Don't sign a thing without consulting me. We'll get you the best deal."

He smiled. "I hope this works out for you. Too bad about Michael and Chantelle. I'm truly sorry they screwed you over."

He looked it. Marcus wasn't often sincere, but he was at this moment.

"I'll get on the phone and get you an appointment today. Wait in the reception area with Candace." He leaned forward and confided, "Her stage name is Candy LaRue. She won't change it to something more sophisticated."

"Can she act?"

"Not worth a damn. Sit with her while I set this up. You'll feel like a movie star again. She'll love to talk to you now that you're *some*body."

Gracie laughed. Just before she opened his office door, Marcus asked, "Do you need money for tonight? Where are you staying?"

"No worries. I have a hundred bucks. I'll find a cheap room somewhere." She shrugged. "If not, I can always sleep on the street."

"You will not," he roared.

"I've been doing it for six years."

"Jesus." He wiped his forehead. "You'll give me a heart attack. You're coming home with me. I'm going to feed you and put you into a warm, *safe* bed. No more streets. Promise?"

"It depends on whether I get a publishing contract."

"You'll get one. People want to know about you, Gracie. They want to know where you went. They were upset when you disappeared."

"Thank you, Marcus. I appreciate your help."

Ten minutes later, Marcus came out of his office. Thank goodness. Candy had been grilling Gracie so hard about who she knew in the business, she finally had to say, "I don't know anyone anymore. I'm of no use to you. I can't open doors. I can't get you roles."

Candy pouted for a while before saying, "I really did love your show."

Gracie smiled. "Thanks."

"Gracie," Marcus said when he joined them. "I have a booking for you in twenty minutes with a literary agent. Here's fifty bucks. Take a cab there. After the appointment, come back here. I'll take you home tonight."

Gracie noted Candy's deflation, but didn't spare her a second thought. She needed to get this appointment over and done with. She was about to sell her soul and didn't like it one bit.

Afterward, though, she would be free. No more hiding. No more running.

By the end of her meeting with the agent, after the man had contacted a few publishing houses, Gracie had the promise of a contract and a sizable advance. Real money and all hers. They hadn't even asked whether she could write. They told her they could set her up with a ghostwriter. She set them straight on that score.

Nobody wrote her story but her.

Everyone wanted to hear Little Gracie Stacey's story.

What they didn't know yet was that the story would be as much about her development from that naive little girl to a full-grown, savvy and cynical woman as about any exposé of her childhood.

Cynical? Maybe not so much anymore. Austin had burned away a lot of her world-weariness, and had softened her hard edges.

She missed him.

THIS SUCKED. Austin wandered the ranch he loved, but felt only emptiness, a gaping hole where fulfillment should have been.

Gracie had devastated him, drawn, quartered and eviscerated him, turned his views of himself and his place in the world upside down. He was a controller, she'd said.

He, who'd always felt controlled by his mother, had become a controller himself. Granted, he wasn't a manipulator, but yes, he needed to control, to force the world to make sense.

He needed straight lines and boxes.

He needed rational thought, not emotion.

Now that he had those in spades, he missed Gracie and how she made him *feel*. He missed how she challenged him at every turn.

Where did he go from here? How did a man get over a woman who wished he were some other kind of man, while he wanted her just the way she was?

Do you?

Yes.

You sure about that?

Yes!

Prove it.

How?

Let her go.

He already had, and it had proven to be the most painful thing he'd ever done.

When he heard a car pull up, he wandered from the barn to the front of the house. Even Sadie's crazy antics, running in front of him, running back to him, jumping around him in her excitement, couldn't coax a smile from him.

He'd invited a bunch of kids out, hoping it would lift him out of his funk.

Six of the town's toughest teens got out of an old van driven by Mrs. Mason, the mother of one of the boys, Joey. Both Joey and his mom knew that unless something drastic changed in his life, he was heading for a life of crime.

"Joey," she said. "Be good today."

He stuffed his hands into his pockets, raised his shoulders defensively and muttered something his mom, thankfully, didn't hear.

"No profanity on my ranch," Austin admonished, but his heart wasn't in it.

Mrs. Mason said she would return in three hours to pick everyone up.

"Come on to the barn." Austin walked along the path beside the house. "I'll get you started on chores."

"We hafta work? That's so lame, man."

Austin confronted the kid. "Joey, what would you be doing right now if you weren't here?"

Joey shrugged. "Nothing, I guess."

"Right. You're getting into trouble because you're bored stiff. You need to keep busy. Might as well do it here and earn some money."

Four days ago, after Gracie had left, C.J. had brought Shadow to the ranch. Even that hadn't relieved the sense of profound loss that had fallen over Austin.

They entered the barn. "This is Shadow. Approach slowly and I'll show you how to handle a horse."

"Can we ride him?" Joey asked.

"Her. Eventually. First, get to know her."

Austin taught them how to check a horse for problems, how to feed her, how to lead her out to the corral. He took them out into the field to teach them about cattle.

This work he had thought would be fulfilling left him empty. Without Gracie, nothing seemed to matter. She'd added a dimension to his life that hadn't been there before. He hadn't known he was missing anything.

Now that she was gone? He knew, oh, how he knew, exactly how much he'd lost.

He brought everyone inside for a lunch of grilled cheese sandwiches and tinned tomato soup.

He missed how much Gracie would enjoy even a lunch as simple as this one. When she was young, she had known only the best yet hadn't grown up spoiled.

Austin had given each of the teenagers a task.

Joey stirred the soup so it wouldn't burn on the bottom. "What's wrong, Trumball?"

Austin had lost track of how many times today he'd told Joey to call him Officer Trumball, Mr. Trumball or even just Austin. He knew Joey did it to get a rise out of him, but at the moment, he didn't have it in him to care.

Joey frowned. "Seriously, man. I mean it. What's wrong? You got like this black cloud hanging over your head."

And running all the way through to my heart.

"It's woman trouble, isn't it?"

Joey couldn't be older than fourteen, but talked as though he knew about *woman trouble* through and through.

Thing was, he was right. Austin had a bad case of woman trouble, so bad he doubted there was a cure.

"It's that chick you brought to town, isn't it?"

Austin realized the kitchen had grown quiet, with a half-dozen pairs of ears listening in.

"Yes. It's about the woman I brought home with me."

"Where is she?" Hailey asked.

"She left."

"Why?"

"I can't talk about it."

"Buy her flowers. All chicks love flowers."

If she were close, he would.

"Give her money," Joey said. "That's all women want."

Not this one.

Hailey snapped a tea towel at Joey. "That's not all women want. They want romance, doofus."

No, what this woman wanted was to be on her own, to find herself. Without Austin. He'd been found lacking in a big way.

Mrs. Mason came back to pick up the kids at one.

"Can we come back next Saturday?" Joey asked, surprising Austin.

"Yes. I'll be here."

"Great." Joey grinned. "Next week I wanna ride your horse."

As the van cleared the end of the driveway, an old pickup truck turned in. Finn was home and he wasn't alone. Someone sat in the passenger seat. Melody.

They got out of the truck, Finn with a grin on his face and Melody with a softer smile.

"Hey, man." Finn hugged him and slapped him on the back.

Austin smiled and hugged Melody. "How did it all turn out?"

"My dad died a few days after I met him."

Austin sobered. "I'm sorry. Did you manage to reconcile with him first?"

"Can we come in for a coffee? I'll explain everything."

In the kitchen, Austin put the coffee on and they sat at the table Mrs. Olsen had left behind.

Until today with the kids he'd had in for lunch, he hadn't used the table. It had been made for a family and the children the Olsens had raised here.

Sitting at it alone, Austin had felt the lack of company.

He'd taken a kitchen chair and had set it up in front of the TV in the living room to eat his meals there.

Melody shared her family's news.

"I'm glad you were able to learn the truth before he died."

"Me, too. Those last three days were beautiful."

"And now?" Austin asked. "What are you doing in Ordinary? Are you and Finn an item?"

"A permanent item." Finn smiled with glee, like a kid in a candy store. "Will you be my best man?"

Austin laughed and shook Finn's hand, truly happy for his friend, but the happiness rang hollow inside him.

Melody watched him with perceptive eyes. "Tell us what happened with Gracie."

Austin ran through the story after he left them in Dallas to drive to Vegas to get Gracie and then bring her home to Ordinary.

"I screwed up. She doesn't want me. She wants a different kind of man."

"Yeah, she wants you," Finn said. "She just wants you to loosen up, to let go of your neuroses, man."

Austin did a double-take. "Since when did you become Freud?"

"I've just been doing a lot of thinking. We both, you and me, need to step up to the plate, because there are a couple of great women who want us. We need to be worthy of them."

Austin peered around Finn. "Who are you and what have you done with the real Finn?"

Finn laughed. "Hey, it sounds strange, but it's true. Get your shit together, man, or you're gonna lose Gracie like I almost lost Melody."

"Pardon me while I stare. Aren't you the guy who hates her?"

"Not anymore. You love her. I almost lost Melody. You need to get a move on before it's too late or you'll lose Gracie. For good."

Too late.

Was it too late? Had he blown his chance at the best thing that had ever happened to him?

"I have to go," he blurted.

Finn stopped chewing a cookie from a bag one of the kids had brought. "You need to take a whiz?"

"No. Not that," Austin said impatiently. "I mean I have to go after Gracie. I need to get her back and keep her. I was a goddamned idiot."

"Yeah!" Melody punched the air.

"Who'll take care of the ranch and the cattle while you're gone?"

"You?" Austin held his breath.

"Okay. I can pinch hit with C.J." Finn grinned. "You got it bad, buddy."

"I need Gracie."

"Love trumps all, Austin." Melody touched his hand. Austin wasn't sure how to work out what was wrong between him and Gracie, but he had to try. By going to her now, he didn't know if he was still trying to control her, or trying to hand control over to her.

She'd been right. Every time his mother had been out of control, Austin had fought to regain it.

But hell, he didn't know what he was doing now. He just knew he had to be near Gracie.

Within the context of his life, taking control made perfect sense. But he'd shifted too far in the other direction. As a kid, his life had been so chaotic, not knowing when his next meal would be, when he would sleep in clean sheets, whether the bank would take their lousy tin can away from them. Then Cash had offered sanity. When he'd left, Austin had still had C.J. and his awesome ranch.

The time had come, though, when Austin had to live with his mom again. No question. She was considered fit, but he never trusted her again. If life were ever going to be good, it would have to be on his terms, and by his hand. He fought every day to keep his life on an even keel.

Until Gracie, who tempted him with her courage and spirit. She'd known more security than he could ever have imagined…and she'd walked away from it, like a pioneer heading into an unknown future. Eyes wide open.

She had done it so she could live life on her terms, and then he'd tried to change that. Had tried to get her to live by *his* terms.

Could a man be any more foolish or arrogant than he'd been?

She needed him to stop giving. The way he felt right now, he wanted to do nothing but take from her, take and take and take, and never stop. He wanted her tenderness, her affection, her love.

Love was pain and beauty and hope and struggle.

"It won't be easy," he said aloud. "Not easy, but worth it."

He ran up the stairs two at a time to pack a bag.

GRACIE HAD BEEN in Hollywood for a week, meeting with literary lawyers, hammering out a deal that would keep her comfortable for a very long time.

She was viable again, but this time on her own

terms. She'd even managed to work out something that had been percolating. The publisher had agreed to buy a novel as well as her autobiography. Once the dust settled down after that came out, if all went well, she could have a life as a writer.

At last, she would be able to put her runaway imagination to good use.

Hollywood offered one more big piece of unfinished business she had to deal with before getting on with her life. Meaning, before returning to Austin.

She visited the old stage set where she grew up. She snuck onto the lot. As a child, she'd learned every inch of the place. She knew her way around. No need to go in through the front gate. She had her back-door ways.

She was certain the stage set would still be here. Many times over the years, her parents had wanted her to start a new show, with her as a grown-up, married and with children, and still living in the same house. Studio execs had agreed and had offered her the moon. As an adult, she'd declined. She didn't doubt that the studio still held out hope and would preserve the lot. They had. It was still here.

She stepped in through the front door of the building.

"Who's there?" She would have recognized Hal's voice blindfolded. Hal had been the security guard who used to sneak her licorice—red not black, because black would have left a ring around her mouth and stains on her costumes. So, they'd kept him on. Good. He must be near retirement age.

"A blast from the past," she answered, wondering how long it would take him to recognize her without bleached hair, bright blue contact lenses and makeup.

"Gracie Stacey." He grinned, still on the ball. "How many years has it been? Ten?"

"At least."

"How are you, luv?"

"I can't believe you recognized me."

"Why wouldn't I? Saw you in this very place every day for years. You've grown up, but you're still you."

Hal's smile welcomed her back with more sincere affection and generosity than her parents had in Vegas. She remembered that smile well. In the old days, Hal could always coax one out of her in return.

"What are you doing back here?"

"I came to L.A. to see Marcus. I thought I'd check out the old set while I was here."

"I shouldn't let you in, but I'm going to. This place was more yours than anyone else's. You're the one did all the work."

His validation warmed her to the tips of her toes. She sat with him in his small security office, waiting while he made her a cup of tea.

"I do security for a bunch of active sets, but I like to take my breaks here where it's quiet."

He pulled out his stash of chocolate-covered digestive biscuits, the same ones he used to serve her when she was a child.

"Are you still ordering these from overseas?"

An ex-pat Brit, he loved his treats from England.

"Yep, still get my monthly shipment in. Look what else I got, luv."

"Shortbread," she squealed. He pulled out thick wedges of it dusted with coarse sugar.

Hal grinned. "Want some?"

"Oh, yes. I haven't had any in years." She still couldn't get enough food. Maybe there was a hole in her belly she would never be able to fill for the rest of her life.

"It's good to have you back. I remember our little tea parties like they happened yesterday."

"Me, too, Hal. I used to love sneaking in here when I had a half hour away from shooting."

"Here." He handed her more biscuits. "We need to fatten you up."

Over the next hour, she told him where she'd been and what she'd been up to. Also, she shared how she planned to make a living from now on.

"I wasn't surprised when I heard you ran away. They put you through the wringer on this show. I worried about you keeping safe, though." He'd brewed fresh tea. He sipped his while she let hers cool. He liked his scorching hot. "Never understood why you didn't break down, they worked you so hard."

She didn't break down because of people like him and because of the crew, who took care of her better than her parents did.

She had treated them as people rather than servants and they had responded to her well.

He told her what had happened to as many people

as he could, all the peripheral characters in the show, as well as those on the set who kept the show going.

"Davey Hedges got into drugs and alcohol. Been arrested a couple of times now. DUI."

"Oh, no." Davey had played her older brother on the show. He was a good actor and a good guy. "I saw that on the rag mags in the variety stores. It was true?"

Hal nodded. "It's a hard business to grow up in."

Understatement of the century. "Charity did all right after she got off the prescription meds," Hal went on. "Got out of showbiz and straightened out. Married a nice guy. Has a couple of kids now."

Charity Hall had played her older sister. See, right now what Charity was doing sounded like heaven. Gracie had done her running, had traveled exotic places when she had money, had seen America without a cent, and was plenty ready to settle down.

She heard about cameramen and sound people who had treated her well, and about stylists who'd moved on to bigger and better things.

"Can I look around?"

"Need to get rid of some old ghosts, luv?"

"Something like that, Hal."

He patted her shoulder. "Take your time."

She wandered through the living room and kitchen, strange and artificial with only three sides, with the fourth open to cameras, lighting and a studio audience. Her character's bedroom was there, too, still juvenile with its pink and white frills. She'd never understood why they hadn't updated it when she became a teenager on the show.

Little Gracie Stacey. America's Little Darling. Heaven forbid that she should ever grow up, should ever become real, with the deep issues that teens had to face. All they ever dealt with on the Stacey show was whether she should kiss the boy she had a crush on or—gasp!—whether she should get braces.

Yet, it had all felt so real to her, because she'd known nothing else. She had assumed real life was like this, until she'd grown older and real life had come barreling in in the form of a young man she had married thinking he loved her.

No wonder she daydreamed. No wonder she made up stories in her mind. Lately, though, since meeting Austin, those stories had taken on real borders. They were no longer fairy tales, but honest love stories sewn with the thread of reality.

She sat in the bleachers where the audience would have sat, up in the middle of the last row, where she had a bird's-eye view of the set.

A house and yet not a house. A home and yet not a home. Fabricated, not created. Built, but not nurtured.

For a real house, a real home, she need only remember Austin's ranch, full of love and happiness. Had she left too soon? Given up too easily?

Could they have worked on his control issues? Isn't that what married couples did—worked things out instead of running away, instead of leaving without trying?

There had still been the issue of her independence to sort through. She'd taken care of that.

With that done, could they get through the rest? They had their differences. So what? She would be hard-pressed to find a better man on earth.

What was she doing here when the best man in the world—and the best life—was waiting for her in Ordinary, Montana?

Shouldn't she give Austin a chance to change and grow? He had only just walked away from his mother a few weeks ago. The man had wings to stretch. Surely that would include change?

Was he waiting? Would he welcome her back?

And what could she do about the press hurricane that would be released the second news of her book came out? Control it, of course.

She rushed back to Marcus's house.

He sat at the dining room table eating alone. "I wondered where you were. I started without you."

"I was at the old sound stage. You can tear it down. I won't ever come back."

Marcus sighed and set down his fork. "Damn."

"I need your help," Gracie said. "I have a plan."

CHAPTER FOURTEEN

AUSTIN ARRIVED IN L.A. wondering how the heck he was going to find Gracie. Why the hell hadn't he given her a cell phone?

Turned out finding her wasn't going to be a problem. The papers and TV news networks were abuzz.

Little Gracie Stacey had returned to Hollywood and was giving a press conference that afternoon.

Gracie? The press? Her worst nightmare come true. Why was she giving a conference? This is what she'd come here for? Hard to believe.

He needed to be there for her, but where was *there*?

Slinging his knapsack over his shoulder, he took a cab from the airport to a hotel in Hollywood. He didn't like this place any better than he'd liked Vegas.

He bought all the newspapers he could find and brought them back to his room. Combing through them and a map of L.A., he figured out where the news conference would be. He checked his watch and swore. If he didn't fly, he would miss it!

Trouble was, he didn't know how to get in. Didn't matter. He would find a way. He hadn't flown all this way for Gracie only to not see her. To not be able to plead his case.

He didn't have a clue how he was going to convince her to return home, to treat his home as hers, too, but come hell or high water, he would find the magic words that would work. If he had to, he would get down on his knees and beg.

Taking another cab, frantic now in his need to see Gracie, he leaned forward, grappling with his own impatience. "Can't you drive any faster?"

"Mister, I don't want speeding tickets."

Austin swore under his breath.

At last, they reached the building housing the press conference. He dodged the crowds in the street hoping to catch a glimpse of America's Little Darling. He scoped out the place.

Security was tight. Damn. He *had* to see her. Had to know she was okay. Had to help her get through this. He pulled up short after that thought. No! He didn't need to help *her,* the strongest woman he'd ever encountered. If she was giving a press conference, she had her reasons and would handle it.

Now that he was here, mere yards away from Gracie, he understood why he'd traveled so far to find her. It wasn't to save her or rescue *her,* but to *be* rescued. *She* had to save *him*—from his long, lonely future, from his neuroses and control issues, form his fear of receiving love, from his vulnerability. He needed her light and love and strength to give his days joy. He wanted to wake up beside her every day, and to share her life and her dreams and her heart's desires. He wanted to *be* her heart's desire.

He circled the building on foot, but there was no way to sneak in.

What else could a man who was crazy in love and in gut-wrenching need do but one crazy, irrational, out-of-control thing? He would have to force his way in.

It would likely get him a night in a jail cell. It wouldn't look good on his record, and would mess up his law-enforcement career, but he'd be damned if he would leave Tinseltown without the woman he loved.

GRACIE CHEWED ON a stick of peppermint gum that Marcus had given her. It helped settle her stomach.

She might have come up with a plan to make her dreams come true, to find anonymity while she wrote her books on Austin's ranch, with Austin by her side, but she was scared to death of this press conference.

She wished he were here for moral support.

"You good?" Marcus asked.

"I think so." She could do this. "Yes. I am good. This will work. I'll make it work."

"Are you sure this guy will marry you and give you his name? Is he worthy of you? If not, you can stay here with me and I'll keep the vultures at bay."

"Marcus, you've been a true friend." She hugged him. "I'll never forget this."

"Do me one favor?"

"Of course. Name it."

"Let me come visit this ranch you're going to live on."

Gracie smiled. "I'll send you an engraved invitation." Gracie crossed her fingers, hoping Austin would take her back and offer her forever.

Marcus made a small adjustment to her wig, a long, sophisticated, grown-up version of the blond wigs she used to wear as a child and teenager. The bright blue contact lenses hurt her eyes. She couldn't wait to take them out and become herself again.

Her eyebrows had been bleached and waxed.

He pulled a tissue out of his pocket. "Gum."

She spat it out into the tissue without smearing her lipstick.

In her future life, she wouldn't be caught dead in the conservative dress she wore. Only another half hour and her real life could begin. After this press conference, Gracie Stacey would disappear. Her book would come out, but there would be no press junket. There would be no late-night TV appearances, no book signings, no blogging.

Nothing but peace and quiet, and the royalties deposited in a bank account that Marcus would manage. She trusted him.

"Showtime, one last time, Little Gracie."

"Thanks, Marcus. Here we go."

The host of a popular local talk show introduced her and she walked onstage. Cameras flashed. Lights burst in front of her eyes. The crowd went wild, clapping and asking questions already.

The feeding frenzy had begun.

The host called the proceedings to order and Gracie took questions as they came, her answers coy.

To many, especially those about where she had

been for her *lost years,* as the press had dubbed them, she said, "You'll have to wait for the book." She was so sweet, so into Gracie Stacey's character, it elicited only moans and laughs.

"C'mon, Gracie," an older gentleman she remembered from the press circuit years ago said. "Give us something."

"Okay," she relented. "I've been traveling *incognito*."

"Where?"

"Across America. I've met wonderful people. Visited awesome places. We live in a beautiful country."

A commotion at the back of the room caught her attention. A man with familiar features, so precious her heartbeat stuttered, burst into the room and ran up the aisle, with security in hot pursuit.

Austin.

He was going to ruin everything.

Crap on a broomstick. Why couldn't the man stay on his ranch where he belonged? She was coming back to him.

He wouldn't have known that, Gracie.

She tried to send him a message telepathically.

She couldn't call him by name, she couldn't say anything that would cause the press to jump on him, to research him, to find out where he lived.

"Gracie," he yelled.

Shut up, she wanted to hiss, but kept her phony smile plastered on her face.

Her decent honest cop was breaking all kinds of rules, was *bursting* out of his self-imposed square box, and she loved him for it! She wanted to run to him and never let go, but the man was going to mess up everything. Why did he have to choose today, now, *here,* to become wild and crazy? To start breaking rules? God, she loved him, but she had to save him from himself.

Thank God he'd had the presence of mind to at least put on a baseball cap.

Do something.

"Help," she said with a laugh. "One of my many fans is trying to get to me. I keep telling you guys, you have to stop following me around. Give my secretary your address and I'll send you an autographed glossy."

The audience laughed.

The press was shooting photos of Austin, but he'd been mobbed by security and they couldn't get a clear shot. Thank goodness for small mercies.

Gracie excused herself and ran to the wings, where Marcus was watching the action.

"That's Austin," she hissed. "He's going to ruin everything. Handle this for me, Marcus. Get one of your own security guys to go out front and pick him up. Take him to the set. Tell him to wait for me there."

She grasped his wrist. "Make sure there are no repercussions. I don't want him going to jail or being charged with anything. And I don't want the press to find out who he is!"

Marcus rushed off.

Gracie took a deep breath, forced herself into character again and returned to the stage. Austin was being hauled outside, still calling her name.

Don't hurt him.

Gracie turned on the charm, amping up her smiles, just like she used to do when she was young. Not a speck of her animosity showed. She was a professional again, doing a job.

When she finally ended the interview, she said, "Thank you all for coming out today. There will be plenty of advance notice about when the book will be out. I'll see you all then."

That was the only outright lie she had told them.

She walked from the stage calmly when all she wanted to do was to run.

Austin was here.

"Did you get him?" she asked Marcus.

"Yep. I told security I would take over. One of my guys drove off with him, but I had to show him my ID before he would believe that I wasn't just putting him off." Marcus shook his head. "He wrote it all down."

Gracie laughed, joy shooting through her veins like a drug. Austin was safe. "He's a cop. He was being careful. He didn't want to get fooled."

"He said if he found out I'd lied about you showing up to see him he was going to come to my house and teach me a lesson I'd never forget." Marcus wiped his forehead. "I believed him. That guy is fierce."

"Really? I've always found him so calm."

"Not about you, Gracie. Trust me. He's in love and isn't leaving this city without you."

"He won't have to. Come on. Let's get to the car. I need to get out of this get-up and go see him."

She couldn't stop thinking his name. He'd come to L.A. for her. Austin was here and all was right with the world.

She'd missed him. She'd missed his voice. She'd missed his touch. She had even missed his bossy ways.

They scooted out through the back door, where a black SUV with tinted windows waited. As they drove away, so did a couple of cars, following them.

"Reporters." Now that the press conference was over, Gracie allowed disgust to creep into her voice. She took off the wig and tossed it onto the floor.

"Karl will lose them." Marcus picked up her old knapsack and held it with a horrified expression. "I don't know why you wouldn't let me buy you something new. Gucci has a great line of backpacks."

"This one has sentimental value." She pulled her fingers through her freshly shorn jet-black hair. "Don't look."

While Marcus stared out the window, and while the vehicle turned corners too sharply as the driver used evasive maneuvers, Gracie changed into a different outfit—black skinny jeans, a red T-shirt and boyfriend cardigan, and black flats.

"Lost them, boss," the driver said.

"Thanks, Karl. Good work." Marcus handed her a makeup bag. "Here. Your eyebrows will eventually turn black again, but in the meantime, use an eyebrow pencil."

Karl pulled up in front of the Gracie Stacey stage and parked. Gracie took out the contact lenses then colored her eyebrows black and used eyeliner to punch up her pale blue eyes, along with a little mascara.

She put four little silver skulls into the four holes she'd had punched into her ear lobes, two in each ear. In the side of her nose, she inserted a tiny diamond. Reckless, yes. She should wait longer for her new holes to heal before taking out the studs, but she had kept the holes clean and had sterilized the new earrings. She wanted her new self, her new person, to begin *now*. Yesterday.

Excitement thrummed through her.

"You're cute," Marcus said. "I like this new look."

He got out of the car. Gracie, no, *Grace*—she had to start thinking of herself as that because that's who she would be from now on—picked up her bag and got out on her side. Marcus walked around the car, his expression tinged with sadness. This was the Marcus she liked, the genuine man, not the Hollywood wheeler and dealer.

She smiled gently. "Thank you, Marcus, for everything."

He hugged her. Held her. Sniffed loudly. "I'll be waiting for that invitation."

He let go of her and got into the car without looking back.

Grace walked into the building.

Hal approached. "Your man is here, sitting up in the bleachers."

"I'm going on stage. Turn on one of the spotlights when I get there?"

"Sure thing, luv."

She came onto the stage from behind and stood in the middle of the living room. One light came on, highlighting her.

She heard a gasp then fast footsteps. Austin was there, taking the steps to her two, three, at a time. She was in his arms, her mouth on his, her heart thundering to match his, and all she could think was *Austin*.

When they finally came up for air, they moved to the bottom row of the studio bleachers and sat.

She couldn't let go of him, touched his face, his throat, his chest, ran her fingers through his hair. "It's already getting long again."

"If I buy you dinner, will you cut it for me?"

She laughed. They had only met three weeks ago, but it had been a long journey to today. She felt changed. New. Ready.

Austin's hands shook. "I can't stop touching you."

"I can't believe you're here. How? Why?"

He ran his finger across her eyebrow, down her cheek and along her jawline. "I had my house, I had my cattle, I had my work with the kids and I had my job." His voice sounded strange, thick and full of banked emotion. "None of it meant a thing without you. I could still live that life, but it's meaningless without you in it. I need you. I want you."

Magical words designed to melt her heart. She leaned her forehead on his shoulder. "I want you, too. I was sitting here in L.A. wondering why on earth I had left the best man I had ever met. I missed you, Austin."

They kissed for a long time before parting. "We'd better stop." Austin's voice trembled. "The security guard probably wouldn't want me hauling you to the floor and having my way with you."

"Hal? Probably not." She tried to kiss him one more time, but he stopped her with a shaky laugh.

"We have to stop, Gracie. I'm serious. I want you too badly and kissing is making it worse."

"I have a new name, Austin. It's Grace. I've grown up. Gracie has been put to bed for good."

"I'm glad. I'll try not to slip up." He pointed at the stage. "Tell me about this place."

"This is the set where the show was made."

"So, this is essentially where you grew up?"

"Yep. The only home I ever knew. It was more real to me than any of the hotels or rentals we lived in. This was my fantasy home, even when the lights were turned off."

She twined her arm through Austin's. "I wanted to live here for real. That was why I worked so hard on the show. I desperately wanted it all to be true."

"And now?"

She sat away from him to look into his eyes. "Now, I want you. I want your house in Ordinary. I want to live on that beautiful land with your animals. With your dog. But mainly, I want you. While I sat here night after night in California, I realized that my home is you. That you are my *true* home. Even if you lost that land, that house, you would still be my home. Does that make sense?"

"Perfect sense because I feel the same way about you. I had achieved my long-term plan, but it was just a house. Once you'd been in it, I knew it wouldn't feel like a home again until I got you back."

He squeezed her hand. "Come home with me?"

She sighed. Surely these were the most beautiful words she'd ever heard.

"I love you."

Those were even better. "I love you, too."

Whatever needed to be settled between them would be, because the truly important stuff shimmered around and through them, and always would. It was here and strong now, and they would work to keep it that way, because it was worth working for.

"For how long? How long will you stay with me?"

"For as long as you'll have me."

"Forever, Grace. I want you forever."

"That's how I want you, Austin."

He stood and hauled her into his arms, up against his solid chest, with her feet dangling above the ground.

"Austin." She laughed.

He didn't. "For forever." His voice shook. "Stay with me forever."

"Yes. A thousand, million times yes."

He spun her around, his breath heavy and warm against the crook of her neck where his face burrowed. She held on with all her strength. She was never letting go again.

"Will you marry me?"

"Yes."

A sigh gusted out of him as he lifted his head to look at her. "Thank God. I missed you so much."

"I missed you, too." Austin's smile was transcendent.

"One thing, though, Austin. Don't get angry, but I will pay my own way. It's important to me."

"I know."

No argument. The man was accepting her exactly as she was.

"I want to make a contribution."

He held her again. "You do. Your love is like gold to me."

She swallowed a knot of very fine emotion called joy. He couldn't have said anything better.

"I will be dependent on you for only a short time and then I'll have my own money."

He pulled back, brows raised. "Why? What's up? What was that press conference all about? You hate the press."

"I signed a book contract with a publisher. I want to write my story. People need to know what the industry can do to children and why so many child stars are screwed up as adults."

"You're going to be published?"

"They offered me a lucrative contract."

Austin hooted. "Honey, I'm happy for you. Awesome!"

"When my advance check comes in, we can use it to buy more cattle."

"You should use that money for *you*. You earned it the hard way."

"I want to share it with you."

"Will the writing of the book be hard on you? How will it feel to rehash everything?"

"I'm not going to write it as an exposé. It won't be titillating or salacious, but an honest look at the industry and how hard it is on children. Then, and the publisher doesn't know this yet, I'm going to write about my life on the road. About America and what I learned about myself, and about the interesting people I met."

Austin squeezed her. "I like it, but leave out the part about you stealing my wallet."

"Yeah, and the date squares, too. Let's get on a plane and go home. I need to be alone with you." They walked away from the stage together. "Do you know what I'm going to do first when I get my money? I'm going to pay you every penny I owe you."

"But—"

"Please, Austin. I need to."

He relented and his smile was gentle. "Okay."

"The second thing I'm going to do is to send that waitress from whom I stole the date squares a check for a thousand dollars."

Austin's smile widened. "I like it."

"Oh! There's more good news."

"What?"

"They're buying a novel from me, too. I wrote up

a synopsis for one of the stories that's been rattling around in my brain forever. They bought it."

Austin's smile looked downright giddy, and probably as silly as hers felt. "You like happy endings, don't you?"

"Love them. Let's go make ours."

Grace stared at the make-believe house.

All of her early wealth was nothing compared to the reality of her love with Austin.

Money was necessary. Greed was not. One way or another, they would get by. They would work hard and would raise a hardworking family, but money would never be more important than family. Money would never be more important than her children.

And yes, she wanted children. She wanted to love the daylights out of them.

They stood and strode off the set together.

After giving Hal a big hug and an even bigger thank-you, she left.

She was going back to Ordinary with Austin.

She was going home.

CHAPTER FIFTEEN

As THEY DROVE from the airport to Ordinary, Grace's heart swelled. *Home.*

Austin held her hand. "I wasn't sure when I flew out to L.A. whether you would think I was trying to control you again."

"No. The second I saw you, I knew something had changed," Grace admitted, "You were different."

"When I was alone at home, I realized it was more than my need for control that had me keeping you close when we first met. You were right about the control part, but there was more. It was *you*. I wanted *you* close. On a subliminal, maybe animal, level I recognized you as mine, my partner, my better half, whatever you want to call it. I'm calling you a part of me. I couldn't let you go."

They pulled into Ordinary and Austin parked on Main Street to pick up groceries.

Grace had been thinking about marriage ever since Austin had asked her.

"Are there any good marriages in the world, Austin? They can't all be as bad as the ones we saw growing up."

They walked to the grocery store holding hands.

"They aren't. Look at Cash and Shannon Kavenagh. I don't think their marriage and parenting skills are smoke and mirrors. I've seen them regularly over the years when they visited Ordinary. It's real.

"Look at Finn's parents. It took them a while to get together. They didn't marry until Finn was twelve, but you should see them now. They love each other and have a great family life. They did a good job raising him and his younger sister.

"There are other families in Ordinary who make married life look blissful. I believe they are real."

They passed the diner. In the window sat an older couple, the man on the homely side and the woman faded but still beautiful. Austin waved.

"That was Hank Shelter and Amy Graves. They've been married for years. They bring inner-city children who are recovering from cancer to the Sheltering Arms ranch. They've been doing it ever since Amy first came to the ranch to get him to sell, only to end up helping him to save both the ranch and his charity. Their own children are rock-solid and have moved into the field of charity work, running or involved in different organizations.

"There are all different kinds of people in the world. You know that old saying that the road to hell is paved with good intentions?"

Grace nodded.

"There might be some truth to it, but I choose to believe it's not completely true. I think good intentions matter in life. I think if we love our children more than ourselves, we will give them everything they need. And that's a real good thing."

Grace hoped he was right, because someday she wanted to be a good mother.

Driving onto the ranch and walking into the house, with Sadie jumping around her barking and begging for attention was the best homecoming she could have imagined.

"I need to do chores before bed. You okay here alone?"

"Of course."

"Welcome home, Grace." He kissed her sweetly, and then with building heat.

"Go," she said. "Get your chores done and then get back here fast."

She waited in the bedroom in a pretty cotton nightgown she'd bought. Half an hour later, Austin walked into the room.

"You're wearing too many clothes," she said.

"Why don't you take them off me?"

"Me?" she whispered.

"What you said about control last time we made love? It was all true. This time I'm giving you control. I need to prove I can do this."

Honored that he would put his trust in her, she undressed him, as he'd asked her to do.

He lay on his back on the bed with his hands under his head, leaving himself exposed to her and ready for whatever she wanted.

This man she loved was beautiful inside and out. She lay down beside him and started to touch, exploring the body she had come to crave. She took her time, fascinated by him.

She skimmed the tip of her tongue along his neck and hard shoulder then down to his nipple. He hissed in a breath. So did she. He tasted good. His nipple hardened under her tongue.

Sitting up, she straddled him and took off her nightgown. Involuntarily, his hands came out from under his head, but he checked himself and put them back.

In the moonlight from the window, his eyes glowed with desire. Sweat beaded on his forehead and she could see what giving her control was costing him.

She loved him all the more for it.

Scooting back onto his thighs, she ran her fingers down his chest and stomach. He tensed. She slipped her fingers around the beating heart of his masculinity.

While she stroked him with one hand, she laid her other palm over his heart, because that was the center of his decency and the part that compelled him to do the best for others, the part of him that couldn't *not* help when a person needed it. And it charmed her.

"Austin." Her voice shushed through the quiet of the room and took on a hallowed note. "Thank you." *Thank you for this gift of yourself when I know it's hard to lie back and let go.* Her hand continued to stroke him, the ferocity of his expression letting her know how close he was to release. His hands came out from under his head. *Oh, no. Don't stop me, please. I will be so disappointed.* But he didn't.

Instead, he grasped the bed sheets in his fists. His knuckles turned white. His arms shook.

He honored her with his discipline, with this simple act of giving in, and then he gave himself over to her control completely. With a long, low moan, he came.

In time, he opened his eyes. "Thank you." He opened his arms.

She lay down beside him and he cradled her against his chest. She listened to his heart pounding.

In time, she asked, "Was that hard for you?"

"Yeah, but I liked it." He ran his fingers through her hair in a rhythmic flow. "I think I could get used to letting go more often."

Grace smiled into the silvery darkness. There was hope for them. So much hope.

"I enjoyed it, too. There's something to be said for taking control."

"Don't go getting power crazy on me. I like your idea of an equal relationship."

"Me, too."

A little while later, they made love, giving and receiving attention in equal measure.

They slept and then awoke in the early dawn.

They ignored the sun rising over the horizon, coloring the mauve-gray room with warmth, and stayed in bed because they still had a couple of hours before they had to be anywhere. Why waste that time with sleep or food?

Times had changed. Her body was no longer starving, her psyche on a journey of healing.

His hands moved, traced the contours of her body, the dips and swells and she lost herself in sensation.

She returned the favor, bolstered by his hums of appreciation. They came together in a union of bodies and love.

THEY LAY IN BED, talking quietly.

"You're looking for something that might not exist, Grace. There's no pot of gold at the end of the rainbow that looks like the perfect all-American dream. Families like the one on your old show might not exist."

She tried to shrug off his criticism until she thought of something. "I dream, Austin. I can't help it. I wanted my show to be real. Every speck of it." She pointed at him. "You, though, try to make it real. You try to force it into existence and it just isn't going to happen. It can't be forced."

He couldn't argue with that. He seemed to come to a decision.

"Let's make a deal. Let's forge a unique marriage, and a unique family."

"They're all unique, Austin."

"Yeah, but we're going into it with our eyes wide open. We know the pitfalls. Let's always support each other. Let's balance each other out. When I try to force things, call me on it. When you start to float into a daydream instead of facing reality, I'll call you on it."

"Between the two of us, we should be good."

"Let's make a pact to check in with each other

every night before bed. Let's ask two questions. How are *you* doing? And how are *we* doing?"

THEY HELD THEIR wedding a month later.

They had already had a private talk with the minister, explaining who Grace really was, and that that part of this union must always remain private in the future. He agreed to call her Grace Travers for the ceremony, so the community wouldn't know who she really was, and it would be legal because they spoke the vows using her name privately with the minister before the public ceremony. When they signed the register, she signed it as Gracie Stacey. Then Gracie Stacey disappeared and, to her unending happiness, Grace Trumball came into being.

Melody and Finn stood up with them for a simple, beautiful celebration, and the small church was full of Austin's friends, coworkers and townspeople.

Marcus flew in from California and gave her away, becoming more emotional than she had thought possible.

She remembered when she'd thought she'd become invisible, that she'd disappeared, that she wasn't leaving her mark on anyone.

That was changing. When she'd returned to L.A., somehow she'd left her mark on Marcus. She wasn't sure how, but he'd changed. He'd even begun dating a woman his own age, wonder of wonders.

And, of course, loveliest of all, Austin had been changed by her.

His mother, Connie, attended the wedding, sitting in the front row as mother of the groom, wearing a dress she'd let Grace help her choose. Their relationship was strained, and sometimes downright difficult, but Grace planned to work on it.

They partied in the parish hall well into the wee hours and dined on chicken wings and burgers from Chester's Bar and Grill. Dessert was chocolate from Sweet Talk.

Music flowed for hours and kids danced with adults.

Teenagers spiked the punch and some got drunk. C.J.'s wife, Janey, drove them home.

Never in her wildest dreams had Grace imagined she would be part of a community, but Austin had given her this, and she could never thank him enough.

Grace and Austin left with the last of the party-goers, staying to celebrate until the very end.

"That was the best wedding I've ever attended," Marcus said when they dropped him off at his B and B.

They drove home to the ranch, where a yellow lamp burned in the living room window. Grace had shared so much with Austin about her old fears and longings. When they went anywhere together, he never left home without turning on a lamp so Grace would feel welcomed by the house when coming home.

Tonight, he insisted on carrying her over the threshold.

"Austin," she protested, laughing. "This is so old-fashioned."

"I know, but I always thought I would do this if some woman was ever foolish enough to take me on."

He set her on her feet and closed the door. "I like your dress. You did a great job."

In her old life, if anyone had ever told Gracie Stacey that she would walk down the aisle in a home-made wedding gown, she would have told them they were crazy.

She had done just that, had made herself a simple white empire-waist dress with modest lace sleeves. No big poofs. No crazy mile-long train. No designer label.

"Grace?"

"Yes, Austin?"

"How are you doing?"

So, he was starting the ritual tonight. Good. Lovely.

"I'm wonderful." Austin turned on lamps and their rooms filled with warmth. Grace remembered on her travels looking into all those windows of all those houses and wanting to be inside, wanting to be part of a family.

She'd thought the best she would ever do was to buy a small home of her own and live in isolation. She would have been safe, but alone.

Here, with Austin, every dream and aspiration of the lonely traveler she had been was realized.

Later, in bed, with dawn creeping over the horizon, Grace whispered, "Austin?"

"Mmm?" he murmured.

"I'm really glad I stole your wallet."

He burst into laughter, filling their home with joy's symphony.

TWO YEARS LATER, Grace and Austin brought a child home from the hospital, a girl named Irene, after Gran.

A yellow lamp shone in the window, welcoming them up the driveway.

Austin walked through their home turning on more lamps.

Grace's book sat on the coffee table, the photo of her on the cover as a precocious, blonde five-year-old no longer painful to look at. What gave her more pride, though, was the book that sat beside it, a story of a lonely man and a lost woman who had come together and found love, written by the promising new romance author Grace Trumball.

She carried her baby upstairs to the bedroom she and Austin had decorated for her.

Grace placed Irene into her crib. She couldn't stop staring at her tiny perfect child.

Austin came up behind her and wrapped his arms around her.

"How are we doing?"

"We," Grace whispered, "all three of us, couldn't be better."

She turned in her husband's arms and kissed

him while their child slept contentedly in the room they'd created for her in the mansion of their love, in the ever-expanding, elastic, laughter-filled home, which could never be called anything as mundane as *ordinary,* that Grace and Austin filled with more children over the years.

* * * * *

LARGER-PRINT BOOKS!

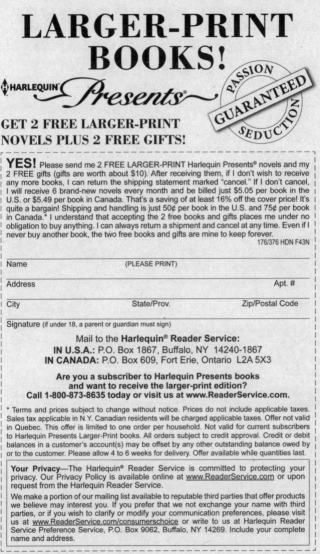

HARLEQUIN *Presents*

PASSION GUARANTEED SEDUCTION

GET 2 FREE LARGER-PRINT NOVELS PLUS 2 FREE GIFTS!

YES! Please send me 2 FREE LARGER-PRINT Harlequin Presents® novels and my 2 FREE gifts (gifts are worth about $10). After receiving them, if I don't wish to receive any more books, I can return the shipping statement marked "cancel." If I don't cancel, I will receive 6 brand-new novels every month and be billed just $5.05 per book in the U.S. or $5.49 per book in Canada. That's a saving of at least 16% off the cover price! It's quite a bargain! Shipping and handling is just 50¢ per book in the U.S. and 75¢ per book in Canada.* I understand that accepting the 2 free books and gifts places me under no obligation to buy anything. I can always return a shipment and cancel at any time. Even if I never buy another book, the two free books and gifts are mine to keep forever.

176/376 HDN F43N

Name _____ (PLEASE PRINT) _____

Address _____ Apt. # _____

City _____ State/Prov. _____ Zip/Postal Code _____

Signature (if under 18, a parent or guardian must sign) _____

Mail to the **Harlequin® Reader Service:**
IN U.S.A.: P.O. Box 1867, Buffalo, NY 14240-1867
IN CANADA: P.O. Box 609, Fort Erie, Ontario L2A 5X3

**Are you a subscriber to Harlequin Presents books
and want to receive the larger-print edition?
Call 1-800-873-8635 today or visit us at www.ReaderService.com.**

* Terms and prices subject to change without notice. Prices do not include applicable taxes. Sales tax applicable in N.Y. Canadian residents will be charged applicable taxes. Offer not valid in Quebec. This offer is limited to one order per household. Not valid for current subscribers to Harlequin Presents Larger-Print books. All orders subject to credit approval. Credit or debit balances in a customer's account(s) may be offset by any other outstanding balance owed by or to the customer. Please allow 4 to 6 weeks for delivery. Offer available while quantities last.

Your Privacy—The Harlequin® Reader Service is committed to protecting your privacy. Our Privacy Policy is available online at www.ReaderService.com or upon request from the Harlequin Reader Service.

We make a portion of our mailing list available to reputable third parties that offer products we believe may interest you. If you prefer that we not exchange your name with third parties, or if you wish to clarify or modify your communication preferences, please visit us at www.ReaderService.com/consumerschoice or write to us at Harlequin Reader Service Preference Service, P.O. Box 9062, Buffalo, NY 14269. Include your complete name and address.

HPLP13R

LARGER-PRINT BOOKS!
GET 2 FREE LARGER-PRINT NOVELS PLUS
2 FREE GIFTS!

HARLEQUIN®

Romance

From the Heart, For the Heart

YES! Please send me 2 FREE LARGER-PRINT Harlequin® Romance novels and my 2 FREE gifts (gifts are worth about $10). After receiving them, if I don't wish to receive any more books, I can return the shipping statement marked "cancel." If I don't cancel, I will receive 4 brand-new novels every month and be billed just $4.84 per book in the U.S. or $5.24 per book in Canada. That's a savings of at least 19% off the cover price! It's quite a bargain! Shipping and handling is just 50¢ per book in the U.S. and 75¢ per book in Canada.* I understand that accepting the 2 free books and gifts places me under no obligation to buy anything. I can always return a shipment and cancel at any time. Even if I never buy another book, the two free books and gifts are mine to keep forever.

119/319 HDN F43Y

Name   (PLEASE PRINT)

Address   Apt. #

City   State/Prov.   Zip/Postal Code

Signature (if under 18, a parent or guardian must sign)

Mail to the **Harlequin® Reader Service:**
IN U.S.A.: P.O. Box 1867, Buffalo, NY 14240-1867
IN CANADA: P.O. Box 609, Fort Erie, Ontario L2A 5X3
Want to try two free books from another line?
Call 1-800-873-8635 or visit www.ReaderService.com.

* Terms and prices subject to change without notice. Prices do not include applicable taxes. Sales tax applicable in N.Y. Canadian residents will be charged applicable taxes. Offer not valid in Quebec. This offer is limited to one order per household. Not valid for current subscribers to Harlequin Romance Larger-Print books. All orders subject to credit approval. Credit or debit balances in a customer's account(s) may be offset by any other outstanding balance owed by or to the customer. Please allow 4 to 6 weeks for delivery. Offer available while quantities last.

Your Privacy—The Harlequin® Reader Service is committed to protecting your privacy. Our Privacy Policy is available online at www.ReaderService.com or upon request from the Harlequin Reader Service.

We make a portion of our mailing list available to reputable third parties that offer products we believe may interest you. If you prefer that we not exchange your name with third parties, or if you wish to clarify or modify your communication preferences, please visit us at www.ReaderService.com/consumerchoice or write to us at Harlequin Reader Service Preference Service, P.O. Box 9062, Buffalo, NY 14269. Include your complete name and address.

HRLP13R